DIVINE
DECEPTION

ELLE MAE

Get ready for the biggest gay panic of your life. You're welcome.

This is a work of fiction. Names, characters, places, and incidents either are the product of the author's imagination or are used fictitiously. Any resemblance to actual persons, living or dead, events, or locales is entirely coincidental.

Divine Deception

Copyright © 2025 by Elle Mae

All rights reserved. No part of this book may be reproduced or used in any manner without written permission of the copyright owner except for the use of quotations in a book review. For more information, address: contact@ellemaebooks.com

Cover design by Seventhstarart
Edits by Leticia Edits

www.ellemaebooks.com

NOTE

This is a work of fiction. Names, characters, business, events and incidents are the products of the author's imagination. Any resemblance to actual persons, living or dead, or actual events is purely coincidental.

Before moving forward, please note that the themes in this book can be dark and trigger some people. The themes can include but are not limited to: mentions of past torture, depictions of torture, deceptions of murder, depiction of attempted murder of a pregnant person, attempted murder, parental death, abandonment, seeing death of parents, blood play, gore/violence , family violence & abuse, voyeurism, murder, stabbing, biting, physical altercations, depictions of corpses being treated poorly, verbal, mental and physical abuse by a parent, ableist language, bullying, implied abuse of an animal, depression.

If you need help, please reach out to the resources below.

National Suicide Prevention Lifeline
1-800-273-8255
https://suicidepreventionlifeline.org/

National Domestic Violence Hotline
1-800-799-7233
https://www.thehotline.org/

Also by Elle Mae

Elle Mae

Blood Bound Series:

Contract Bound: A Lesbian Vampire Romance

Lost Clause

Blood Royale:

Eternal Captive: A Dark Enemies-to-Lovers Sapphic Vampire Romance

Divine Decption

Winterfell Academy Series:

The Price of Silence: Winterfell Academy Book 1

The Price of Silence: Winterfell Academy Book 2

The Price of Silence: Winterfell Academy Book 3

The Price of Silence: Winterfell Academy Book 4

The Price Of Silence: Winterfell Academy Book 5

Winterfell Series Box Set

Short and Smutty:

The Sweetest Sacrifice: An Erotic Demon Romance

Nevermore: A Deal with a Demon

Stolen Demon Brides:

Taken to the Deadlands

Taken to the Shadow Realm

Taken to the Demon Court

Eden Emory

The Ties That Bind Us

Don't Stop me

Don't Leave Me

Don't Forget Me

Don't Hate Me

Two of a Kind

Hide n' Seek

Queer Meet Cute Anthology

Patreon Only

Wicked corruption: An FF Mafia Romance

Watch Me

Tales of the Stolen Demon Brides

DIVINE
DECEPTION

ELLE MAE

Aurelia

Vampires didn't sleep. We didn't dream.

Losing consciousness was akin to hell for us, when all the ugly thoughts and memories that we wanted to hide came rushing to the forefront and we were unable to fight them.

After being alive for so long, there was a chance that the mind would rot. All the memories. All the pain. All the torture we put ourselves through.

If we didn't push it to the back of our mind, we'd go crazy.

That's what never sleeping protected us from. It gave us the ability to live in the now, building steel walls inside our heads to keep the memories locked in.

But losing consciousness was like ripping a hole in the armor, letting all the evil inside loose.

I had many dangerous evils behind my walls. Creatures with fangs bared and drool dripping from their lips as they waited for the opportune moment to strike.

And, as it would turn out, getting stabbed in the heart would render even the most powerful vampire unconscious. It should have killed me. But my spite, my fury, were too strong for that.

I didn't realize what had happened at first. I thought I was still in the palace, wandering the halls like any other day. It was no different from when I was awake, and nothing raised my suspicions.

I didn't remember Vesper. I didn't remember the crusade my father was on. There was absolutely nothing on my mind. For a few moments, I was free.

Until I heard the gurgles.

And then in an instant, everything changed. Instead of the sun shining through the windows, it was raining. Hard droplets thundered against the glass. The entire hallway darkened. Froze.

Fear crawled up my spine, an invisible clawed hand traveling up my body until it had its fingers around my throat.

I had been here before.

I knew the sound of the gurgling. Knew who it was coming from. But I didn't want to follow. My feet had other plans, though. They pushed me toward the sound. My mind knew what was going to happen, but my body was acting like it did that night.

I stopped right at the open doorway to the throne room.

No—this wasn't right.

She hadn't been in the throne room. She had been in front of Krae, reaching out to the goddess for mercy.

Yet there she was. My mother. Gasping her last few breaths at the feet of my father while he sat on his throne without a care in the world. He looked at her as if he was bored. And when she held out her hand for him instead of the goddess, he smiled.

I tried to scream for her, but it was lodged in my throat. I tried to run to her, but my legs wouldn't move.

Muffled voices were coming from all around me, but I couldn't make out their words. All I could focus on was the pooling of my mother's blood as she desperately tried to get Father to help.

The image shifted.

Another woman had taken her place. She was wearing the same gown as Mother, but her hair was blonde, her eyes a beautiful hazel. Fear filled them.

My heart twisted.

I knew her...

Familiarity tugged at my senses, but her name and who she was didn't come to mind.

But what was the most alarming wasn't the blood pooling under her, her terror-filled face, or her silent cries.

It was her belly. Round and swollen, her hand splaying across it protectively.

My head felt like it was going to be split in two.

Father looked at her with a cruel sneer.

He hated this woman, maybe even more than my mother.

She reached for me. Me. The hand that had once covered her belly was now stained with blood.

Help her. I needed to help.

The space between us stretched out as my feet moved. Each step that should have brought me closer to her seemed to be pushing me farther and farther away. Light flooded my senses. I instinctively raised a hand to cover my eyes, or at least I tried, but it didn't move. My body was frozen even as my mind was spinning.

I blinked rapidly, another scene coming into existence.

My room.

Lighter than I usually had it. No, it wasn't the room. My eyes were fixed on the shimmering chandelier above me, but that wasn't what was burning my vision.

My gaze followed the light to meet the redheaded witch. Her brows were pushed together, her lips settled into a frown. The light came from her.

That's when I felt the burning.

Pain like I'd never felt before exploded through my body. I wanted to writhe, to try and curl in on myself, but again, my body wasn't listening to me.

It was a different sort of hell when your mind and body were disconnected. I had no control over it. I could do nothing but sit there as the witch's magic burned me.

If I'd been in less pain, I might have had the energy to feel anger. But all that was there was agony, panic, fear, and more pain.

A groan left my throat, calling someone else into my line of sight.

Vesper. It didn't come back to me right away. My first thought was to reach for her. She was covered in blood, her eyes watery.

Why? Why did she look like that?

I never wanted to see the silver-haired girl look like that. I wanted to fix it. Wanted to destroy whoever made her feel that way.

And then a burst of pain shot through my chest, bringing the memories of what happened before I passed out.

It wasn't the witch's magic that was burning me.

It was the giant hole in my chest.

Krae, help me. I was going to kill her.

"*You fucking stabbed me, you bitch,*" *I forced out.*

I didn't know it was possible for Vesper's face to look even more griefstricken.

"Finish with the blood, then open the windows," Cedar barked. Her tone was harsh. Anger and something else shone in her eyes. Her face was a hard mask. "If we move fast enough, your scent will be gone, but the magic will stay."

Vesper tore her eyes from me, nodding at Cedar before leaving my side.

Heaviness pulled at my eyelids. Cedar's lips moved, but the words never reached me.

Darkness wrapped around my consciousness and violently pulled me back into my nightmares.

Vesper

Pain shot through me, a reminder of where the claws slashed across my calf.

The distraction had me tripping over my feet and plummeting to the soft, damp earth below. Dirt mixed with the blood in my mouth from the narrowly missed kill shot from earlier.

I grabbed my sword from its sheath and turned just in time for a vampire to pounce on me. He grabbed the blade with his bare hands, his face unchanging and his crazed bared teeth still the same since he'd started chasing me.

Hot, thick, dark vampire blood seeped from his wounds and dripped onto my face, chest, and neck.

I tried to kick him off, jerk him to the side, but nothing seemed to work. Not when he was so far gone. He didn't feel the pain—all he knew was that he needed to *feed*. He wouldn't stop. His skin could be cut, his legs broken, but even so, all it meant was that he would have to crawl to his target.

The forest around us was thick enough to block out most of the moonlight, making it difficult for a mere human like myself to see the vampires coming. The air was cool against my heated skin, each inhale freezing my lungs. The only reprieve was how fast my heart was beating, warming up my body.

His eyes were bloodred and glowing in the darkness. His fangs seemed painfully enlarged. And he was desperately trying to take a bite out of me.

Aurelia's father was getting desperate. At first, he'd sent vampire guards, predictable and sometimes a pain, but overall easy to manage. I had lost count of how many we had killed during the few months after leaving the palace.

And believe it or not, things started to fall into a pattern—the constant killing of the vampire guards was a job and started to lose its sense of danger. No matter how much the Castle family paid them, they still valued their lives. They hesitated. Some even begged for mercy.

Then they started sending the crazed.

I cursed when I heard the sound of another to my far right.

This makes it four.

I wanted to look, take stock of the next one coming, but I couldn't. Not when this one was pushing the sword closer and closer to my neck with his enhanced strength. More blood dripped down, sending a wave of disgust through me as the sword threatened to slice right through his hands.

It made no difference.

That's why the crazed were so dangerous. They would stop at nothing to get blood.

Humans, vampires, and witches alike were all possible victims of the crazed.

The king must have been keeping them around for a while, carefully starving vampires for months and months on end until he could send them on our trail, which meant he was no longer playing around.

He wanted revenge.

He wanted what he was owed.

He wanted his daughter.

I smelled it before I saw it.

A burst of raw, unfiltered magic filled the air. The smell of burning wood and herbs filled my senses before bright red vine-like magic circled the vampire. This made him pause. When the sound of sizzling flesh reached my ears, for the first time that night, it looked like the vampire might awaken from his state.

But it was too late. The red vines squeezed him, cutting through his body and rendering him useless.

Dead.

I pushed the corpse off me with disgust, my attention shifting to the other crazed waiting for me.

With a single throw, I sent my short sword flying through the air and straight into his chest. Red vines held him tightly in place, but it was the sword to the heart that ended up being his demise.

"Getting rusty, hunter."

I let out an annoyed huff, shooting Cedar a death glare as she appeared between the trees. Her auburn hair was pulled up into a half bun, her face free of blood and dirt as she had been standing on the sidelines during the fight. She gave me a smirk as she took in just how much of a mess I was, her gaze running the length of my body until it got to my face.

Her green eyes glittered with something akin to amusement.

"There were *four* of them, and you didn't even think to help 'til now?" I grumbled and stalked over to the corpse.

"Don't get your panties in a twist," she said. She crossed her arms and leaned against the tree, a few strands of her hair falling into her face. "I can't just come in here and save the day. This is *your* job. Plus, if I did all the hard work, you'd never get back into shape."

I muttered obscenities under my breath as I grabbed my sword from the vampire's chest and yanked. It came out with a sickening wet sound.

The last few months had been hell. I had never pushed my body harder than in the short period of time we had been hiding. My muscles ached constantly. My body was leaner. The scars all but doubled, though.

But it wasn't enough. I still had to rely on Cedar every time we went on one of these patrols. It was the only time I even saw her anymore. I never would have thought I'd miss the witch, but I was starting to get a bit of hay fever from being stuck in the cabin for so long.

These days, it was either being locked in there or getting beat up by crazed vampires that had picked up our carefully laid trail until they got to the forest where magic would turn them around.

Oftentimes, that gave us enough time to take out a few, but these new crazed ones were different. Once they homed in on a scent, there was no stopping them.

I looked up through the trees. The stars were slowly disappearing, and light blue seeped into the inky blackness of the sky.

"Time to feed," Cedar reminded me with a playful tone. "Don't want to make her royal highness wait."

Another complication.

Even so, my chest squeezed, and a sort of excitement ran through me at the thought of seeing her.

Vesper

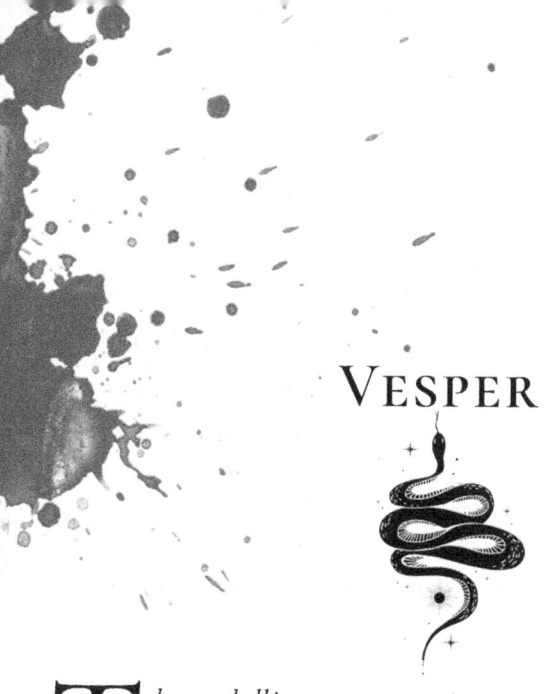

The medallion was warm in my pocket. The urge to contact Atlas was weighing on me, but I couldn't—not until we at least made it out of the palace.

Things were happening so quickly that if I even so much as hesitated, it would put us all in danger, with me definitely losing my life.

Night had fallen long before, giving us an uncharacteristically cool night for the season. The sky was pitch black, not a single star shining as if they too were hiding.

Cedar was in front of me, acting as a lookout, leading me through a path out of the palace that she seemed all too familiar with. Aurelia was thrown over my shoulder. The bleeding had stopped, and Cedar had done what was medically necessary for the time being, but we needed to get her to a safe point sooner rather than later.

Thank whatever god was out there for the witch.

I could tell she had a million questions running through her head, and she no doubt wanted to lecture me on just how much I was risking, but as soon as she saw Aurelia, she jumped into action.

Cedar made a motion for me to follow her against the back of the garden wall. The forest wasn't far, but the open space between the palace and our freedom seemed too exposed for comfort.

My chest was aching since Aurelia had given me that betrayed look when she regained consciousness. I didn't want to do what I did. But I needed to get us out of there and get the secret organization off our trail. I needed to at least make them think that I had completed the prophecy. Even if just for a few days. Hours even.

They would find out at some point; they were at least smart enough for that.

But it would at least give us enough time to run.

Aurelia's father, on the other hand, would be a completely different case. We could hide with magic, but not for long. And knowing him, there would be hell to pay once he caught wind of us.

We needed a place even he didn't dare go. That no vampire would.

It wasn't enough to hide in some random clan up north. We needed protection. Atlas couldn't offer that, at least not right away.

But the witches could.

Our footsteps were muffled by the dirt as we stalked the distance to the forest. Both of us were looking over our shoulders, just waiting for even a hint that we had been caught. Awareness crawled up the back of my neck.

It was quiet. Too quiet.

Aurelia had more guards than I could count, each of them on a rotation. The grounds alone had hundreds of them.

Yet we hadn't run into a single one.

They should have noticed us, but they hadn't. They had somehow been catching handfuls of assassins, but no alarms sounded for us. No vampires showed up. Nothing.

We made it to the safety of the forest without so much as breaking a sweat—save from my own anxiety.

Cedar and I shared a look. Her eyebrows were pushed together, her lips in a thin line. There was a bead of sweat falling down the side of her face.

Without saying anything, she motioned for me to follow her through the densely packed trees. The temperature was dropping steadily, cooling my heated skin. I hugged Aurelia's body close.

Cedar said she was stable for now, but with the time it had taken to set up her room in a way that looked like a murder had taken place and with how long it would take to get us to wherever the hell we were going... I wasn't sure what type of condition she would be in.

Finish the prophecy.

It's what I needed to do. Or at least I needed to make people believe I had.

But just when I thought we were in the clear, I heard the distant sound of people fighting. Groans. The sound of bodies dropping to the ground. Bones breaking.

But not just one or two people. It sounded like a full-on battle.

Cedar moved closer, pausing before turning sharply to the right, in the direction of the sound.

"Where are we goi—"

"The wind will conceal our scent, or most of it, but there is a stream over here that will help," she murmured, her eyes searching the dark forest for any sign of guards. Aurelia had mentioned the same thing. "The fight should keep them preoccupied. My guess is your time is up, hunter. The cavalry has arrived."

I was about to deny her claims when we pushed through a small section of the trees that opened into a clearing and saw not one, or two, or even five, but ten more of the people sent by my organization. They were a few yards away, but the light from above was enough to make out exactly what was happening.

They weren't hiding anything. Fully dressed in battle garments, their tattoos shining in the moonlight, they outnumbered the guards, but with their vampire abilities, they were evenly matched.

Cedar's hand was around my wrist, pulling me along the side. The secret path that only she could see was still unclear to me, but I followed her anyway.

It was too late to go back. There was nothing waiting for me at the palace other than death.

I needed to make it through. I didn't care if we had to walk for miles. If I had to fight my own people.

I was getting Aurelia out of here, even if it killed me.

"Halt!"

My blood froze at the yell. My body pushed me to obey it, but my mind told me to run. To keep going without looking back. So, I kept marching on.

Cedar did the same. She cast a glance behind us but kept her steady pace. As if us getting caught was nothing. Like the person following us was some sort of annoying salesperson you'd pass in the mall.

The sound of the river was faint, but it meant we were getting closer and closer to where we needed to be. If only we didn't have company.

Footsteps rushing toward us hit my ears. My grip on Aurelia tightened. My mind ran through scenario after scenario.

I would have to put her down to fight. Or maybe I could throw my sword at them. Talking was obviously out of the question.

They wouldn't take her. I wouldn't let them. But they were getting closer.

Fuck.

I tensed and turned. Two palace guards were making their way to us, weaving in and out of the trees. Their eyes were narrowed in our direction, and with one look at the body over my shoulder, they knew exactly what was happening.

My free hand reached for my sword.

"Let the princess go—"

Their shouts were cut off as bright, magical red ropes wrapped around them. They slithered up their bodies, tightening against their limbs and wrapping around their throats so hard they drew blood.

Cedar tried to pull me along, but I was too stunned.

Cedar hadn't done that.

Another person appeared from the tree line. A witch. One with bright pink hair and a shit-eating grin that showed her fangs.

"To think you actually made it out alive," she said with a laugh as she stalked toward our group. "The gods heard my prayer."

Levana. The witch that had helped me hide my tattoo the first time I came to the palace. The witch that had been helping me throughout the years despite knowing what I had done to vampires and witches alike.

I had never been so relieved to see a witch in my life.

"Not in the clear yet," Cedar said with a huff and yanked me forward. "Hurry up. We have people to meet."

***

I never knew the sheer amount of restraint it would take to let the witches look over Aurelia. They wanted to take her away from me. Somewhere where I couldn't see what they were doing. But Cedar saw the look in my eyes, and with an annoyed huff and a dismissive hand, she ordered them to finish what they needed to in my presence.

She ordered them.

The dynamic became clear as I sat next to Aurelia's unconscious body, two witches on either side of her, their hands glowing as they ran them over her wound and heart.

"It's not hurting her," Levana said as she sat on the ground next to me. "Our gods held compassion for the vampires when they infused us with magic. Healing won't hurt. Not if we don't want it to."

There it was again. The mention of their gods. The entire time I had been with Cedar, she hadn't mentioned them. Just like most witches, she kept her mouth shut about them.

Levana was given a hard look from a few of the witches in the room, which she ignored. Even with the hard feelings of betrayal growing inside me, her trust of me with this meant something.

Cedar, on the other hand...

The hardwood floor below us was already putting a strain on my back, but I was glad to be out of the forest. Even if it was a small single-room cabin that looked like it hadn't been updated since before my organization had been created.

The windows were boarded. The wood had been covered in dust before the witches did something about it. And there were only a few lamps placed throughout that provided very little light.

"She's the one who stabbed her. I think she's feeling worse about hurting her than the witches doing it," Cedar said, her arms crossed over her chest. She remained standing, her eyes digging into mine.

"I thought vampires were weakened by magic," I told Levana, ignoring Cedar completely. "I never really imagined they could be healed by it."

I felt betrayed by both of them, but more so by Cedar. What else had she been keeping from me?

She sent me a strained smile.

"Two things can be true at once."

"Like Vesper having some weird crush on the princess yet still digging her heart out—"

I shot up, lunging toward Cedar. "You were the one who told me I had to fulfill the pro—"

"You don't think I should have gotten a heads-up?" she asked with a raised brow. "You're lucky I was around, or the other hunters would have had you surrounded. Then you would have never gotten out."

The sureness in her voice caused me to freeze.

"You are a seer," I hissed.

"I told you; you don't have to be a seer to know—"

"About the prophecy?" I asked. "That was for the organization only. How did you even know about it? How did you know I was there? What the fuck is your goal?"

The other witches went silent, tension settling over us. It made the air thick. When it cracked, I realized Cedar's magic was spreading out from her. It washed over me with a cool feeling. I could feel...something connected to it. Like it was taking stock.

I had never experienced anything like it before.

Cedar looked me up and down, and a slow smirk spread across her face.

"What, you thought this prophecy shit was like a one-prophecy-per-seer thing?" she asked with a scoff. "Seers across the country, maybe even the world, know about this. It's up to them whether they want to keep their mouth shut or have a stake in the game. Evidently, we chose the latter."

My blood froze.

"Who are you exactly?"

Just as Cedar opened her mouth, a loud gasp came from Aurelia.

We all turned to her, but before I could even get a good look, I was knocked to the floor, my head bouncing so hard off the hardwood that spots covered my vision. Long, delicate fingers were wrapped around my neck with an unimaginable strength. Aurelia's red eyes dug into mine, her teeth bared. Fuck. I couldn't keep my eyes open. My consciousness was quickly fading.

But all I could think was how relieved I was to see her up again. Even if it made her hate me even more. Even if it made her resent me. I would gladly take the punishment if it meant she would live.

I was fucking screwed.

Aurelia

She was in my nightmares.
  With that cold look of hers and those gentle caresses. Bursts of fire lit under my skin where her fingers trailed.
She was confusing me. I had never seen her look so heartbroken before.
Maybe once I would have been happy to see the almighty vampire assassin brought down a peg, but her expression caused me more sorrow than glee.
It had been one of the only few times in my life I wanted to take away someone's pain. I didn't want her to hurt. I wanted my silver-haired vampire assassin back.
Until I felt the pain.
It started in my lower ribs and then extended straight through to my heart. It was blinding. Father would punish me. Hit me. Starve me, even. But nothing had ever felt like that.
Then the memories came back. Her tear-filled eyes as she looked at me. Her kiss as she stabbed me through the chest. Her whispered apologies.
But whatever was happening in my nightmares hurt far worse. It was like the wound was being torn open and burned with fire.
It was unbearable.

Made even more unbearable with Vesper's pity-filled face as she watched me like she hadn't been the one who had caused the pain in the first place.

Fucking vampire assassin. A fucking hunter if I ever saw one. How could she? How could she do this to me? I had been willing to do anything for her. To leave everything I knew. To risk my palace. My life. For her.

And she had fucking stabbed me in the chest as a reward.

Not just that; there was something tying us now.

I thrashed against the pain. Tried to fight my restraints as invisible forces held me down. Magic. I could smell it. I felt it crawling against my skin and invading my body. Tearing apart my atoms and putting them back together.

When my eyes opened, just like before, being pulled out of my unconscious state was painful and disorienting. But this time I was able to see around me. Hear the voice. Smell the witches. Sense Vesper.

Sense. I could sense her.

She wasn't far, but there was something else that hadn't been there before. Something that pushed through my veins and tied me intrinsically to the unashamed hunter.

Our hearts were yearning for each other. My body was begging me to get close to her.

We were one.

I became enraged when I realized what she had done.

How could she do this to me?

How could she just take it?

My body moved on its own. The room blurred around me as the invisible red string that tied us together pulled me forward like a steel cord. She was on the ground with me straddling her before she even knew what was happening.

I didn't think about her fragile human life, or how my claws wrapping around her neck could have ended it.

All I could see was red.

I wanted to hurt her. Wanted to make her pay for hurting me. But another part of me was sad, sad enough to doubt if I should have even been attacking her in the first place. My rage was stronger though.

But just as she was about to lose consciousness, a wave of pain ran through me, and I was forced to let go.

I shot a look at the source. Cedar. The fucking redheaded witch who couldn't keep her nose out of my business.

Her hand was out and glowing softly. Only then did I realize how unbearable the scent of magic was in the small room.

"Behave," she warned.

"Or what?" I hissed at her. "Do you know what she fucking did to me?"

Vesper was coughing below me, the sound of her lungs filling with air far more relieving than it should be.

"She tried to kill you, I know. I was there. But listen, there wasn't—"

"She blood-bonded me!" The words that left my mouth sounded downright hysterical.

A heavy silence fell over the room. Even Vesper's heart stopped for a bit.

"I didn't. I wouldn't. I—"

"You did." I looked back at her, seething. She met me with a wide-eyed stare that made the boiling rage inside me die down just a smidge. "Can you feel me? Can you feel the ties connecting us? Has it been hard to leave me? Hard not to touch me?"

Understanding flashed across her eyes, but there was still a healthy ounce of doubt in them.

"But that's not because of the bond. I didn't even know we—"

"You," I corrected. "I would have never agreed to it. This will tie us together for eternity; did you know that?"

"A few months at most," Cedar interrupted with a huff. "I know you're angry, but don't scare her—"

"Don't scare her?" I asked with a laugh. "Blood bonds are serious. It's how people like my father keep a tight leash on their families. And the worst part? It will always feel stronger for me. Humans are too weak to experience the full effects of it."

Cedar's eyes shifted to Vesper, who still hadn't moved from under me.

"Rumors say that a blood bond may last longer than a few months, but you have to redo it every so often for it to remain strong. It's likely that it will fade away if you don't nurture it."

I looked down at Vesper. Her face was unreadable. Then, finally, she said the words I never expected to hear.

"I'm not like him," she whispered, her gaze meeting mine. It was so sharp, so serious, that I was pinned by it. "I never meant to do that against your will. I can't take it back, but know that I regret hurting you that way. I'm sorry."

Listening to her was like being doused with ice-cold water.

How could I be angry at a statement like that?

How did she know so easily why I was upset about the blood bond?

It was sacred to vampires. Cedar was right—it would fade—but I never wanted to blood-bond unless it was for love. If that was ever in the cards for me.

It was too intimate. Too powerful.

Many of the corrupt leaders, like my father, used it to control people. But Mother had taught me differently.

It was meant to be Krae's gift to us. The gift of a love no other species could feel.

Even as I sat on Vesper, my hands around her throat and about to take her life, I could feel it thrumming through us. It was glad that we were close. It wanted us even closer.

I was still hurting with a dull kind of pain that spread throughout my body. But it was less painful with her.

Which is why I had never wanted a blood bond.

I didn't want to be tied to anyone. I wanted to be my own person, never having to worry about another being beside myself. Yet even before the blood bond, I had been worried about her.

When I saw the way Father beheaded the assassins with the snake tattoos, I saw her face instead of theirs.

It was what had made me want to run away.

While I was lost in thought, a warm metal chain was slapped on my ankle. Magic vibrated against my skin, but it wasn't enough to pain me.

I hissed and looked back at the witches suddenly inside the room with us, but they averted their gaze.

Except one. A younger witch with bright pink hair. She didn't look away. She met my glare head-on with a fierceness that annoyed the living hell out of me.

But there was something different about her. The way she smelled...

Was she some type of witch hybrid?

"Are we done with this?" *she asked and cocked her head to the side.*

"Who the fuck are—"

"She's a friend," *Cedar answered.* "And an important part of the coven that is so graciously allowing you and Vesper to stay."

I didn't pay her any mind, too annoyed with the pink-haired hybrid. I could rip her head off, I was yearning to, but she didn't look scared at all.

"After the probation period," *she said with a smile, fangs glinting in the dim light. Vampire-witch hybrid. Not something you see every day.* "Which has been extended to two months thanks to your tantrum."

"Tantrum?" *I echoed and pushed off Vesper.* "I was fucking stabbed and taken against my will. I don't even know where the fuck we are or trust any of you witches. Where do you get off? I'll show you a fucking tantrum—"

Vesper's hands were on my shoulders in seconds, keeping me in place.

"She's half vampire," *she whispered, her voice scratchy from my assault.* "Be careful. Not only that—we also need them."

Something prickled at my senses.

"How do you know that?"

The pink-haired vampire let out a huff.

"Remember your place. She just saved you from another—"

I lunged forward, wrapping my hand in her shirt and baring my teeth.

"You're getting on my fucking nerves," *I growled.* "I don't need you. I need to get the fuck out of here—"

"There is nowhere to run, Princess," Cedar said from behind me. I turned and hissed at her.

"Don't call me that."

She merely raised a brow at me.

Vesper stepped forward with her hands up. "Let's talk about this. Please. It's truly just so we can be safe."

"You should listen to her before getting your panties in a twist—"

I turned on her, my fist smashing into her face before the witches had a chance to stop me.

"Not so fucking strong for a vampire-witch mutt now, are we?"

My entire body seized as I was hit by a blast of magic. And I knew the scent of it.

Cedar. There was something so potent about her magic, unlike anything I had ever felt before. It attacked every cell in my body. Boiled my blood. Stopped the inner workings of my brain.

My vision went black.

I could hear Vesper's screams, but the longer they went on, the more muffled they became.

Until I was sent back to my world of nightmares.

Vesper

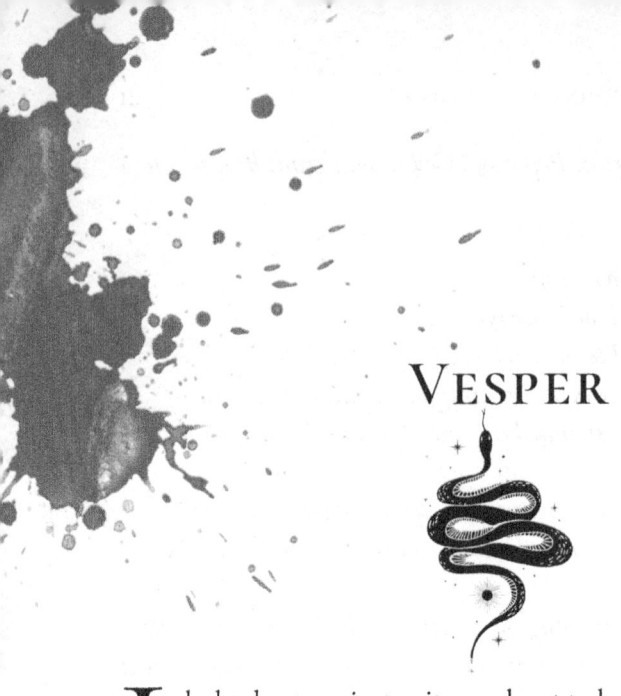

I dodged a stone just as it was about to lodge itself into my skull. It flew past me and out into the yard of the cabin, crashing to the ground with a thud.

I gave the culprit a look, but all it did was earn me another stone thrown my way.

"You're late!"

I didn't blame her for being mad. I *was* late, if only for a few minutes. But if I were in her position, I wouldn't be too understanding either.

Aurelia stood toward the far end of the room, her hair a mess from her constantly running her hands through it. She wore a simple red dress, but that too was torn at the ends. I had caught her trying to rip the seams on multiple occasions, though I never knew what she planned to do with them.

Since we'd arrived at the small one-bedroom cottage, her face held a permanent look of distaste. She had every right to be angry; I did stab her in the heart after all.

But what hurt me the most was seeing the magical chain wrapped around her wrists and ankles.

It extended enough for her to walk around the room, but often she just stayed in her little corner until it was time to feed, glaring at me whenever she got the chance.

The only time she dropped the anger was once she was done feeding. She would make sure to humiliate me. Force me to submit. She took pleasure in it, and due to the overwhelming guilt eating me alive, I never stopped her.

At least I could give her that much.

"Your father sent four more crazed," I explained, shooting a look at the open door where Cedar held my blood-stained weapons. She looked at us with an amused smirk.

"He'll get in sooner or later," she said with a frown.

"He won't," Cedar replied from the doorway. "Though he is getting anxious. And the more he sends, the less the others want to let you—"

"And that's my fault?" She bared her teeth and tried to step forward, but her chains wouldn't allow it. "What about the fucking human mercenaries? They're also coming after us, but I don't see you locking up Vesper!"

A stillness fell over the group, and Aurelia's reddened eyes flashed blue before they met mine.

"Still?" she asked, her voice softer.

I pushed my lips into a thin line, unsure how I wanted to answer.

Still meant that, while he had a good idea of what happened, the king hadn't told the world. He kept it a dirty little secret that his daughter had been taken. He'd rather have people think she was dead than believe someone got a one-up on him.

Instead of raging or calling all the forces he could muster to save his daughter, he quietly sent them after us.

Sending the crazed was different. There was no way they'd be able to take her back with them, so what he was really after was obvious.

Revenge. Showing up whoever decided to take her.

Something else wasn't that obvious, though.

He wasn't trying to rescue her. This was nothing more than damage control.

And no matter what Aurelia's father had been like, she seemed to still have hope he would act like a decent being and not the cruel vampire she knew him to be.

"Seems like maybe Daddy's motives aren't so clear after all, huh?" Cedar's words hit Aurelia right where it hurt. I didn't need the watered-down bond to tell me anything. It was written all over her face.

"Leave us," I snapped at Cedar.

She sent me a look, her face dropping slightly. Almost as if she *regretted* those words. But I doubted it.

She concealed it quickly by letting out a huff before closing the door. It was only seconds before Aurelia was in front of me, her hands on my shoulders, pushing me to sit on the ground.

Her expression was complicated and hard to dissect, but I could see the hurt in it. I immediately felt guilty.

Even if I had been out to take care of the vampires her *father* sent, I had still been out. Aurelia hadn't so much as been able to open a window without a witch in her face, watching her every move.

She was a prisoner here.

I imprisoned her after I ripped apart her heart.

After she had given in to me so fully. So trusting.

I shifted so she could straddle me. When my heart skipped a beat and heat ran through me, I didn't try to hide it. Didn't try to deny how even the simplest of Aurelia's touches made me feel.

I had given it all up for her. My legacy. My family. My whole life up until then had revolved around killing people just like her. But *for* her, I changed our path. *For better or worse.* There was nothing left to hide.

"They're stupid if they think a bit of blood and a missing body mean I'm dead. How can they be so gullible?" she muttered under her breath. Her eyes reached mine before her hand tilted my face not so gently to the side. "You smell."

They weren't looking for me. Not yet at least. They had taken the bait perfectly, and since the king had decided to keep his plans to get Aurelia back hidden, there was no way the secret organization my family was a part of would know anything other than what the spies in the palace reported back.

That the princess is dead and the hunter is nowhere to be found.

In the meantime, her father kept trying to find us. He wasn't as believing as the organization I came from, but how he was still keeping it hidden from the spies in the palace was somewhat of a mystery.

"Vampire blood will do that to you."

The quirk of her lips caused my heart to skip another beat. But she didn't sink her teeth into me—not yet.

She was teasing me. Asserting the only control she had. She was a prisoner, but when we were alone, she could do whatever she wanted to me, and I'd gladly take it.

She could tear into my skin. Drain the blood from my body. Make me cry. Make me beg. None of it would change how I felt about her or what I owed her.

She leaned forward, her lips centimeters from mine, and I couldn't stop myself from trying to meet them, even though I knew she would pull away with a smirk like she always did.

She was taking advantage of the small bit of bond that was left in us. It pushed me to keep going. To please her. To strengthen it.

But she wasn't letting me. She wanted to watch me yearn for her.

Ruthless.

I winced as she dug her teeth into my neck, her fangs slicing through my skin like a knife through butter. Some days, I barely registered the pain. Others, it seemed like the ultimate punishment. A burning reminder of her true nature and her feelings toward me.

My hands gripped her hips to steady myself.

"He doesn't want to admit he failed," I said through gritted teeth. The venom was working its way through my system, but it was too slow for her ravenous gulps of blood. "They will find out sooner or later."

She didn't answer me, but she did slow down her pace. I wrapped my arms around her and inhaled her scent. She let me. She was letting me touch her.

Boldly, I ran my hand down her back, then up again. A comforting gesture I once used on Tate when he was a child so focused on throwing a tantrum that he forgot to breathe.

She felt much like that—crazed, unable to think of anything else but how unfair the world was—and took it out on me. Drinking to forget. Drinking so viciously, my head started spinning as blood ran down my neck.

I once felt as though she was treating me like a lover when her fangs tore through my skin. She would caress me. Take care of me. Make me feel good.

But at times like these, I felt more like an object again.

I guessed it was a way to put space between us, but I wasn't the only one affected by the bond.

Her drinking slowed. She leaned against me, resting her body weight on me, and inhaled deeply through her nose. She became calmer, her grip loosening and her jaw unclenching just enough to give me some relief while still allowing her to drink.

That's it. That's my princess. Words I wanted to say aloud, but I buried them because I knew it would only ruin whatever little moment was happening between us.

But it couldn't stay like that between us for long. The universe didn't want us comfortable together. It wanted violence. It wanted hate.

And it would do anything in its power to remind us of that.

Aurelia

I knew she had been out on patrol. Patrols were part of the terms for staying in the safe house. They obviously didn't trust me to handle them, so Vesper was constantly out.

Every day. Every single fucking day. Mostly early in the morning, I heard her leave with an assigned guard and walk outside, probably checking the perimeter. This happened over and over again.

She was either with the pink-haired witch, Levana, or the redheaded one, Cedar. They all seemed so chummy, bonding over killing the crazed vampires my father was sending after me.

Which Vesper killed. Over and over.

She looked tired. But I didn't care.

I couldn't care.

I heard her take a deep breath before walking into the room I was being held in. She knocked quickly, even though she didn't have to.

My first reaction was to bare my fangs.

"For you," she said, offering me a small, delicate bird in her hand. It looked at me with curious eyes, its black orbs trained on me as if it could see into my soul. The feathers were dark brown with a white underbelly. "I know how much you loved animals, so I thought—"

"Thought you'd let me decorate my cage a little?" The spite in my voice was strong, and even though I shouldn't care, I could feel her disappointment.

"I'm still here too," she reminded me. "I just thought it would be a nice present."

"A nice present would be getting the fuck out of here," I spat back.

"I can't do anything—"

"No, you can't," I hissed. "You can stab me in the fucking heart. You can go out every night on patrol. You can flirt with the witches. But you can't do the one thing that would make me happy."

She had no answer for that. She looked stuck, mouth open, bird in hand, with no idea how to proceed.

"It reminded me of your hair color. And how upset you were when yours died."

I had hidden the bird feather necklace she had given me. I knew she noticed it. I didn't care.

I was hurt. I didn't trust her. I couldn't.

"Did I come at a bad time?" The suddenness of Cedar's voice as she just barged in had me glaring at her. Anger took over me. Even more when Vesper looked...relieved to see her?

They were all liars. They were all keeping me here.

I huffed, annoyed.

"You and your fucking witches," I said and slammed the door, but not before grabbing the bird out of her hand.

※

I listened and waited for Cedar and Vesper to start talking.

"It's getting worse," Vesper whispered. "We need a plan. The vampires will be too overwhelming soon."

"Can't handle it, hunter?" The flirtation in the witch's voice had me frowning, but not as much as Vesper's heart. It gave the slightest little skip both then and when she first saw her.

Not just Vesper's; Cedar's as well.

Both of them were so excited yet so nervous to see each other it was ridiculous.

Their faces didn't show it, but their hearts were in sync. Both reaching out, eager to feel the other but neither willing to make the first move.

Every shift forward Cedar took had Vesper taking one back. One heart would race, the other would skip, intertwining in a complicated waltz.

Neither was willing to admit it out loud, though.

A heavy feeling fell over me.

Not only would this complicate things...it would be dangerous. Vesper and I were the bonded ones and tying both of us to a witch we couldn't trust was a sure way to get us killed.

Multiperson bonds weren't very common, especially in the romantic sense. Most of the time, they were useful for people like my father. To control those who took it.

But it could be done.

Bitterness exploded across my tongue. Vesper shifted outside the door, likely feeling just how enraged I was at them together even through the dulled bond.

The urge to go out there and tear her from the witch came over me. *She's mine. My little mouse. My hunter.*

Even if she tried to kill me. Even if I was still pissed.

"I'm skilled, but not against six of them," she growled. "Especially when you send those useless guards with me."

Cedar let out a warm chuckle. "Come on," she said. "I don't like being spied on."

I heard her footsteps walking away, Vesper's shortly after.

Damn it. They left the house and went out back, far enough away for me not to hear them.

The bird let out a small chirp, calling my attention to it.

Did she think I was some lovestruck idiot now that we were bonded?

I looked at the poor thing in my hands. It was nothing like the beautiful one I kept before. The one with its wings clipped. The one in the *gilded cage that was forced to stay by my side until the step bastards cruelly murdered it.*

I should do that to this one. If not to send a message, then to just get the damned thing out of my sight.

I had removed the necklace Vesper had made from the other bird's feather long ago. I wanted to throw it away or destroy it.

But I couldn't bring myself to.

So I wrapped it around my ankle so that she wouldn't see how weak I still was for her.

But another one? A living creature? One that is utterly common and not at all a gift worthy of my stature?

I was a princess, for Krae's sake. This was an insult really. Boys growing up who'd hoped to gain my favor had been better at giving gifts than she was.

It was inexpressive besides the back-and-forth movement of its eyes as it looked me over. It was a bit standoffish, wings spreading as it steadied itself. For some reason, I had a feeling it liked Vesper more.

"*She gave you up, you know?*" *I taunted.*

The bird tilted its head to the side and folded its wings back in.

"*I should kill you.*"

No response. With a grumble under my breath, I got up and opened the window to the room.

The magical chain around my ankle stopped me from going too far, but it was enough for me to place the bird on the sill.

I couldn't bring myself to throw it out even though I knew it could fly.

It was a stupid gift.

But it still made my heart pound. Made my skin heat.

I could feel the emotions through the bond, even if they were dwindling every day since we arrived here.

She had been hurt at my reaction.

I wondered just how much humans felt through the bond. If she could feel that, even though I had implied that I hated the gift, inside, I actually...

"Get out of here," I growled at the bird. It turned around, its black, soulless eyes narrowing on me.

My hands gripped the sill on either side of it. My nails dug into the wood, splintering it.

But the bird was like Vesper in the way that it wasn't at all scared of me. It watched me curiously like she did at times. There was something going on in its brain, but just like the vampire hunter, I couldn't figure it out.

Emotions leaked through the bond, telling me that even though she was disappointed by my reaction, the conversation between her and the witch was going well.

Jealousy burned inside me.

When had she become so buddy-buddy with all the fucking witches?

I had heard her and the pink-haired witch talking. I hated whenever they interacted, mostly because I hated that specific witch with a burning passion.

She was my official babysitter when Cedar was off doing god knows what.

It had been a whole fucking month. A whole goddamned month that I had been stuck in this rotting wood cabin.

I hated every moment of it.

I had traded one cage for another, and there was really no telling if it was worth all the trouble.

Vesper had saved me from being married off, but only causing more trouble than I ever imagined.

Was she worth it? Was the bond?

My hand came up to my chest.

Sometimes the scar where her sword had pierced my skin still ached. Phantom pains, shooting out and down my body as a reminder of what she had done.

And the dreams. I was still haunted by them. The memories of them, at least.

There was nothing to do inside this room besides stare at the fucking walls, so I had no choice but to remember. Over and over again. Each day was the same.

I was going to lose my mind in here.

I thought of cutting her loose. Of leaving the coven—and her—behind. But that caused an even more distressing emotion to rise in me. One I violently pushed back into its cage at the recesses of my mind.

No fucking time for that.

A knock at the door jolted me from my musings and had the bird finally flying out the window.

I felt Vesper on the other side. Something similar to dread was filtering through the bond.

And suddenly I wanted to play with her.

I quickly brought my wrist to my mouth and used my fangs to tear up the skin, quickly smearing the blood across my hands and face before turning to the door just as it opened.

I took in her appearance. Her silver hair had grown longer in the month we'd been here and was just disheveled from the patrol she'd just come back from. The dark circles under her eyes seemed permanent, and she had lost weight. She might have been a worker at the palace, but we fed her well. The same couldn't be said for the witches.

She thought they were our saving grace, but they barely gave her the time of day. If there was one thing I liked better than having things go my way, it was being proven right.

Witches were on my do-not-fuck-with list, and she was slowly learning why.

And then I saw the look in her eyes when she saw me.

"What did you do?" she asked with a sigh.

Her body sagged forward, like my actions were just another stone on top of the weight she was carrying. But regardless of her appearance or how much I was pissed at her, my stomach still did strange things when she was near.

My body yearned to be close to her. To feel her warmth. Smell the blood just under her skin. I hated how much I still wanted her. She was a weakness.

But I still took in a silent, deep breath just to indulge in her scent.

"Thanks for the treat," I said and licked my blood off my fingers.

"You could've just let me know you were hungry," she replied, a frown marring her face.

I gave her a smirk. "What's the fun in that?" I almost regretted it as her face dropped, even if I knew keeping her at arm's length was the right thing to do.

I hated how awful it felt when her emotions rushed through the bond. How much I wanted to take back my words.

It should have been easy to talk to Vesper this way. To rebuild the wall between us that should have been there from the start.

But it was damn hard.

And in truth, no fun.

I could terrorize her. Bend her to my will. Feed on her. Fuck her. Make her beg for me. But there wouldn't be any fun until I was out of the cabin and of this fucking hellhole.

We both knew it, and anything she did up until then was just a Band-Aid put on the gaping wound that she ripped through my chest with her own sword.

Vesper

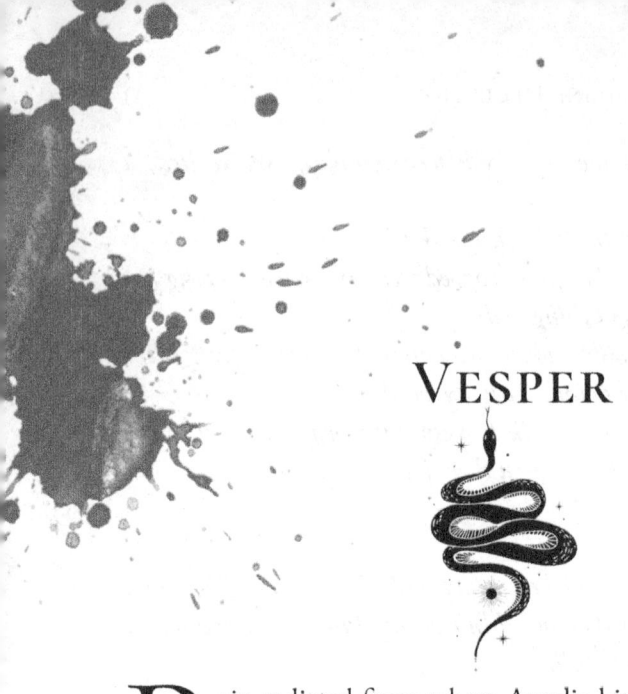

Pain radiated from where Aurelia bit me, shooting down my arm. Each moment took more and more out of me, leaving me breathless.

I am getting weak.

In her rush to finally be out of the safe house, she had forgotten all about coating it with her venom. I didn't care for how it made me feel. I had gotten over being her fuck toy a long time ago.

I just wanted it for the healing properties.

It was one of the perks of being a vampire and how they kept their victims more or less...well, *alive*. It didn't fare well for humans if they risked actually dying each time a vampire fed on them.

This way the vampire could keep them for longer and the human had a better experience overall—the universe's fucked-up way of making it so humans were at the mercy of vampires.

You're not complaining, a little voice whispered in my head. *You quite like it when Aurelia sinks her fangs into you.*

The voice was annoying. *And right.*

I could suck up the less-than-ideal side effects if it meant making her happy. It was just a moment. One where she would lean into me, let me wrap my arms around her...When the world would fall away and it was just the two of us again.

For that, I would take it. But even with my hardened resolve, each step on the uneven ground caused more and more pain to shoot up to my head.

I was lagging behind them. My excuse was that I was covering the back, but the fight from earlier in the day combined with the blood lost left me almost completely drained.

Hold on just a bit longer.

Aurelia hadn't been the only one held up in that safe house. *Four months.* Thanks to her tantrum when she first woke up.

Witches weren't trustworthy, regardless of my previous relationship with Levana. Though her crassness toward the princess didn't sit right with me either. I expected her to at least give the vampire a chance. I had never seen her act so rudely to another being.

Maybe I was missing something, but every time I saw her, I hesitated. *Should I ask her? Should I leave it?* At the end of the day, I was mad too.

"Just a few more feet," Cedar called from up front. She was wearing an all-black outfit, a loose shirt and pants with something akin to a cloak over her shoulders with slits in it for her arms. There was embroidery on the two front pieces and across the back hem in gold thread. It looked like some type of language, but nothing I'd seen before. Something that had me suspicious the first time I saw it.

She usually wore a variation of the same outfit—a loose shirt and jeans. Sometimes I saw a crewneck. Other times, when she joined a hunt, combat-ready pants but never anything...*like that.*

Aurelia perked up at her words, her blue eyes widening and a smile spreading across her face. She still wore the red dress the witches gave her, and it flowed behind her as she picked up her pace, getting closer to the redheaded witch.

My heart skipped a beat at the sight.

But the closer we got, the more confused I was.

There was nothing in front of us except for dense forest. We had been walking in an incline for what felt like miles, but there was nothing in sight, just the fresh breeze, the sounds of animals scurrying as we passed, and the sound of my own labored breathing.

"I didn't realize we were so close to the coven," I muttered, slowing my movements.

Cedar looked back at me with a smirk. The mischief that once seemed to be a permanent addition to her facial expression back in the palace was back.

I missed that look.

The thought surprised me and had me freeze completely. There was no reason to miss the witch. It's not like we were friends.

But even the thoughts had a bitterness laced in them.

She took one more step before her body completely disappeared from view.

Aurelia came to a halt.

"What the hell?"

Even through my tiredness, I smiled. I could play along too.

"Not something you see every day, huh, Princess?" I passed her, grabbing her wrist and pulling her forward.

She huffed but didn't correct my usage of the title.

I had seen the magic witches used to keep people out of their covens, but never one so advanced. Most would make you confused and make you turn around, but this one had a full-on cloak.

The magic let us pass, its heat cascading over my body as we entered.

There was no forest behind the curtain. It was an entire city, and we were right in the middle of it.

Cobblestone was lined beneath our feet. The strong smell of magic and herbs surrounded us. Buildings were erected all up and down the street with the same dark-colored brick and vines winding up the walls and through the cracks. Every now and then, a colorful flower bloomed.

The windows were high and mostly curved, giving us an easy view into the shops. Some type of language I couldn't recognize was carved into the stones of stores and walkways. I stopped to look at them.

Just how much are the witches hiding from us?

But the odd thing was...there was not a soul around.

"I guess I'm not the only one that's seeing something for the first time," Aurelia said, pulling her hand from mine as she moved toward Cedar, waiting for us up front, a small prideful smile on her face.

I had never seen a coven so isolated before. It looked otherworldly and nothing like what I thought I knew about witches.

Have they always been hiding in places like these? Is this the coven Cedar and Levana come from? If so, what the fuck are the other witches?

Seeing the hidden town made me realize how little I knew about them. About where they resided. How they lived their lives. After four months, I didn't even have an ounce of knowledge of where their power came from or how they formed their covens.

"Come on. If the high priest accepts you, you'll have all the time in the world to explore."

High priest?

I had never heard that position before.

"I thought I was in the clear?" Aurelia asked.

I hesitantly followed them, my eyes scanning every single surface as we walked through the empty downtown. It wasn't likely that there was no one inhabiting the town; it looked well-kept, and the shops were overflowing with goods ranging from books to herbs to dried meats.

My steps faltered when I saw two pairs of eyes peeking out from a bush. They were green just like Cedar's. Small. *Children.* When I caught their gaze, they disappeared in a small ripple.

Are the children in this coven this powerful?

It made me uneasy about what the hell I had forced us into.

But they were hiding. Which meant they were scared of *us*.

My eyes shifted to Aurelia and Cedar, getting further and further away in my distraction.

Her.

They were afraid of the random vampire that we brought into their homes.

I couldn't blame them.

Aurelia

High priest. And I thought the vampires were the extravagant ones. Even with just the little glimpse I was getting into the witch coven, I had a feeling that they too had a thing for flair. Or at least they used it as a way to control their witches.

The trail through the ghost town ended at a gothic cathedral covered in vines and foliage.

Vampires and witches had their own gods, but while we had a single deity—one who had made vampires who they were—witches had a bunch of made-up gods and goddesses they prayed to and worshipped for their powers.

At least that's what I gathered from the rumors.

They were even more elusive than the most powerful vampires. For some reason, they thought they needed to protect themselves. Or maybe it was just a show of how much better than the rest of the population they thought they were.

Either way, it left anyone facing them at a huge disadvantage.

That meant that going to see something so powerful to their coven wasn't sitting well with me. The structure looked powerful, so what did it say for the people inside?

I was no witch, but I could feel magic radiating off the place.

And it fucking reeked of it.

If witches smelled like burning trees, then this building smelled like a fucking forest fire mixed with an abundance of herbs that had me plugging my nose. But after a quick jab from Vesper, I moved my fingers away with a scowl.

When my eyes searched her frame, I realized I hadn't healed the bite on her neck. Reaching for her, I caught a few drops on my thumb and spread her blood across my lips, trying to at least dampen the smells around us.

Cedar's scoff had me growling at her.

"Can you have a bit more decorum?" she asked.

Annoying witch thinking she can tell me what to do with my bonded.

Because as much as I hated to admit it, Vesper was mine. And if Cedar even so much as forgot it, I'd rip her fucking throat out. Magic be damned.

Maybe I'll make her watch as I take what she can't have.

Now *that* was a sinful thought so sweet I had to control myself so I wouldn't show my hand.

"A scary vampire like me?" I replied, giving her a smirk. "Evidently not."

Vesper walked forward with a huff.

"Let's get this over with," Vesper said, her eyes on me. "We need them."

We need them? I wanted to laugh. *Maybe we wouldn't need them if you hadn't stabbed me in the fucking heart.*

But even as the bitter words ran through my mind, I realized that the anger I was feeling was barely a spark of what it should be. I blamed the bond for making me go soft on the hunter. Or maybe it was the excitement from actually getting out of the fucked-up safe house.

I thanked Krae for helping me make it out of there alive. One or two more days, and I would surely have pissed off the witches again somehow.

I didn't like to praise the witches, especially since their kind was known for hating mine for hundreds of years, but the way they'd hidden this city was an incredible feat of magic that I'd never seen before.

I could give credit when credit was due. *But I sure as hell won't utter a word of it.* Especially not at the risk of having it go to Cedar's already too-big head.

Vesper held my gaze for a moment in warning before walking to Cedar. But instead of leading us inside, the witch stopped her with one hand on her shoulder and the other on her neck.

My hackles raised when Cedar's hand lit up and the smell of magic cut through the air.

"Poor hunter; your vampire left you bleeding. Maybe you should get one that treats you better," Cedar murmured, her eyes on Vesper before moving to me.

She's taunting me.

So the witch wanted to fight. That was fine by me. All the fucking nice things I thought about the coven were already forgotten.

It's time to teach her a lesson.

I took a step forward, ready to tackle the witch, knowing that would get me locked up in the cabin again but not giving a shit, when the doors of the cathedral opened and the pink-haired one made an appearance.

I should have stayed in that prison. At least then I wouldn't have to deal with her.

She glared at us, obviously showing just how unwelcome we were even after my punishment had ended.

"They're waiting." Her voice carried over the space between us.

Cedar's face shifted, and then, without another word, she led us to the front entrance. Vesper didn't hesitate to follow her this time, and like a good little prisoner, so did I.

The interior was vast, but there were no chairs or pews for people to sit and worship like in a normal human cathedral. It was all empty except for a group of four standing on the stairs leading up to the altar. They were dressed in the same black robes as Cedar.

Behind them, statues were carved into the walls. There was an overwhelming smell and power to them. The eyes were carved from stone, but they glowed softly with magic. Many were smiling, probably supposed to look soft and caring, but they creeped the hell out of me.

They are looking right at us.

That caused the hair on the back of my neck to raise.

The urge to flee was strong. It held my body captive and made my movements jerky.

I looked at Vesper to see if she was feeling the same, and based on how pale she had gotten, it was safe to say that I wasn't the only one affected by the weird statues.

Cedar walked forward with a powerful stride, her eyes on the person in the middle. He looked younger than I assumed a high priest would be, maybe in his mid to late thirties, wearing an all-white robe that seemed to be embroidered with patterns of leaves and plants.

His hair was a wild red, not unsimilar to Cedar's, and his face was scarred. His eyes were a stark light blue, and they homed in on Cedar as she approached.

Is he blind?

Despite his eye color, he didn't seem to be, especially when his eyes followed Cedar as she knelt before him.

The three other figures behind him seemed to be watching. *Guards? Right hands?*

Vesper gripped my arm and pulled me forward to do the same as Cedar.

I let out a growl. I could feel her pleading through the bond, but it wasn't enough to sway me.

"I don't bow to wit—"

His eyes shot to mine.

"Princess Aurelia." The priest's words came out like a purr. "What a pleasure to finally meet you. I've heard a lot about you."

I hate him. The gross feeling washing over my skin at his voice told me that automatically disliking him was probably the correct option.

What the hell are they doing in a place like this?

"No doubt from those who'd wish me dead," I said, my eyes pointedly going to the pink-haired witch now standing beside him.

I could see two more witches now, both in smoke gray robes, their faces hidden. The pink-haired one was the only one showing her face.

"That's an understatement," she muttered, then froze. I didn't catch whatever happened between her and the priest, but his eyes shot to her for a split second before coming back to land on us. No, on *Vesper*.

"The legend," he said. "The one who is set to end one of the vilest vampire families out there. I've heard your future, hunter. We are delighted to have you walk our halls."

Vesper's back stiffened.

"You're the seer?"

"In due time," he replied. "I'm the coven leader. Reid. You may call me such."

I don't like this guy. Not one fucking bit.

"How long have you been planting people in my life?" Vesper asked, her words cutting through the pleasantries.

Pride spread through my chest, especially when Cedar gave her a panicked look. *That's right. Show the witches they can't control us.*

"We will get to that later," he said with a smile. "First, let's talk about the conditions of your release. Obviously, we can't protect you here without getting anything in return."

"I never—"

"They understand," Cedar said, cutting me off. "Please continue with the requirements."

Reid's lips twisted into a grotesque type of smile.

"We protect the area and the surrounding covens," he explained. "We go out and take care of...troublesome vampires—hunters too, but it's more the former. There has been an uptick in *issues*, so having a vampire and a hunter on the team to dispose of those would be rather helpful. Go on these missions, and we will give you room, board, and safety as long as you complete the missions and stay within the barrier walls. If you choose to leave the safety of our coven—"

"I don't work," I hissed out, meeting the priest's gaze head-on.

He tilted his head, the smile never disappearing. An eerie chill passed through the cathedral.

"A princess who doesn't work; who would have guessed?" Pinkie teased.

I'll kill this fucking witch the first chance I get.

"Then you can leave," he said. "Vesper, on the other hand—"

"She will do it," Vesper answered on my behalf. "I will convince her."

I couldn't help but snort.

"How about a trial mission first?" Cedar offered. "Not only for the princess to see exactly what these missions entail, but we can also use it as a test. Nothing good will come from putting them on missions if they suck."

Excuse me?

Anger was boiling under my skin. The slight was too much for me to take. I stood taller, baring my teeth at the group in front of me.

"You really think I'll just sit here while you—"

The doors to the cathedral opened, drawing our focus. A tall man with bright silver hair and a snake tattoo on his neck walked in, dressed in black with weapons strapped to his thighs.

He looked familiar, but even without knowing exactly who he was, the resemblance was undeniable.

"Gabriel..." Vesper breathed.

My gaze shot back to the priest, that smile still on his face. *How long have you been planting people in my life?* Vesper has asked. And she had been right.

I might have been the target of the prophecy, but Vesper's life had been molded to fit it. People everywhere had been watching her. The witches. Her own people.

And now her brother?

None of this was right.

It felt like Vesper had these carefully placed enemies all around her, waiting for her to turn her back. It had me baring my teeth. My hands itched to grab her and her brother and run. Back to the city. To the fucking vampires.

I didn't care. It was just all too fucking...wrong.

Especially that weird-as-fuck priest with the smiling statues behind him.

Vesper

It was like seeing a ghost.

It had been years since I'd seen Gabriel, and most of what I remembered about him was the immense void he left when he went off to do whatever it was he was doing.

The adult version of him was a mystery. But my memories of him—the younger, kinder version—were warm. He was trustworthy. He was someone who had tried to protect me. Tried to reason with our parents.

I had put him on a pedestal. But as soon as he walked through those doors, the perfect image of him started to crack. The rose-colored glasses shattered, and I fell back to earth with enough force to destroy every warm memory between us.

I had trusted him with Tate. So, how was he here? Why was he here? Better yet, how did he know I was here?

"About fucking time," Cedar whispered under her breath.

"Way to make an entrance," Levana commented.

My eyes drifted from Gabriel to the others and then to the high priest. No one even flinched at his entrance.

They were expecting him. They know him.

"Gabriel has been working with us for some time now," the priest said, his voice cutting through the tense silence. "I thought it might make for an easier transition if you learned from someone you knew."

When the priest's eyes met mine, we shared a thought. An acknowledgment. It was in the slightest twist of his lips—an answer to the question that had been plaguing my mind.

I was lied to. Again.

They had plotted my life, my future, all behind my back. Everyone knew what was going on—except me.

I could feel Cedar's gaze on me. Memories of our time back at the palace flashed through my mind. How she had helped facilitate the handover of Tate.

I remembered her words.

I saw him meet with Gabriel. Or at least I think it was him. Same hair as you with the snake tattoo. Not many people out there look like that on purpose.

It hadn't been that long ago, so they had to have been working together even before then. Why hadn't she told me? She had stood there, looked me straight in the eyes, and pretended like she didn't know him.

I couldn't look at her now, so I chose to turn my gaze back to Gabriel instead.

He had grown more rugged since I last saw him. His once clean face had a slight stubble. His hair was shaggy. His clothes had some obvious wear and tear from the battles he'd been through.

"Where's Tate?" I all but growled.

I entrusted him with *one* thing—the safety of our younger brother. I thought that with him, at least he wouldn't be at the mercy of our parents. He wouldn't have to be groomed to be an assassin meant to carry out the plan *I* failed.

I had wanted him as far away from this mess as possible. Away from the Castle family. Away from the witches. Just *away*. Far enough that he could live whatever life he wanted.

If that ended up being something to do with vampires and witches, then so be it. But I wanted it to be his choice.

If Gabriel had brought him to the coven, right in the middle of the prophecy, he had destroyed that future.

My heart broke for the young boy. My chest puffed. My hands clenched.

I felt something faint race through the dull blood bond between Aurelia and me. Suspicion, maybe? Had she felt what I felt?

It would have made me feel a bit better, a little less alone, if I hadn't been so fucking angry.

Gabriel's expression faltered before he answered, "Close. You can see him—"

"This was *not* what I had in mind when I sent him to you. You were supposed to keep him safe," I hissed, standing straight so I could stalk closer to him.

"Ves—"

Cedar attempted to reach out and grab my hand, but I jerked it away as if her touch burned and sent her a glare. Her face crumpled before she schooled her expression.

But of course, the vampire saw it.

"Oh, do tell... How does it feel to be cast aside, witch?" Aurelia snarked.

Maybe I should have cared about whatever kind of face-off was happening between them; maybe I should have been happy that Aurelia seemed jealous. But all I could see was red. All I could feel was anger. *No.* Anger was the reaction, something to disguise the real emotion hidden underneath.

Fear.

I feared for us. Feared for what it meant that everyone around me had their own secrets.

Everyone I knew had been connected. Had been working together. Just like the secret organization ran my family, the coven had been doing something similar.

Except I still had no idea how far the web of lies went.

"Are you stupid?" I hissed. "How could you think *this* was the safest place for a child? I gave him to you for safekeeping because I wanted him *away* from all this. What else have you been hiding from me?"

Gabriel went pale.

"I think it's better if we talk about this alone," he said, his eyes shifting back to the crowd behind me. "I can explain."

"No need for any more secrets," Aurelia called. "Just come out with it, why don't you?"

I didn't know what Gabriel would think of Aurelia, but his reaction to her comment made it clear.

He despised her.

Looking back, maybe it wasn't so surprising that Gabriel decided to work with the witches. He might have hated the organization our parents forced us into, but he always held a resentment toward vampires.

He was what they called a hunter, through and through. It didn't matter whether he was part of the organization—he would still be out there in his uniform and daggers taking down any vampire that so much as caused any issues for humans.

And witches, I guess.

"Nice to meet you in person, Castle," he said with a sickly-sweet smile. "But to be frank, this is none of your fucking business. You're nothing but a leech that my sister decided to take pity on. If you know what's good for you, you'll shut up and do what the coven asks of yo—"

I crossed the space between us in seconds. Rage heated my skin, pushing me forward, controlling my moves. Before I could even comprehend what I was doing, my hands were grabbing his shirt and jerking him to me, shaking with the urge to pound into his smug-looking face.

My brother.

It was his unchanging smile that had my reason ramming back into me like a freight train.

What am I doing?

"Is my little sister blood-bonded?" he asked. "I refuse to believe you'd do something like this to your own blood if you weren't being hypnotized by the Castle leech."

"Stop calling her that," I said in a low voice. "I was the one who brought her here. Don't take this out on her."

His eyes lingered on my face, searching for any tell. But there wasn't one.

"Let's talk outside, Ves." The old nickname he had for me as a kid caused my chest to twist.

I looked back at the crowd, where Aurelia was giving me a warning glare. *Don't you fucking dare leave me here.*

She was a lone vampire in a den full of witches that wanted nothing to do with her. Levana alone seemed ready to tear her head off.

Leaving her would be a betrayal. The bond between us, no matter how light, was begging me to stay.

My gaze fell to Cedar. It was hard to make out her true feelings under the mask she was wearing. I didn't trust her. No matter how helpful she had been in getting us here, I couldn't even begin to unravel just how much she had been keeping from me.

But even then, what I was asking her was clear. *Watch her.* She gave me a stiff nod and inched closer to Aurelia.

"This better be worth it," I told Gabriel.

"Tate is safe here," Gabriel said and leaned back against the mossy wall of the cathedral. The temperature had dropped while we were inside, and a chilled wind brushed across my exposed skin. "I've been working with the coven for years. They wouldn't hurt him. It's the vampires they don't like."

Surprisingly, a part of me was hesitant to believe it. Especially given the cult-like show we'd just witnessed.

I gritted my teeth and clenched my fists, trying desperately to fight off the nasty words running through my mind.

"It's the prophecy, isn't it?" I asked, my eyes shifting to him. "That's why they've been planting people in my life. Watching me."

Gabriel was silent for a moment, his eyes traveling to the darkening sky. I wished the circumstances were different. I wished I could rely on him. At least before, I truly thought Tate would be safe.

I was ignorant, but ignorance kept the weight off my shoulders. Knowing the truth only doubled the weight. Tripled even.

I didn't know where to start.

I need to protect the princess. I can't see the prophecy through.
But everyone wants me to. Everyone has a stake.
I need to get Tate out of here. Convince Gabriel it's not safe.
And what about Cedar? I need to know what she knows.

All these thoughts ran around in my head until it was pounding.

"No one hates Castles more than them," he said, his arms crossing over his chest. He got antsy when he was nervous. "They have a long history, longer than any of us have been alive."

"And you knew," I accused. "But you never thought to tell me."

His eyes fell to the floor as he tapped his foot against the stone ground.

"The less you knew about them, the better. I thought you'd be in and out, not turn your target into your fucking pet."

Rage simmered below my skin. *I'm so fucking tired of people undermining me.*

"She's not my *pet*," I hissed.

A smile pulled at his lips.

"You're right; you're hers."

"I'm going back in," I spat and turned on my heel. Gabriel's strong hand on my wrist stopped me from moving any further.

"They may not want you dead," he said. "But that doesn't mean you're safe. Or your vampire. Do what they say, but when you get the chance, you need to get out of here."

The seriousness of his tone had alarm bells ringing in my head. We were supposed to be safe. Or at least protected.

Did I make a mistake?
Fear ate at me. Regret started to swirl deep in my belly, making me nauseous.
But what other choice did we have?
"What do you know?" I asked, turning back to him.
"The missions. They're dangerous. They are hunting rogues. Rogues who have killed thousands and have injured a fair share of their own witches. They don't want you dead, but your vampire..." *The prophecy needs to be completed.*
"I appreciate the warning," I said and pulled my wrist from his hand, but as I was walking away, his voice rang out again.
"They're quiet. Not because they believe your lie, but because they are regrouping. The organization, I mean. Don't underestimate them just because the Castles have more flair."
His words only solidified the suspicious feeling that had been holding me hostage since the night Aurelia's father first attacked.
Maybe I'd fooled them for a moment, but I knew they would eventually catch on. It had only been a matter of time.
"I've missed you, Gabe," I said, looking over my shoulder. "I wish we could have met again in better circumstances."
He gave me a forced smile.
"Tate and I will be waiting for you when you're done. Let's go for dinner or something."
My gut twisted. I wanted to take him up on that offer more than anything.
"Just with Tate," I replied. "It's better that way. Better for now. Until I...come to terms with a few things."
He didn't fight me as I made my way back into the cathedral where the entire group was seemingly waiting for me in silence.
The priest was the first one to meet my gaze.
"So, do we have a deal?" he asked. The smile that spread across his face sent shivers down my spine.
Aurelia was glaring at me. Her gaze like daggers cutting deep into my skin.
But there was something behind the mask of rage. Something that

reminded me of that vulnerable girl who curled in on herself when the cruelty of the world seemed too much for her to bear.

This is the Aurelia I fell for. She's still in there.

Beyond it all, she was still *my* princess. She might have been taken out of her palace, but she was still locked in that gilded cage of hers, everyone else around her choosing what to do with her life.

It only added to my guilt. I wanted to break her *out*, not force her back in.

But this was the best option. The only option to guarantee her safety.

Even if she hated me, there was one thing I cared most about in this twisted world.

Her.

"We do," I said, straightening my shoulders. "We'll start immediately."

Aurelia

"So we're fucking stuck with you now?" I hissed, looking back as Cedar leaned against the walls of our new place.

The meeting with the high priest had ended quickly after Vesper practically signed my life over to them.

Well, my labor at least. They got what they wanted and provided us with a better cabin inside the wards than the one we had been using as a safe house. It was small, but slightly larger than the other, with two bedrooms, a living room, and a kitchen.

Even our servants had had better quarters than these. The guards had been another story, but we had made sure every part of our palace that was visible to the public was kept clean and presentable.

The cabin's walls were cracked. The air smelled of decaying wood. It's like they chose the most disgusting one to give us. Probably just to spite me.

The longer I was imprisoned by the coven, the less and less I liked them. And it wasn't as if I liked them at all to start with.

But I had no choice in the matter. It was meant to keep me safe, or whatever. So, with a few words of warning and a walk to our cabin, we were *set free*.

But freedom meant different things to different people. To me, it was to come and go as I pleased. To be able to leave coven grounds if I wanted to. It's not like I was going to go running back to Daddy after everything. At least not without a plan.

I wanted to go back to my people. I wanted to kill my father for what he'd done to Mother. To *me*. And save the people she tied to him. Even if they had originally been there because of Mother, I felt like I owed them. But I wasn't fucking stupid.

The witches' definition of freedom was simply to be able to roam around the coven. On one condition, of course. Cedar and the pink-haired witch bitch were our babysitters, even though it seemed like the latter answered to the former. Something that gave me just a twinge of joy.

But it was short-lived when the redheaded one stuck around.

Their version of freedom tastes like shit.

"That is the condition," she replied, crossing her arms over her chest. "You want to leave this house? You have to bring one of us."

I narrowed my eyes at her. Vesper shifted by my side but said nothing. As annoyed as I was with her volunteering me, I was pleasantly surprised she was letting me take the lead with the witch.

Maybe I'll reward her later.

"So why are you still here?" I asked pointedly. "I doubt we're going on a field trip today."

"Actually," she said and stood straight, stretching her long legs. I'd never noticed how tall the witch was until she was standing right in front of me. I had to tilt my head back to look at her as she towered over me. "I'm offering Vesper a tour of the coven grounds."

I tilted my head to the side. *Does everyone think they can lie to me and get away with it?*

Not only was it out of the ordinary for Cedar to offer to do anything of the sort, but every time the witch lied, her heart would race. Her face was pretty blank, but her body gave her away.

"You could just say you want to talk to Vesper instead of lying," I grumbled with a pout. "Besides, no one wants to see this run-down village."

She gave me a smirk that had my stomach flipping. I had seen it a hundred times before when it was directed at Vesper. But when it was directed to me?

My slow-beating heart picked up. My skin heated. My blood rushed through me.

I'm angry. I'm fucking pissed off. That's why my body is reacting this way. Stupid witch.

"Okay, fine. I want to talk to Vesper," she admitted. "Alone."

Annoyance prickled at my skin. *Alone? Again?* What was so important for them to talk about that I couldn't know? And only the two of them?

I shot Vesper a look. *Don't fucking say yes. Don't fucking say—*

She nodded.

I put my hands on my hips and let out a huff.

"I'm tired of you two going back and forth! Whatever you want to say, you can say it in front of me. Stop treating me like I'm some damn child."

Cedar's face twisted with just the slightest bit of irritation.

"You're not in charge here, *Princess*." Her voice was harsh, her stance guarded. "We treat you like a child because you have tantrums like one. Maybe if you were better behaved—"

"Cedar, wait—"

I held up my hand, motioning for Vesper to back off.

"You want to see a tantrum?" I warned. "A tantrum would be slitting your throat. A *tantrum* would be sneaking out in the middle of the night and letting the vampires in. A *tantrum* would be killing you and your coven for keeping me locked up. You don't even know what type of *tantrum I'm* capable of."

"Oh, I know what you're capable of, Princess," Cedar countered, closing the space between us. She had to bend down to look me in the eyes. Mischief swam in her gaze. "But why don't you show me anyway, hm?"

There was a sultriness to her tone that had me jerking back. I schooled my features, trying to hide the effect she had on me, but judging from the satisfied smirk on her face, she'd seen it.

"She's *my* bonded," I growled, stepping closer to Vesper. I even went as far as to wrap my fingers around her wrist. Her pulse was thundering under my grip. My words seemed to shock her, so she stood to her full height again to look down at me.

"Oh really?" Cedar coaxed with a raised brow. "Didn't you throw a fucking fit when she did that? Now you're saying it like it means something?"

"It does mean something," I said, my chest puffing. "Vampires hold blood bonds in high regard. I may not have chosen her to be mine, but it happened, and where she goes, I go."

Cedar shook her head.

"Sounds like a good excuse to get what you want. Come on, Vesper. Let's go—"

"What do you want, Cedar?" Vesper asked, and the witch stopped moving, her eyes flashing to mine.

I gave her a triumphant smirk. *That's right. She chose me.* Maybe there was still some doubt in me that she wouldn't. But that was overshadowed by the confidence I had that Vesper would do anything for me after the sword incident.

"I wanted to apologize," she admitted with a sigh of defeat. "I didn't mean to catch you off guard."

There was a sincerity in her tone that I'd never guess the witch was capable of. It caused me to pause.

All of it was fucked up.

I had been locked up in the palace, my power had been taken away, and I had been forced to marry some asshole prince. But at least the people around me were who they said they were. Even if they wanted something from me, they never hid their true intentions.

Vesper had been the first.

But realizing that my family and friends had wanted things from me and had stuck around only for that my whole life, like Vesper? I think I'd slowly go crazy.

I was not one to forgive and forget, but this made me sympathize with my little mouse.

"I don't want it," Vesper said. "At least not for that reason."

Cedar's face fell.

"You could apologize for, you know, planting people in her life. Lying to her. Keeping things from her every chance you got," I offered.

Pride burst through the dulling bond so strong it felt as though it was my own. *Krae, this had to be some sort of praise kink or something.* My head was swimming. My body warmed.

Vesper being proud of me was its own special kind of drug.

"That wasn't my call," Cedar said with a frown.

"Thanks for the offer," Vesper said. "For the tour. Maybe I'll take you up on it some other time."

Cedar got the hint, but even so, her gaze lingered on the two of us. Her tone from earlier was still swirling around my head.

She's not afraid of me. At the same time, she doesn't underestimate me.

What a contradiction.

With one last sigh, she turned and left Vesper and me alone in the cabin.

I couldn't stop the smile that spread across my face as I grabbed her hand.

"Come on, let's feed—"

She pulled it away. My gaze snapped back to hers. It was like, as soon as the door shut, she became a different person.

"Don't mess this up for us," she warned. "I know you hate them, but tone it down. We need a place to stay. Even if it's just for—"

"Are you seriously telling *me* not to mess this up?" I asked with a scoff. All the warm and fuzzy feelings she had given me had gone up in a cloud of smoke.

I am too damn hopeful.

"You were the reason we were on probation for so long," she pointed out.

"You don't think it's freaky?" I asked, throwing my hands up in the air in frustration. "They seem like a fucking cult!"

She pressed her lips in a thin line.

It was more than that. The gods they worshipped. That freaky priest that gave me a slimy feeling. I knew the witches would do anything to keep their place in the coven, and I *really* didn't want to find out just how far they'd go.

"I won't have this conversation with you if you won't listen."

My jaw dropped at her attitude. If I were any less surprised, I'd fuck the attitude from her until she was writhing and begging me for release. But before I could recover, she took one last look at me and turned around with a sigh.

"Three days," Vesper reminded me as she walked into one of the rooms, making it clear that it was hers and I was not to follow. It was so dismissive and... unlike the Vesper I knew back at the palace. Ever since coming to the coven, she had lost the bite that I so loved about her. I wanted her to fight me. Wanted to see that anger in her eyes again. But I got none of it. "Be prepared to get your hands dirty."

I crossed my arms with a pout.

Like hell I will.

Aurelia

I'm *not fucking doing this. I'm a princess, for Krae's sake!*
I just knew that if the goddess was looking down at me now, she would pity me.

"That priest dude's manipulating you," I hissed as Vesper rushed ahead of me. "We shouldn't even be here, let alone risking our lives for—"

Vesper turned on her heels, anger twisting her face. It was enough to take my breath away. Beautiful. Tempting. Vicious. I knew the little mouse had it in her. It was still there. I desperately wanted to see her let it out again.

The tension skyrocketed between us. Electricity zapped at our skin.

Fuck.

Since the night she dismissed me three days ago, I wanted nothing more than to teach her a lesson for getting all annoyed with me. I wanted to remind her of what she did to me. Make her beg at my feet for forgiveness.

But this angry version was just too delicious. Maybe if I was bad enough, she'd fight me like she did during that first party.

"This is the only thing saving us. Do not ruin this opportunity."

I love it when my little mouse lets her emotions get the better of her.

If we weren't in such a dire situation, I would have sunk my fangs into her right then and there and made her ride my fingers while she told me how much she hated me.

I missed the days when I could feel her. When I could taste her without this wall between us.

Now that I was free, my pink-haired babysitter insisted I could only feed on Vesper and that I couldn't just run off and find a random human to drain.

Like I'd feed from anyone but my little mouse anyway.

I fucking hated it when people thought they could control me. They acted as if the freedom they gave me would change anything, but after three days, I was still stuck in the coven. I couldn't go out alone, and I sure as hell didn't want to ask any of the witches to chaperone.

And it would seem Vesper was a hot commodity to the witches. In the few days we had been free, she was always either taken by the coven or with her little brother Tate, leaving me alone to pace in a dark room. It was infuriating, and I was left hungry.

Vampires didn't need to eat every day, but if it went on any longer, I was bound to go insane. Not to mention that having her so far away made me...lonely?

As if someone like me could ever feel something like loneliness. But it was heavy and had me aching to be near her the moment she was out of sight. My heart even raced when she came back.

And then the missions started.

"This *opportunity*?" I asked and motioned to the wet, stinky concrete jungle around us. A rogue vampire was said to be living here with two others at most. The coven had told us they had just finished a killing spree of three more, bringing their total to fifteen. "This isn't an opportunity. It's cleanup. It's dirty work. It's a *fucking insult*, and if you can't see how they're playing you, I am really starting to doubt what I ever—"

"Yes, just scream and announce our presence to every rogue vampire in the area," Cedar said, appearing from the shadows. "Didn't know you were so eager to get the job done, Princess."

I hated when Cedar called me *princess*.

It lacked all the fiery emotion Vesper gave it when she said it. If anything, it felt more like she was mocking my little mouse.

Vesper looked at her with a frown.

"You could help a bit more, you know?"

Cedar gave her a wicked grin and raised her hands in surrender.

"I'm on babysitting duty; this is *your* mission."

This was another complication.

I had seen Cedar more times in the past few days than I'd ever wanted to see her. Her obvious flirtation with Vesper only angered me more, and ever since Vesper dismissed her, she seemed to be coming back even more.

As if the pink-haired hybrid one wasn't a nuisance enough.

The dripping of water broke the tense silence between the three of us. The old, moldy, abandoned construction site was dark. The floors were covered in scrap metal and splattered with blood.

Even if I hadn't known what lay ahead of us, I would have easily smelled the old blood that painted the place. Vampires themselves had a specific smell. They didn't have the rotting smell the crazed did, but it was close. The crazed didn't care about where they got their blood and often tried to feast on many until the craze subsided, leaving them smelling like dead bodies and rotten blood.

These vampires' place smelled damp. They had been hiding out for a while, so they left only to hunt and came back stained with blood.

The cracking of rocks against the concrete was the only warning sign I got before a hard body slammed into me and threw me to the ground.

My head hit the dirty rocks. Pain ricocheted through my skull, dulling my senses enough that I couldn't stop the vampire when he forced his hands around my throat.

"Is that royal blood I smell?" The vampire's voice held a teasing tone to it. His breath reeked of his victim's blood. "Why, I'm honored you came all the way out here to see me, *Princess.* I heard your father was making some big moves in the north. Maybe we'll have some fun with you before we let him know we caught you—"

I let out an enraged scream and grabbed the man's neck before using his body weight to flip us over.

The sounds of Vesper and Cedar fighting not far away from me forced me into a panic.

I am on my own with this one.

I used my nails to claw at him, used my fists to punch his nose with enough force to crack it open and have his dirty blood splatter all over my face.

But he wouldn't give up that easily. He fought like a wild animal, launching himself at me, sending us back to the dirty ground.

The smell of my own blood had fear clawing at my throat. An ice-cold chill ran through me as I watched the vampire climb on top of me, a random metal pole in his hand.

I'd never been in a situation where my life hung in the balance and I literally had to use my fists to free myself. My inexperience meant that I was at a disadvantage.

"You're pissing me off," he sneered. "I guess we don't need you alive to have a little fun, hm?"

My hands flailed to stop him as he brought the rusted pole down to my chest, but he was too strong. He had been aiming for my heart, and even with all my strength, I was only able to move it a few inches before it pierced my skin.

The screams that ripped from my throat didn't even sound like they belonged to me. They were panicked. Scared even. Something I'd never let anyone else see before.

"Vesper!"

Bright red lights flashed across my vision, knocking the vampire off me. The redheaded witch was the first to show herself in my blurred vision, followed by Vesper.

"I told you not to draw their attention, didn't I?" Cedar hissed, her hands on me, pulling me up. They sent warmth shooting up my chilled arms.

I took in a sharp, pained breath.

"Lecture me later," I spat back, pushing the witch away. "Vesper, make yourself useful and give me some blood."

"She's right," Vesper said as she lifted her wrist to my mouth. "You need to be more cautious on these missions if you want to live—"

"I didn't want to come on these missions in the first place!" I slapped her hand away from me and reached up with a shaky hand to tangle my hand in her hair to force her neck down. "And where were you while I was getting beat by that fucker? Huh?"

I didn't let her try to defend herself before I sank my teeth right into her neck. She let out a pained groan.

"Careful, Princess," Cedar warned. "Vesper's hurt too."

Cedar was getting on my nerves. I wanted to swipe at her. Wanted to tear off her head from her shoulders.

Especially for how her eyes shifted to Vesper when the venom finally reared its head and had the little hunter struggling to contain herself against me.

I get it now.

The realization of what was happening between them had two emotions running through me.

Excitement was one, especially when I saw just how much what I was doing to Vesper affected the witch.

And *jealousy*. I didn't like how the witch looked at her. Didn't like how she thought I wouldn't notice how much she had come to care for the hunter.

I caught it in the safe house before by listening to how their hearts sped up when they saw each other. I had been blinded by my own anger and sometimes even caught off guard by Cedar's flirtatiousness, but now that I could see what was happening between them... it clicked.

This wasn't just some sort of nervousness because of lingering anger and betrayal. These weren't two *friends* dancing around each other as they figured out where they stood.

There was something sweeter brewing there, and I wanted to taste it. Badly.

So I did what any sane vampire would do when someone looked at their blood-bonded the way she did.

I grabbed Vesper like my life depended on it. Drank gulp after gulp while pumping her full of vampire venom.

"We're not here to play, *Aurelia*."

Cedar's voice had a dangerous tone to it. How exciting. I couldn't wait to see how she would react to my obvious disrespect.

Playing with Vesper was one thing, but Cedar? I hadn't felt this excited since Vesper had first shown up in the palace with a calm heart and warm honey eyes.

"Tell me, Little Mouse," I whispered after pulling my teeth from her neck. "Tell me what you want. Do you want this to stop? The vampire venom will heal you. Don't you want to feel better?"

I could smell her blood. The sweet scent filling the air had caused my mouth to water. I licked my lips, ready to taste even more.

"Not here," Vesper said quickly and pulled away. Her pupils were blown, and her face flushed. I could smell her arousal, but her face made it clear that I would have to take a rain check.

And she knew I wasn't very patient.

"Hurry up, witch," I grumbled as Cedar lit the vampire's body on fire. "He's dead, you don't have to wait that long."

Her magic had already done a number on him, tearing up his skin and even an entire arm off.

A bit overkill if you ask me.

Her entire body was tense. The muscle in her jaw was more pronounced as she clenched her teeth like she was angry at the whole situation and not just a failed mission.

Maybe she's mad I got hurt.

Right. As if.

The smell of Vesper's arousal as the venom worked through her was distracting and such a delicious tease. It had my mouth watering and my body vibrating with need for her.

She was inching closer and closer to me as Cedar cleaned up. Each moment that passed, her breathing grew faster. Her heart raced. The wetness between her thighs got more and more obvious.

I can't wait to get her back into the car and have the witch watch as I fu—

"He's done, we can go—"

I pulled Vesper away from the scene even before Cedar had stopped talking and didn't stop until I had her in the back of the beat-up coven-assigned car.

I ignored Cedar as she slipped into the front seat. She was grumbling under her breath, but I ignored that too.

I was straddling my little mouse before the witch had even started the thing.

I couldn't help it anymore. My fangs were aching. My cunt was dripping. I *needed* Vesper as much as she needed me, and knowing that the witch would be watching only excited me more.

I could feel her eyes on us. Could hear the racing of her heart as she watched us.

"You know most serial killers get caught because they violate traffic laws," Cedar grumbled, her hands gripping the steering wheel tight enough the material squeaked.

"Is that what we are now?" I asked as I licked the length of Vesper's neck. She rewarded me with a shiver. *So good.* Even when she tried to push me away, we'd always end up right back where we belonged.

Me and her. My fangs in her neck. Her hands on my hips.

"It means I need you not to get us in trouble," Cedar shot back, but we both ignored her this time.

"You need to be more careful," Vesper soothed. Her voice was low, her breathing shaky. She was trying to appease me while still getting her way. *Too bad.* I was having too much fun. "This is only the first mission."

She was missing a carefully placed *princess* in her sentence. The absence of it made me feel something uncomfortable in my chest.

"And you almost messed it up." Cedar was quick to add on the little bit Vesper left out.

"I wouldn't be in this situation if it weren't for you," I whispered in her ear. "You remember that? Sometimes I can still feel when your blade just barely missed my heart. Do you know how close you were to actually killing me? Now I'm here. Getting my hands dirty and getting disgusting vampire blood in my hair."

I pulled away to watch as guilt flashed across the little mouse's face. Finally. The anger from the coven meeting and almost failed mission disappeared from her expression.

"Yes," she muttered, her voice low. I almost felt bad about it. But the enjoyment of what was happening between the three of us overshadowed it all.

"Yes, you remember, or yes, you know how close you were to killing me?"

"Aurelia," Cedar admonished from the front. When I didn't say anything, she pumped the brakes quickly.

If Vesper hadn't had her arms wrapped around my waist, I would have been flung against the back of the seats.

"Both," Vesper answered softly.

"So you owe me," I said. "Which means you'll let me do whatever I want to you."

Her gaze hardened.

"You know the answer to that."

I did. I could hear the little skip of her heart every time I touched her. Could hear just how excited she got whenever my hands roamed her skin.

I could smell it too.

But it was all heightened. Because this time, we weren't alone.

The parties I had taken her to were all for show. Other people's gazes had some weight, but nothing like the venomous one that Cedar was giving me. I could feel the heat of it on the back of my neck.

"I bet you'll let me do just about anything to rid you of that nasty guilt that's been eating you alive."

"Don't test that theory," Cedar warned.

"You've done good for a babysitter, but this doesn't involve you," I hissed, turning to send her a glare through the rearview mirror.

Her green eyes met mine, and her body betrayed her. She wanted me to believe she was angry. That she was annoyed with what we were doing in the back.

But I could smell her too.

Vesper pressed her hand against my cheek, pulling my gaze back to her, and my head was spinning.

"Just drink, Princess," Vesper said in a soft tone. "We're both hurt. Spill some venom on the wounds and let's be done with this, hm?"

The nickname. The one that caused stupid irrational feelings to sprout.

"I want you to drink," I said and lifted my wrist to my mouth, sinking my fangs into the flesh before offering it to the silver-haired hunter. "Show me just how willing you are to be used by me."

A silence fell over the car.

"This is insane. Can you make up your mind with this bonding shit? First you hate her for bonding you, then apparently bonding is important to you, and now you are asking her to drink your blood. Do you even know what the blood does to humans—"

"Enough. I'll do it."

Vesper's voice was strong; her gaze held conviction.

She would do it. For me. To erase the guilt inside her. A part of me wanted Vesper to do it because *she* wanted to instead of just out of guilt.

But I'd take what I could get.

There was a thrill of excitement shooting up my spine at the prospect of her drinking my blood. Even more so when the annoying witch was asking her not to, and she was doing it anyway.

That's right, Cedar. This should show her that no matter what, Vesper would always be siding with me.

Vesper's lips wrapped around the wound on my wrist. A pleasure like I had never felt before ripped through me. The act itself was nothing more than a simple feeding, but because it was *her*, my body was reacting in all sorts of ways.

I could feel the wetness of her mouth, the swipe of her tongue, and all of it reminded me so much of our time together back in the palace.

I want to feel it again. I want to have her mouth between my legs as she swears her loyalty to me.

With a wicked grin, I leaned forward and sank my fangs back into her neck. Her moan was obstructed by my wrist, but it was loud enough for our babysitter to hear.

Her hands grabbed my hips, pulling me closer as we drank. I couldn't help but grind down on her in response—not when her blood was that sweet. And especially not when she took gulp after gulp of my blood.

The bond between us roared to life.

I hadn't realized how much I missed it until it made itself known. I imagined it was what it felt like when you came home after a long time away. Warmth. Comfort. Happiness. All of it swirling together. All of it feeling like *her.*

I hadn't even noticed Vesper's wandering hand until it was slipping into the front of my pants.

I gasped against her, dislodging my fangs from her throat, and greedily licked up the spilling blood as her fingers ran circles over my clit. All the while, she never stopped drinking from me. She was determined to show me that she was ready to do anything to get back on my good side.

I'll fucking take it.

She slipped her fingers lower and lower and lower until they pushed into my wet entrance. The witch was long forgotten at that point. I was running on a high of Vesper's blood and asserting control. My hands dug into the back seat, using it as leverage to grind against her, meeting her pumps as she led me into a quick orgasm.

How long has it been since she touched me like this?

I couldn't even remember. My mind was so blurred by the events at the palace and the coven, I couldn't remember the last time she got me off. I didn't realize how delicious it would be to do it with a fresh bond. I could feel everything. I could feel her. She was all around me.

Inside me. Never once had I felt so close to someone in my entire existence. The fact that it was my little mouse made it even better. I was going to come, and fast. Embarrassingly fast. Normally I would care. Would hate that it would inflate the hunter's ego. But everything was so powerful at that moment that I couldn't stop myself from chasing it.

Just when I felt the first wave of orgasm take hold of me, two hands grabbed me and yanked me back. One was tangled in my hair, the other gripped my wrist. Something that should never have happened.

I had been too distracted to realize the car had stopped. Or that the redheaded witch had left the car to open the backdoor and pull me and my bleeding wrist away from Vesper.

My first instinct was to snarl at her as she glared down at me. But I couldn't bring myself to. Not when Vesper's hands were still between my legs and the orgasm was taking over my entire body.

Perfect timing. Even more perfect was that Vesper didn't stop.

"Like the show?" I forced out through my orgasm. Her gaze darkened before her eyes flashed to Vesper. I followed her gaze.

Beautiful. Vesper looked absolutely ethereal with blood all over her mouth. Her pupils were wide, her chest rising and falling sharply with each breath.

She would look glorious as a vampire.

I leaned into Cedar's hold on my hair, using it to steady me as the orgasm finished its rampage.

I had never seen anything so perfect. I had once thought that having Vesper kneeling between my legs and swearing herself to me would be it, but there was something much more intoxicating about watching the witch see what Vesper and I were like together.

And then my mind went straight into the possibility of the three of us together and how the witch would look...

Stop.

I locked the image of the three of us away for my personal late-night fantasies.

Instead of replying to my question, Cedar let go of my wrist and reached in to grab Vesper's jaw, forcing her gaze to hers.

"Does it hurt? Are you okay? Vampire blood isn't safe for humans to consume. Let alone that much."

I let out a scoff that was ignored.

Vesper didn't pull away from her hold. She gave her a stiff nod.

"I'm fine. The blood has never been a problem for me."

The shock wasn't evident on Cedar's face, but I felt it in the quick way she jerked away from us.

"Very well."

With no other words, she slammed the door closed.

Cedar

My entire body was sensitive to the touch. Aching. Heat ran through me and straight to my core with every flick of my fingers against my clit. I arched against the mattress, even just the brush of it against my bare skin lighting it on fire.

I covered my mouth with my hand, muffling my noises as my fingers moved through my slickness, fast and without hesitation. I *needed* to come. My entire body was shaking as I forced myself closer and closer to the edge.

More. More. More. I needed more. My fingers weren't enough.

I needed *them*.

I couldn't help myself. Not after what I witnessed in the car.

Vesper, her head thrown back, pleasure written all over her face. Aurelia looking up at me with a wicked smile as Vesper made her come.

I couldn't help but groan, all alone inside my studio apartment. The walls were thin, letting the music from the bar downstairs filter in, which meant I had to be careful and not get too carried away.

But it was hard with the show they'd given me.

They were magnificent together.

I once thought it was just Vesper that called to me—a silly little crush—while Aurelia was a thorn in my side. An annoyance.

But just as my feelings for Vesper had grown into something more solid and undeniable, my thoughts on Aurelia had changed too.

She was still annoying at times. Stuck up. *Spoiled.*

But I wanted her—*them*—so badly it was unlike anything I'd ever felt before.

I could still feel her hair in my hand when I grabbed it. The slope of her neck down to her breasts was so vivid in my mind, it was like I could just reach out and feel her soft skin.

And Vesper...

"Fuck," I hissed and slipped two fingers inside my cunt. I pumped them into me with zero gracefulness. I was clumsy, hurried, rushing to get myself to the finish line.

More.

I imagined myself on the other side of Vesper, my hands trailing her body as she fucked Aurelia.

I imagined her little gasps as I twisted her nipples. How she would lean into me, her body seeking mine. I could still smell the mix of their heady arousal in the air.

I heard Aurelia's chuckle in my mind. Teasing me. It sounded so real, it had the hair on the back of my neck rising.

My orgasm was coming fast. It had taken hold of me and refused to let go until I submitted.

The last image in my mind as I came was the two of them, looking at me. Vesper covered in her own blood. Aurelia's mouth smeared with it.

The blood—hell, the sheer idea of ever being with a vampire or letting one bite me—should make me nauseous. Our kind weren't supposed to even be near each other, let alone fucking each other. At least that's what I always thought. Never once had I looked twice at a vampire.

Until Aurelia.

With her, it was just the opposite. And adding Vesper to the mix?

The sheer memory of them together was already an addiction, and it made me itch to watch them again.

I sank into my mattress with a sigh, taking my fingers out of my over-sensitive cunt and wiping the wetness on my clothes. I had to wash them anyway. But I was too tired to get up, and my mind was still back in that car.

I lay there in the aftermath, my eyes homed in on the dark ceiling, images of them running around in my brain. It was like a broken film reel playing over and over again in my head.

By the time my body had gone cold, I had memorized every second of our interaction. I covered my eyes with my hand and let out a deep sigh.

The blood has never been a problem for me.

Vesper's words echoed in my head. They bothered me. *Worried* me. There was so much about Vesper I thought I knew, but that bit of information shocked me the most.

How could a mere human not feel the effects after consuming the blood?

Yes, the bond would be there...but nothing else? No pain? Any other human should have been writhing on the ground, especially with the amount she'd drunk.

But Vesper displayed not one ounce of discomfort.

This was beginning to feel like too much. I didn't know how to protect them.

I'd brought them both here for protection, but I noticed the sinister look that came over the high priest's face as soon as he saw them.

I don't like it. I don't trust him.

They were never supposed to be here anyway, and it was all my fault.

Aurelia's little tantrums were not helping, and they seemed to be getting worse as the days went on. I could see right through her. I knew what the spoiled brat was doing, and I fucking hated it.

Vesper didn't need any more of her shit. She had gone through hell and back, fought for her when no one else would, and all Aurelia wanted to do was make her bow to her? Humiliate her?

Vesper didn't seem very humiliated, the voice in the back of my head reminded me as images of them together in the back seat flooded my mind again.

She hadn't been humiliated. Vesper had acted like I wasn't even there, her entire focus squarely on Aurelia.

That alone should be enough to make me stop wanting them both. And then with the blood situation…

I didn't know what to do. Didn't know what to tell them when—

I sat up abruptly and let out a groan.

What did I get myself into?

I would have loved to say I had a good life before they came crashing into it, but that would be a lie.

My apartment was cold and barren, and I spent more nights than I'd like to admit down at the bar downstairs. I didn't have friends. The other witches resented me because of the trust the high priest placed in me when I was still so young.

I had no future. No plans. No dreams.

Until I saw Vesper.

She awoke something in me. She made me care. Something I hadn't done for anyone but myself before.

And Aurelia? *Fuck.* She riled me up, fought me in ways no one else had. It was playful. Fun. *Addicting.* And when she didn't get her way? Annoying as hell, but I wish I didn't find it as amusing as I did.

I closed my eyes, thinking of my favorite god. Helma, goddess of conquest. She was underrated, as most witches prayed to Life or Death, Vivus or Exos, respectively.

Help me, I whispered in my mind, infusing my being with magic. *Show me the path. Show me what to do.*

I repeated the words to myself over and over again, praying for an answer, but none came, leaving me alone in my dark apartment, the evidence of my shameful obsession smeared between my legs.

"And your mission, Cedar?" The high priest's voice cut through my haze.

I had all but drained my magic while praying to Helma the night before and was now paying the price.

My body felt heavy and was getting heavier with every passing second. My eyes were dry, my lids droopy. It took all my concentration to even stay awake.

And it had been for nothing. No path had been shown to me yet. Helma's statue was behind the priest, but I fought the urge to look at it.

I blinked quickly, my mind focusing back on the dark ceremony room hidden under the cathedral. We were all in a circle, dressed in our black robes with embroidered golden runes. The priest had on his white ones.

I had been so out of it I didn't even know who the other four members in front of me were.

"The princess almost got herself killed the other day," I said. There was a murmur around the group.

And gave me a fucking heart attack, I thought to myself. I shouldn't be worrying about her, but when I saw her under that vampire, my heart skipped a beat. And the brat had the gall to use what happened to bond Vesper again.

"Almost?"

"Damn, it would be nice for it to happen that quickly, huh?"

"Give her one more. I'm sure she'll fuck it up and get herself killed in the process."

"Quick and easy. The prophecy would be complete."

I gritted my teeth as the voices rang out. My own feelings on the matter were at war inside me.

Had the witches always been this heartless when it came to vampires?

I knew they had been, and maybe I had been too. Before.

To them, prophecies were like a to-do list, nothing more. Even when they were about life and death, we were taught never to assign feelings to them since they would almost always come true.

"*Almost,*" I repeated, sending a glare to those who interrupted me. "But it was taken care of. Vesper saved her. Something we can expect going forward. They also reignited their blood bond."

I could hear the chorus of whispers that followed, but I kept my eyes squarely on the high priest. The information somehow didn't seem to faze him.

Does he know? Did the seer tell him?

It made me panic. Especially when I left out the information about what they did in the back seat of my car. And that I had intervened.

I wasn't supposed to unless it was to protect Vesper's life. Strict orders. Something his gaze was reminding me of.

But I had. I had actively changed the future they'd seen.

Stop panicking. Keep breathing. He'll sense even the smallest falter.

"Keep us updated," he said after a few long moments. "I'll have another mission for them soon. Let them know."

I gave him a slight nod.

"Oh, and do push the hunter to meet with her brother. He's rather agitated that we've somehow turned her against him."

"That's his fault for not telling her in the first place," I muttered.

A stunned silence fell over the group.

Shit. That was supposed to have been an internal thought.

This time, I couldn't stop the panic from taking over my body. I froze in place, ready for whatever punishment was awaiting me. But nothing came.

Instead, his lips curled, and he let out a small huff before motioning for the next person to start their report.

Levana was across from me, her pink hair slipping out of the coat. Her gaze was on me, calling me on my bullshit. She hadn't been on that mission with us, but the girl had a knack for figuring out where to poke and prod.

I didn't want any of it. Not the attention and certainly not the responsibility that came with seeing this through.

For the coven, this prophecy meant more than anything in the world. It was one of the prophecies we were tracking that could end up having a huge impact on the future of the clan.

Whether it was as small as a single witch's death or as large as war between witches and vampires, we had to get involved.

And my job just so happened to be them. Well, Vesper.

The image of her angry, betrayed expression as she asked me if she'd been my real target all along still haunted my mind.

Because it was true. It had been her all along. My job had been to protect her. To make it so she could see the prophecy through.

But then she decided to go and fuck the princess.

For the first time in my life, I didn't really know what to do. The high priest was watching closely—far closer than ever before. I had failed the first round and should have never brought them here.

Yes, I had pushed her to finish the prophecy, but I couldn't have imagined she would do what she did.

She was playing with the gods. Cael, god of wrath, would have a field day with her. The others wouldn't find it amusing when they saw how she evaded their prophecy.

"That rogue struck again, this time killing twelve in three days' time. One vampire and two witches were caught in the crosshairs."

I perked up at the new information, my gaze falling to the hooded figure in front of me.

"We should send the hunter after them—"

"No," I hissed, glaring at Levana. "They are proving themselves with the lower-level cleanups. Something that big is unnecessary."

My interruption surprised even myself. I usually listened to what they had to say before shutting them down.

You're giving yourself away.

"Is it?" she asked, tilting her head.

"We all know the hunter should have died anyway. She's a liability. If you ask me, we should just send them. Tie up loose ends."

My head snapped in the direction of the vile words, and my feet moved that way of their own accord as a flash of red covered my vision. I quickly jerked back, ice-cold panic flooding my veins.

All eyes were on me. We had strict rules in the White Lotus, the small group the high priest had handpicked and trained to protect our coven and see prophecies through. The debriefings were more like ceremonies, with all of us gathered on the runes, carefully carved in the stone beneath our feet. Long ago, they had been painted with our ancestors' blood as they prayed to the gods.

It was the same place prophecies were handed out. The same place where we were initiated. And if necessary... The same place where our bodies would be given back to the earth.

Me stepping foot outside my assigned spot was unheard of. The last time I had witnessed someone doing that, they had been running for their life.

But hadn't gotten very far.

"Oh, someone's a bit too involved, is she?" A man in a cloak to my left jeered.

"Vesper is the most skilled to kill the last Castle," I said through gritted teeth. "That's been decided long ago. Gabriel was too selfish and walked away. Vesper is the last and only option."

There was silence again. I looked at the high priest, but his eyes were too busy searching the group. The members were casting the same hesitant glances at each other.

It was Levana who spoke up first.

"I like Vesper too," she admitted. "I don't think we should kill her, but..."

Don't say it. Please don't say what I think you're going to say.

Her gaze met mine, something akin to pity in her eyes.

"The humans were the ones who picked their warrior. We have a chance to pick ours as well. Especially since we have all of them in the confines of our coven."

"Gabriel is an awful choice," I hissed.

"Gabriel isn't the only choice," the high priest offered.

No. No. No. I can't let them do this to Vesper.

She would be crushed.

But what could I do? The high priest was looking at me as if he could read every single thought in my head. Like he knew just how much I disagreed and was waiting for me to cause a scene.

I swallowed the knot in my throat and stood straight.

"I will defer to you, High Priest, to make the decision you feel is right."

The smile that started to slowly spread across his face had my gut twisting. He had once looked so charismatic. When I was a child, I looked up to him and felt comfort in his presence. But ever since I'd been initiated into the White Lotus, I had started to see just how dangerous he really was.

The warm smiles that once had happiness expanding in my chest now caused fear to sprout instead. His kind gaze now had me rooted to the ground in fear as opposed to running to him with my arms wide open.

"Let's not step out of the circle next time, yes?"

I could do nothing but hang my head and nod.

Vesper

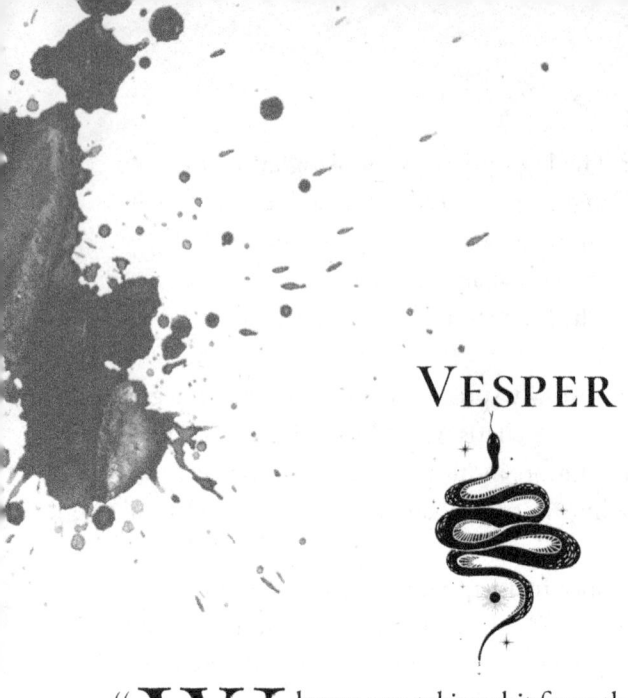

"Why are you taking shit from them?"

Tate's usage of a curse word had my head swiveling to him. He merely raised an eyebrow at me as I paused my skinning of the latest rabbit the coven had caught, looking down at the bloodied dead animal with a frown.

The day was still young, sun shining down on the common area. When I was asked to come help, I couldn't say no. After all, our relationship was already strained with what Aurelia had done to get us on probation.

If there was any chance of us staying here, it would be because I smoothed things over. Even if that meant doing the coven's dirty work.

It was barely eleven in the morning, and I was already on my third batch.

Apparently, hunting rabbits was all the hunter's section of the coven did all day.

According to Levana, they got food imported from the nearest town, but their gods promoted living off the land as much as possible, so they tried to stick with it.

"You never used to cuss around me before," I muttered. "Maybe Gabriel's a bad influence."

Tate let out a scoff. "I'm not a kid anymore, you know? You can't expect me to grow up in our fucked-up family and think that cussing is a bad influence. Maybe killing innocents is what you should be more worried about."

I bit the inside of my cheek.

Not all of them are innocent.

For years I had been slowly coming to terms with just how fucked up the organization that controlled my family was. Throughout school, I still had hope we were doing the right thing. I'd been naïve; hadn't seen the world. It all changed when I started taking missions.

When the vampires begged me not to kill them.

It was all a game to my parents. Something to build up my experience as I awaited to fulfill the prophecy.

I thought it would all end once I did that. That maybe if I just listened a little while longer, I would be in the clear.

Obviously not.

"You're right," I said, ripping the rest of the skin from the rabbit and adding it to the pile before grabbing the next one. "I don't give a fuck if you cuss. I was just caught off guard."

"So why are you doing it?" he asked, kicking the bucket to my left that had all the skins in it.

"They needed help. And I had nothing to do," I lied.

The small courtyard had a fountain Tate and I were sitting on. My eyes drifted to where Levana and Aurelia sat, just in front of the few shops that decorated the area, both looking like they were ready to strangle the other.

Aurelia sat on a bench with her arms and legs crossed and a pout on her face, sending me glares. It was one of her first times out since she was let off probation, but it looked like she'd rather be back in the cabin than with the pink-haired witch.

Levana, on the other hand, was sitting on the back support, her feet on the bench next to Aurelia, as if being at the same level was an insult. She had her chin propped on her hand and was watching the witches that passed by, her discomfort obvious.

I had never seen this side of her. It only reminded me just how much she had been hiding.

She might have insisted it wasn't all fake, but the more I watched her, the less sure I was.

"No wonder you failed your mission; you're a shit liar."

His words had a bubble of laughter falling from my lips. I had forgotten how much I missed Tate. Even in the coven, where witches watched our every move, this was the most freedom the two of us ever had together—the first time we could really be ourselves together.

I missed out on watching him grow because of my missions, and I wouldn't make that mistake again. I would force Gabriel to take him out of the coven as soon as I could, but until then, I would soak up every moment with him.

"Right again," I said and paused to look at him. His gaze was trained on the grumpy vampire. "I want them to trust us. To like us. We already started on the wrong foot, and if we stay that way, there is no guarantee we'll be able to stay here."

It doesn't mean I have to trust them, though.

Something still felt... off.

"We should go north," he said. "Me, you, *her* too if you want."

My heart skipped a beat in my chest. Was he saying what I think he was? The child that grew up in the vampire-killing family was willing to run away with one? The very one I was supposed to kill?

"You don't like staying with Gabriel?" I asked with a raised brow, not wanting to address just how giddy his words made me. "He's the safest person for you to be with."

"I'd rather be with you. I don't know him that well, and you're more important to me. You were there for...everything. He just abandoned us," he said. Eyes the same color as mine looked back at me, but they had something I rarely saw in mine. *Determination.* "Even if it means putting up with that vampire."

My heart twisted. While I was mad at Gabriel, I didn't want Tate to dislike him so much. Though my heart still soared at his admission.

More than anything, I wished I could take him away to a safe place where no one would bother us, but...

"What's with the hunters and their hate for me, huh? Do you guys not have anything better to do?"

Aurelia's sudden appearance had me jolting. The bond hadn't warned me of her, but it sure did tell me how amused she was at my reaction.

Even days after we had reignited it, it was far stronger than I was prepared for. The first blood bond had been weak in comparison—a joke. But this one had my body positively thumping to life every time she was near.

Cedar's reaction in the car told me I had consumed a dangerous amount of blood, but I didn't truly feel the consequences until we were back in our assigned safe house and I couldn't even sleep in a separate room.

I should be fine as long as I didn't die. Now *that* would be a consequence I wasn't willing to face.

I might have been okay with vampires, but I wasn't sure I'd choose the life myself.

Aurelia was pleased. She had been pissed at me for leaving her to do odd jobs for the coven, so this was the perfect opportunity for her to take advantage of my need to be with her.

"It would take me literally all day to list the reasons, and even then I doubt you'd fully understand—or care." Tate's scathing response had my jaw dropping in shock.

"Tate."

"Wow, so insolence runs in the family, hm?" Aurelia said, a wicked smirk spreading across her face, her hands resting on her hips. If Cedar or I made the same comment, she'd be enraged, but with Tate... Well, they seemed to have met each other's match.

"It sure does," Tate answered, meeting her grin with one of his own. "What? Don't tell me the spoiled princess can't take it."

If there was one thing I was starting to notice about Aurelia, it was that she hated when people called her *princess*. I didn't exactly know when that had changed—I distinctly remembered her *asking* me to call her that once upon a time.

It was her status symbol. Even if she wasn't *real* royalty, it meant something in the vampire world.

"Vesper, get the little shit on a leash."

Her obvious annoyance only excited Tate more. I couldn't help the groan that escaped my lips. They were too similar for their own good.

I sighed and went back to my skinning, trying my best to tune them out as they bickered.

It was cute. Almost like she and I were in a real relationship. Like I had introduced her to my family and Tate had accepted her as an annoying older sister that he loved to tease.

And that hurt. It hurt to imagine what a normal life could have been like with the two of them.

All the while, Tate's voice rang through my head.

So why are you doing it?

It was a good question. Maybe not one I had even fully thought about until he asked it.

Why did I go through all that for Aurelia?

A vampire who didn't give two shits about me and saw me as a plaything. A vampire whose entire existence had made my life a living hell. A vampire who only continued to make my life harder as I desperately tried to outrun a prophecy that was threatening to get us both killed.

Except that, when she looked at me, I felt something through the bond.

Beyond the hate, anger, and even guilt, I felt something warm. It reminded me of how relieved she had been when I pushed my sword through her fiancé's chest.

And yet she still fought me. Knowing what was out there. Knowing the risks. Knowing all that we had gone through.

I felt her eyes on me, even as she and Tate continued to squabble, but I wasn't ready to meet her gaze.

"I'm going to find Cedar."

Tate tried to stop me as I got up and walked away, but I merely gave him a strained smile and told him to behave before disappearing.

As much as I would have liked to stay with him, I couldn't handle having Aurelia's eyes on me, especially when her emotions were attacking me through the bond.

"Does this mean I'm forgiven?" Cedar asked with a smirk, handing me a glowing glass of something I had never seen before.

She hadn't been hard to find. I stopped and asked one witch, whose cheeks blanched before she quickly gave up her location. As if the witch was scared of me or thought I had a disease or something. Either way, she scurried away immediately after like she couldn't get rid of me fast enough.

Cedar had been hiding out in a small pub on the outskirts of the shopping district. It was relatively empty with only a few tables occupied, hers being one of them.

The pub overall seemed clean and smelled of fresh herbs. The barkeep even smiled at me as I came in—the only witch to do so since I got there.

Cedar did a double take when I arrived before motioning for the waitress to get her another glowing drink.

"I don't believe in forgiveness," I lied and pulled out the chair across from her.

I stretched my legs under the table and took the drink with a small nod. I realized I should have asked what it was before taking a large gulp when heat erupted from my belly and shot out to my limbs. My face was on fire, and my body ran so hot I was afraid I might faint. I choked on it as I gripped the table for dear life.

What the fuck?

But then it subsided, leaving me with a pleasantly warm and tingling feeling that was similar to a buzz. That or a hot bath on a lazy weekend night.

When was the last time I was able to enjoy a bath?

"Even for yourself, my dear hunter?" she asked and took a sip of her own drink.

I hadn't realized when I first walked in, but she was impaired. Even if just slightly. The magical alcohol had been working its way through her system and had her leaning against the chair for support.

My foot hit hers under the table as I was getting comfortable.

I eyed her warily.

"Did something happen?" I asked. "Or is this how you act after all your missions fail?"

She let out an exaggerated gasp. Her cheeks were slightly pink, her lips reddened. I caught myself staring at them for a little too long.

My face heated when I realized that this was the first time we were seeing each other since the moment in the car.

Why does the memory of her gaze make my stomach flip?

I had been pumped full of venom, high on the feeling of my and Aurelia's bond reigniting, and enjoying the hell out of making the sassy vampire come apart on my fingers.

But her heated gaze and how it made me feel was something new that had me floundering for an explanation.

"Coming out swinging today, are we?" she asked. "I could remind you how your mission failed as well." She leaned forward, invading my space. I held my breath. "Or I could remind you that you're at the whim of the coven." She leaned even closer, dropping her voice down to a whisper. *Why am I leaning closer as well?* "Or I could remind you that if you had just fucking trusted me in the first place, we wouldn't be here. And I wouldn't have to—"

She cut herself off with a frown. I leaned back, searching her face.

She was hiding something. Again.

"Wouldn't have to what?" I asked with a raised brow and took a sip of my drink. The warmth was doing weird things to my body. Or maybe it was the bickering with Aurelia from before. But I *wanted* to provoke the redheaded witch.

"I'm bound too, you know?" she said. "I have a job here. A role. Things that are expected of me."

"I know," I whispered. "I see you with the other robed people." I leaned forward, seeing my chance to get some more information out of her. Hopefully she was drunk enough not to remember in the morning. "Who are they?"

"*We* are the White Lotus," she said. "Just like the humans have their hunters, the vampires have their council, the witches—my coven—have the White Lotus. They are different. Special. Chosen."

"And they—"

"Are fucking dangerous."

She shook her head as if she realized she'd said too much and downed her drink. Red crept up the column of her neck as she gulped down every last sip. My eyes were drawn to her skin, and I imagined what it would have been like if I had decided to kill her that first night at the palace.

When she slammed the drink back down on the table, the cup shattered. I jumped at the sound.

"Cedar! Stop breaking shit!"

The waitress came by with a trash can and shoved it into Cedar's hands, forcing her to clean up her own mess.

"We don't have much money to replace them anymore—not with the donations."

Cedar grumbled under her breath but did as she was ordered. The only sound between us for some time was the clinking of glass as she cleaned up.

"Donations?" I asked after the silence became too much and looked at the barkeep.

She was an older witch with a busty figure. Her dark blue hair was pulled up into a messy updo, her face splattered with freckles and some dark spots. But her eyes were kind. She had seen the world. Been places.

She seems nice.

"The high priest," she replied, lowering her voice. I looked around to see if one of the other patrons looked over, but they were minding their own business. I pulled my attention back to her. "Every year we're supposed to give him a certain percentage of our profit."

"An offering to the gods," Cedar murmured.

The barkeep took the trash can from her and patted her on the head like a child.

"And do they take it?" I asked. "The gods?"

Both of them looked at me like I had said something I shouldn't, so I cleared my throat, heat racing up the back of my neck, and asked instead, "How much?"

"Sixty percent?" the barkeep asked in an inquisitive tone, almost like she'd forgotten. "Yeah, I think this year's sixty."

What the hell? That can't be right, can it? But the expression on her face told me she wasn't joking in the slightest.

"They keep us safe," she said with a sigh and placed her hands on her hips. "But I remember when it used to be twenty."

And with that, and a meaningful glance at Cedar, she left us alone.

Were all shops forced to do that?

"That's highway robbery, Ceda—"

"You're not a part of the coven," she all but hissed. "You wouldn't understand."

The hostility in her tone took me aback.

"I may not be a witch, but I can see when people are being treated unfairly."

She raised an eyebrow at me. "And now you *care* about the people here?"

I pushed my lips into a thin line.

The drink and her attitude told me something had happened, but Cedar didn't seem very keen on talking about it.

I wanted to push. I didn't want any more secrets between us. Between any of us.

But more importantly, I wanted to respect her privacy.

"So, hear anything about a new mission soon?" I asked.

Her eyes flashed to mine, suspicion building.

So that's what her sour mood is about.

"I won't push you to talk about whatever it is you're trying to hide," I said quickly. "At least not yet."

"That's very generous of you, Vesper," she said sarcastically. "And out of character."

I rolled my eyes and sank into the hard chair.

That's what I get for caring.

"I'm tired," I admitted with a sigh and took another sip of my drink. "I've been skinning rabbits all day. Tate and Aurelia have been arguing. And Levana has been the most hostile babysitter we've had. I just want some—"

I cut myself off, unsure of what I was about to say.

What do I want?

So many things. I wanted to start over. I wanted to sleep. To rest. To go out with Tate and have a normal day with him. I wanted Aurelia to be safe.

There were just too many unrealistic things I wanted and not enough time or resources in the world to make them real.

Maybe if Aurelia's dad just up and disappears, we'll be free.

But there was still the matter of the organization my family belonged to.

"It's heavy, huh? The burden of it all?"

I swallowed thickly and shifted my eyes to the table. I preferred sober Cedar. *I'm too vulnerable for this.*

"I didn't come here for therapy," I muttered. "I'm tired, that's all, and I thought you'd be good company."

When my words were met with silence, I looked back up at her, but she was already staring me down.

"Good choice, hunter," she said, slipping back into herself. "Visit me next time and maybe we can have even more fun."

Heat crawled up my neck at what sounded like innuendo.

What's happening to me?

I was going to respond but shut my mouth when Cedar started to stand. She stumbled slightly and grabbed the table for balance. I reached out to steady her.

"Are you okay—"

I barely had enough time to catch the witch as she fell unconscious, just as her head was about to hit one of the chairs.

"I really should have cut her off sooner," the barkeep grumbled. "Hey, do me a favor and take her up to her room, will you?"

I looked up at her in shock.

"Me?"

"Who else?" She threw me a set of keys that landed on Cedar's lap. "She's upstairs; just leave the keys under the mat when you're done, and I'll retrieve them."

I looked down at the peacefully sleeping witch and let out a sigh.

"Let's get you out of here."

Her apartment was...sad.

The walls were bare. There were no pictures. No keepsakes. Barely enough furniture for one person.

The only thing that dampened my worries was the plants she kept around. All of them were still alive and looked well cared for.

I placed her on her well-made bed, making sure to turn her on her side. She let out a sigh but didn't wake and snuggled into the thick blanket.

Just as I was about to leave, her hand shot out to hold mine. Her simple touch had my heart skipping a beat and heat exploding across my face and neck.

"I'm glad you're safe," she mumbled without opening her eyes.

A smile pulled at my lips. Aurelia would be mad that I'd abandoned her for so long, but I couldn't bring myself to pull away from the witch.

I sat back on her bed.

"I thought you'd die in the palace," she continued. "When I saw the blood, I—"

"I'm okay," I said. "We all are."

Her face twisted.

"None of us are."

My heart stopped in my chest.

"What do you mean?"

She opened her eyes, those green orbs staring at me before pushing herself up into a sitting position, her face getting incredibly close.

My mouth went dry and my breath hitched when she brushed a hand over against my cheek.

"Vesper..." she said on a breath.

I couldn't find the words. I should have pushed her away. Should have left before this could even happen between us.

But looking at her, her face flushed, eyes red, mouth slightly open, emotions pouring out of her like an endless waterfall—it was like she was begging me to stay.

Red eyes and dark hair filled my mind.

Aurelia should be here.

I *wanted* her here.

I wanted to know what she would feel through the bond while she watched us like Cedar had in the car.

The venom might have dazed me, but I know what I felt. There had been something between the three of us. Something charged. Something that connected us.

Something that made all three of us want more.

"Cedar... What's going on?"

Her eyes fell to my lips as she ran her tongue over hers. Something soft brushed against my lower one.

Her thumb.

Her breathing had deepened. Electricity ran between us, urging me to lean forward.

How did this happen? How did I go from hating her to...this?

She moved forward, and I didn't stop her.

Time slowed, but all I could think about was what it would feel like if her lips met mine while Aurelia's hands were roaming my body. I imagined the vampire's lips at my ear, telling me what to do. Imagined what the two of them would taste like together.

Being locked in a room alone with her was dangerous. Especially with Aurelia waiting at the empty cabin for me. *She should be here.* It wasn't just about the two of us anymore.

"Aurelia—"

A knock at the door caused us both to jump apart.

"I don't see a key, so either you're still in there or it was stolen! You better hope it's the former!"

I quickly stood and raced to the door.

"Good night, Cedar," I said quickly as I pulled the door open and gave the key to the awaiting barkeep.

"Good night, Vesp—"

I shut the door and was already at the end of the hallway before she could finish her sentence.

Cedar

I was so fucking embarrassed.

Maybe we can have some more fun? I couldn't believe I'd said that.

And then I tried to kiss her?

I had a fucking death wish.

It had been days since our moment in my apartment, but every time I saw her, I wanted to shrivel up and die.

The outcast duo hadn't had a mission in a while, so Levana suggested she take Vesper out to the weekly market. And now I was stuck with them as I tried to forget just how goddamned embarrassing I'd been.

Aurelia was not helping either.

She wasn't invited and threw a fit as usual, so in order to keep the peace, I had been forced to come. I walked behind Levana and the hunter, Aurelia at my side with her arms crossed, anger radiating from her.

"You trade for things," Levana said. "We don't have a lot of money in the coven, so it's easier this way."

Vesper turned to give me a look. *Damn the old wench for complaining about it in front of an outsider.* But it was more shame than anything that filled me. She was right to complain and Vesper just had been there at the wrong time.

The market itself was on the main road. Witches who rarely ever visited the town center would come out, many with fruits and vegetables they grew themselves—all trying to make some extra money.

The coven was suffering, but it wasn't something I wanted to tell them about. It was better if that little dirty secret stayed hidden.

The plain truth was that no one had money. The high priest took it all.

As a member of the White Lotus, I got more than my fair share of coven coin, but even then, it was barely enough for my room above the bar and a drink.

We passed one of the old-timers, George. He had a wife with a bad back and two kids, both still in the coven's elementary school. He opened his mouth to call to me but shut it when he saw the vampire at my side. My eyes lingered on the pitiful excuse for carrots he was selling.

I left Aurelia's side and handed him two coins. He gave me a hesitant smile and bagged a few up with shaky hands.

I could feel the vampire's eyes on my back.

"See you next week," I said and took the bag from him.

"You-u too, C-cedar."

I tried not to wince at his obvious fear.

They were used to Levana being a hybrid, but she was bubbly and very likable.

Aurelia, on the other hand... Her stare alone could cut someone.

"You're not going to eat those, are you?" she asked, cringing.

"No," I admitted, my honesty shocking us both. "I feed them to the wild hares that linger on the border."

"Cute."

Her tone had my skin heating.

I turned back to see Levana still dragging Cedar along. The silver-haired hunter looked uncomfortable, especially when the witch hybrid got too close.

I don't believe in forgiveness. That's what Vesper had said in the bar, but even if she wasn't at ease around her, it seemed like maybe she had forgiven the pink-haired girl.

At least she didn't really seem to hate her anymore.

She should, though. Especially after what she brought up in the meeting.

To use Tate? A child? Levana was more like the high priest than I thought.

She had grown up rough, an outcast because of her hybrid status. Something the high priest liked because it made her so easy to control.

But she had always been so sweet that I never thought I would hear words like those come out of her mouth.

"She's so annoying, isn't she?" Aurelia asked in a whisper by my side.

Yes. But I wouldn't say it out loud. Even if they were too far away to hear me, I didn't want to start shit with anyone in the White Lotus. Especially not after what they wanted to do to Aurelia and Vesper.

I felt like if I wasn't careful, they might do something to hurt them just to spite me.

Vesper and Levana stopped at one of the booths selling pink and white striped candy. The person at the stall coaxed them over with an offering of a free sample, and Levana grabbed Vesper's arm in excitement. Something that sent an unexpected burst of annoyance through me.

Can she be any more obvious? I knew they were friends back before Vesper knew anything about our jobs, but really?

Aurelia let out a low growl.

"Calm down," I told her but was unable to look at her. My eyes were trained on Levana's fingers as they trailed from Vesper's elbow to her back.

My jaw ticked.

"Don't lie. It bothers you too, I know it," the vampire whispered.

That got my attention. She looked at me with an unreadable expression, like she could see right through me. Like she knew what I did in the darkness of my room and the names I moaned when I came on my own fingers.

I don't like it.

If there was anyone I'd like to hide my fantasies from, it would be her.

But even so, she wasn't as angry as I thought she'd be. Vampires were territorial with their bonded. Rightfully so. If she could read me that well, she should be threatening to cut my head off.

"But it doesn't bother you that it bothers me," I pointed out.

She gave me a sinister grin that had my heart skipping.

"I like you watching you want something you can't have."

Annoyance pricked at my skin. *I can have her if I want to.* It was a dangerous thought. Where the fuck was Helma and her path out of this?

At the same time, her words spurred something in me. I wanted to prove her wrong. Maybe that was the whole point. Maybe the vampire princess wanted to play.

"Can't I?" I asked, lowering my voice.

Aurelia shot me a look. Her eyes twinkled, telling me that I had fallen right into her trap. But I couldn't help myself.

I'll play your little game.

"Oh? You really think she'll choose you over me? Her bonded?" she asked, inching closer to me. My heart skipped a beat when her shoulder brushed against mine, reminding me of the look she'd given me in the car that night.

My gaze automatically went to her neck and then down...

"Hm."

"What?" I asked her, suddenly feeling like I'd been caught doing something I shouldn't.

"Just how lonely are you?" she asked.

All the warmth I was feeling for her vanished.

Very.

Images of me alone in my apartment fucking myself while imagining being with them hit me like a slap to the face.

Embarrassing.

"Want to help relieve some of it?" I asked with a smirk.

Shock coated her features before she gave me her signature pout. She was getting annoyed, and it was kind of...cute.

I felt a stare on me, so my eyes went to Levana and Vesper. The silver-haired hunter was looking at us with an expression I couldn't read.

"Your deflection tells me everything I need to know. They keep you locked up in some tower here only to be let out for missions, don't they?"

Aurelia had no idea how right she was. Images of a wet, cold, dark cell flashed through my mind. I suppressed the shiver that ran through me.

"You're close," I murmured, unable to take my eyes from Vesper. "More like a dungeon."

"Maybe you and I aren't so different after all," she said and walked past me, her shoulder hitting mine. "I still don't like you, though."

"Sure you don't, *Brat*."

This caused Aurelia to pause, and I swore I saw red creep up her neck.

I couldn't help the chuckle that left my lips.

Aurelia

Sneaky little hunter.

She had locked the door to her room, kicking me out, citing that she needed some time to herself and not to bother her. It wasn't the first time she had a little pity party, so I let her be. Since I wasn't chained anymore, I could go anywhere in the house while Vesper had a human moment.

I never heard the window opening. Even though it hadn't been long, the bond was weakening, so any deceit I should've felt was muted.

I made a mental note to rekindle it when she got back. I didn't like not feeling her all the time. It got too quiet. Too lonely.

The only reason I found out that she was gone was because I got bored and opened her door to check on her. She wasn't there. The bed was neatly made, and the only thing telling me what had happened was the slightly ajar window.

I let out an unbelieving laugh and strode toward the door. I wouldn't degrade myself by going out the window.

It was unfair. Not only could she go out whenever she wanted, but she decided that she needed to sneak out to get away from me.

I wasn't some type of controlling little girlfriend—I was a prisoner in the witches' land, for Krae's sake!

I stormed the door, ready to follow her scent, but as soon as I pushed it open, a random cropped-haired witch was standing in front of me. His brown eyes glared into mine, and he lifted his arms to create a sort of barrier.

I could feel his magic vibrate in the air, blocking the exit. There was no doubt I'd get sliced to pieces if I tried to force my way through.

As if that could stop me.

I could tear off his arms in seconds.

"Let me out," I ordered.

"You must stay in the safe house if there is no one to escort you," he replied. "Plus, it's past curfew."

"Vesper left; you didn't stop her," I noted and placed a hand on my hip.

The more special treatment she got, the angrier I got.

"She doesn't have the same restrictions you do," he said. I smelled the magic flaring to life before I saw the red strings spreading across the door frame, stopping me from leaving. I jerked back, fear rushing through me as the magic got just a little too close for comfort.

Why am I afraid of this little rat?

It was embarrassing how meek and small I had become since Vesper stabbed me to skirt her prophecy.

"Let me talk to that priest person," I demanded. "It's not fair to lock me in here while she—"

"Rules are rules," he deadpanned. "Don't make me call Levana."

I let out a growl of frustration and slammed the door in his face.

Levana this, Levana that; I was going to explode if I had to see her one more time. Since she took us on that stupid outing to the market that was totally supposed to be some type of date between her and Vesper, I had trouble fighting back the urge to tear her head off.

Stupid coven. Stupid pink-haired witch.

Stupid Vesper.

Where was she going this late at night anyway? Better yet... Who was she meeting?

I doubt she was meeting Levana given how annoyed she felt at the market. Her feeding those feelings through the bond had been the only thing keeping me sane. That and...

Brat.

My skin heated at Cedar's pet name for me. It was worse than being called *princess*, and yet it made my stomach do weird things.

She's with Cedar.

Jealousy burned through me. I hoped she felt it through the bond.

How could they do this without me?

Whatever had been stirring between the three of us was too much to ignore, and as annoyed as I was at them, a burst of need ran through me when I thought of what this could mean for *us*.

I couldn't bear it. I wanted to be there. Wanted to see it. I wanted to see Vesper's reaction as the witch touched her. As she brought her pleasure. Wanted to see how the witch would react when I went in to play. I imagined we'd make a fun game of it.

Fuck, they couldn't wait for me?

If Cedar was that lonely, she could find a witch to fuck. Vesper was mine first. If she wanted a part of this bond, I should have been asked first.

Maybe she was afraid you'd say no, a little voice in the back of my head whispered.

I should. There was no good reason for *me* to allow the witch in. And at the end of the day, I was the only one who could bond us all, so I had all the power.

Power to say no.

And the power to say yes.

But I wouldn't make my move. Not until Vesper came back. She still needed to pay for this.

Acting like a good little prisoner was hard. It took more strength than I thought I had to stay put inside the cabin and wait.

I paced. Paced an entire hole in the middle of the beat-up cabin all while waiting for Vesper to come back.

It's not fucking fair.

I was going insane. Slowly but surely.

The palace had been huge with a garden, and the blood parties I was let out for gave me enough entertainment and sex to get my fix. The cabin they forced us into was minuscule in comparison, not to mention I hadn't fucked Vesper in days. Since our moment in the car.

Are they fucking?

I smelled them together when she came home the other night, so all signs pointed to it.

They obviously wanted each other, but...

Maybe she keeps sneaking away because they don't want you.

I wanted to smack that damn voice in my head. Maybe ramming my head into the wall would shut her up.

When had I become this needy little thing? And why was I not tearing the witch's head off for being with my bonded?

Because you want her too. You want them both.

Fuck.

The voice is probably right, but I won't voice that out loud.

When an hour had passed, I went back to the door. The same witch was there, and he gave me an exasperated look.

I couldn't take it anymore. I couldn't take being looked down on anymore.

They were keeping me in the house because they thought I was dangerous, even though I gave them no reason for it.

So what if I lost my temper and attacked the witches when we first arrived? I had just been stabbed in the heart and had woken up to witches using their magic on me. Any sane vampire would freak out.

I was tired of it. I was tired of being trapped my entire life. Controlled. I was not going to leave one cage just to be put in another.

And Vesper... She belonged to me.

She belonged by my side.

I would show her.

I would show them all.

Fuck the witches.

Fuck my father.

Fuck Vesper for leaving me here alone.

"Why does your royal highness not listen to orde—"

"I'm bored," I said in a sultry tone as I leaned against the wall. "Entertain me?"

He raised a brow at me before looking around and then bringing his gaze back to mine.

"Me?" he asked. "Why do I think you'd be more likely to kill me than fuck me? What about your vampire hunter?"

This is almost too fucking easy. The witches should really reconsider who they put in charge of these things.

"She's annoying me." I motioned for him to come in. "Let's just say she's not meeting my *needs*."

A smile spread across his face before he cast one last glance over his shoulder and stepped into the house.

My lips curled. *Fucking dumbass.* Like most men, he was gullible, and unfortunately for him, that would cause his untimely death.

As soon as he me baring my teeth, he tried to backtrack, but his body had already come over the threshold. I was quick, my hands on his shoulders pulling him to me before my fangs tore into his neck.

I took a gulp of the witch's blood, but it was bitter and tasted almost burned. Pity.

He made a noise as one of my hands grabbed the back of his hair, and the other grabbed his arm. Splitting his body in half was as easy as ripping a petal from a flower.

I let his body fall to the ground, blood seeping into the wood floors.

Satisfaction unfurled in my chest. It had been a while since I killed anybody, and if I was being honest, it felt fucking good.

Vesper wanted to go out and have some fun time without me? Leaving me all alone, bored to death?

I wanted to play too and it wasn't fucking fair that she was able to leave and do whatever she wanted.

And *lie* to me about it.

I don't want to be alone anymore. And if that meant getting their attention through killing a useless guard? So be it.

I'd play the cruel vampire part for them. Gladly.

I stood a few feet away from my victim and waited.
Let the show begin.

Vesper

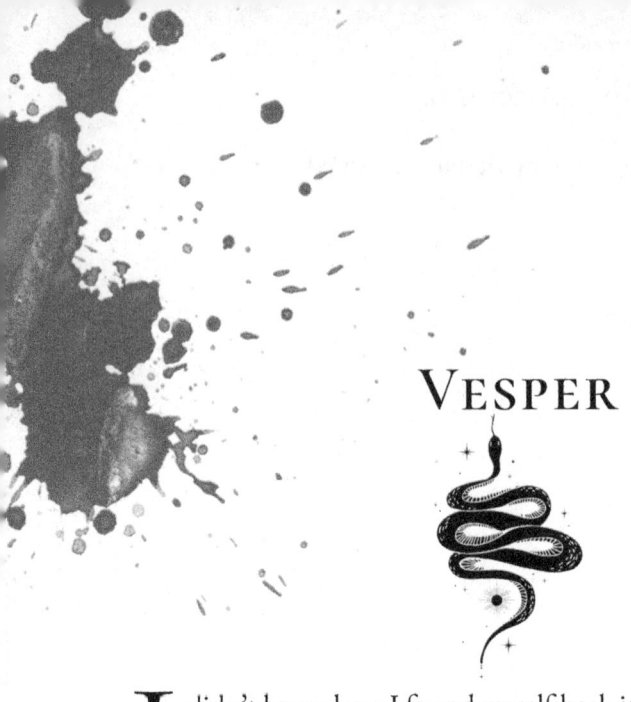

I didn't know how I found myself back in the bar. Or how I knew that Cedar would be there waiting for me.

But she was there. And I had *willingly* snuck out on Aurelia.

I could just imagine how angry she would be at me when I came back.

She'll probably throw another pillow at me. Or worse.

I shuddered at the thought of what she might do.

But I couldn't help it. There was something that kept drawing me to the bar. That kept drawing me to Cedar.

The same something that told me leaving Aurelia on her own was wrong. The same something that kept giving me these mental images of the three of us tangled together.

Impossible, because witches and vampires don't mix. Especially those two.

But I wanted it more than anything. And maybe if I was lucky, I'd make it happen.

As soon as I entered, a few of the witches in there turned to look at me, obviously surprised to see me a second time.

Cedar stiffened before she made any movement to look at me, which was oddly out of character for her. Her wavy red hair was fully down, covering her face and her eyes. Hiding her.

I like it better up. I like seeing her face. Being able to read her.

The thought shocked me, but I didn't have enough time to process it before she turned, her green eyes meeting mine. Piercing.

Just like that day in the market.

There was so much tension in them. So many unanswered questions. Some of them undoubtedly having to do with Aurelia.

I wanted—no, I needed—to know what was happening with Cedar. It had become an obsession. Something that kept me awake at night. Something that had me on edge.

What were we? Why did I feel this pull that kept me bouncing between the two?

And how did I know that, while Cedar seemed fine, something was off?

There's something happening. Whatever it was, it had been happening for a while. Each time I saw the witch, she was more and more tense.

Eyebags told me she wasn't sleeping well. The sinking of her cheeks told me she wasn't eating well. Her facial expression couldn't hide it—it told me how much whatever it was was weighing on her. How much she didn't want to tell me.

I'm scared to know what it is.

But all of that disappeared as the same warm smile she always had when she met me graced her face. She waved me over to the table.

"Finally got the balls to leave your vampire?" she asked, a slight teasing to her voice.

I sat down with a scoff, all the questions I had about whatever was plaguing her suddenly vanishing.

This is the Cedar I used to know.

It was sort of comforting to realize that she was the same person I met at the palace—not the fake persona she had put on just so she could infiltrate my life.

Levana had changed. It wasn't easy to talk to her anymore. And every time I faced her, I couldn't help but think just how many of our interactions had been fake. And just how many she had been feeding back to the witch coven.

But Cedar...

"I feel like I just make it worse sometimes," I admitted, keeping my voice low. "Stabbing her was probably the wrong move. Especially when I had just gained her trust."

Cedar let out a scoff.

"If it were me, I'm not sure I'd forgive you. Maybe she's just biding her time until she can escape."

I balled my hands into fists on top of the table, unable to keep my reaction hidden.

My heart dropped.

Would Aurelia do that?

My stomach lurched. My skin heated. I didn't want to think of what it would be like to lose my princess.

Cedar's hand nudged mine, calling me back to her.

"She will forgive you one day," she said, a surprising sincerity in her voice. "She cares more than you think."

Something tugged at my chest, urging me to go back to Aurelia. *The bond?* It wasn't as strong as it had been, but it felt like it was telling me something.

"Seems like you know her better than I thought," I noted. "I didn't think you cared enough to notice."

Cedar's eyes fell to the table before meeting mine again.

"She's amusing," she admitted. "Sometimes annoying. Bratty. But she's strong and, well... simple. It's not hard to tell that she wants freedom and the attention of her bonded."

I sat back with a sigh. Cedar was right, and it left me unsure of what to do.

"You coming out here won't make it better. I suggest you scurry back or else risk punishment."

"I'm a glutton for it," I murmured, imagining the feeling of her fangs sinking into my skin. The anger, the fury, the pure need it pulled out of us. I loved it all.

"Or maybe it's you punishing yourself," she said. "Don't think I didn't catch what was happening in the car. You'd let her do anything to you, probably even kneel in front of her, begging her to kill you if it made her happy."

Her words had my back straightening. Her gaze was telling me she saw right through me.

"You sure seem to pay a lot of attention to us."

"It's my job." She shrugged, as if it were nothing, but there was more to it than that.

"Really? Does *your job* specify you have to watch us fuck in the back of your car?"

The smile that spread across her face was real. Her eyes widened slightly as if she couldn't believe I had just insinuated what I had.

"There she is," she said with a small chuckle. "Show this version to the princess instead of the whiny, depressed one, and maybe she'll forgive you sooner."

"Or I could just bring you back as an offering. I'm sure she'd be thrilled to know you and I like to get drunk at a witch bar together. I'm sure she'd love to punish us both."

"Be careful, or I might wind up with fangs buried in my neck. But unlike you, I would much rather *not* become her pin cushion."

She made an exaggerated face of disgust, and I rolled my eyes at her.

"Right...Probably for the best. She hates you and all the other witches anyway," I commented, baiting her.

"Don't be too sure about that," she said with a smirk, and I smirked myself.

It was just the reply I was expecting. Because I had seen them at the market. Oddly close, and Aurelia had looked...amused? Interested? So maybe...

Maybe it didn't have to be this violent tug between the two. If I could only bring them a bit closer...

Hope sprang in my chest. Maybe whatever gods out there were listening. Maybe they didn't hate each other as much as I thought.

Maybe they don't hate each other at all.

Cedar motioned for the barkeep to give us another two glasses of whatever she was drinking, but when it arrived, instead of taking a sip, I only held up the glass, swirling the glowing liquid inside.

"Something on your mind, hunter?" Cedar asked.

So many things. The cult-like coven. Aurelia's anger. Tate. Gabriel. The missions. How the entire time we had been in the coven we hadn't heard even a whisper of the crazed vampires that we had been fighting before.

But that's not what I wanted to talk about in that moment.

"I should hate you," I admitted. "I want to. Trust me, I do."

"Ouch," she muttered, the smile sliding off her face.

I merely shrugged. It would be easier if I could hold on to my anger like Aurelia did. But she had practice. All the years in the palace had fortified her heart; she forged steel around it, protecting it from anyone and everyone who dared hurt her. It's why she was able to keep it inside until it burned so hot she had no choice but to let it out.

My heart, on the other hand, felt like it was bleeding out right on the table in front of us and there was nothing in the world that could fill the wound.

The bond tugged again. I wanted to go back to my princess, but something was keeping me rooted to my spot.

"I mean, you did lie to me," I continued.

She gave me a look.

"You were on a job. I was on a job too. I tried to warn you so many times. Just like you, I'm obligated to keep certain things to myself."

"I know," I said with a sigh. "Another reason why I can't hate you. I thought we were good friends at the palace. You helped me more than once."

Cedar shook her head and let out a scoff-like chuckle before she brought her drink up to her lips and took a heavy gulp.

"*Friends.*"

She slammed the glass down on the table, earning a shout from the barkeep.

"I know, I know," Cedar said, raising her hands in a guilty gesture and sending the lady a smile.

It was the same blue-haired witch from before. This time, after she glared at Cedar, she sent me a smile.

The action caught me off guard. Most of the witches were still wary of us, but she felt so warm. My chest started to ache.

Cedar waited a moment before turning to me, her eyes serious and her lips pressed into a thin line.

"Listen, Vesper, I—"

The door to the bar burst open, magic filtering through. The invisible tendrils crawled across my skin, winding around my arms and legs.

It was so powerful, it choked the air from my lungs and sent light shocks through me.

Danger. I stiffened, my hands coming to grip the table. *Are we under attack?*

Not one, not two, but *five* witches filtered in, all of them wearing cloaks and masks over their faces.

I looked back to Cedar for an explanation, but all the color had drained from her face, and for the first time, I thought I saw real fear in her expression. But it lasted only a second, and then the same cold mask I had seen when I first came into the bar was back in place.

"Well," she said, a bitter smile spreading across her face. "It looks like your vampire has thrown another little tantrum."

It wasn't just a tantrum; it was the biggest fucking mistake she could've made while we were still on the witches' land.

Shock and anger could not describe the multitude of feelings that attacked my every being when I entered the cabin and saw the blood splattered all over the doorway and the dismembered body of a witch lying on the ground. All his blood had soaked into the floorboards.

This was what the bond had been trying to tell me. It was trying to stop this. And I failed her. Again.

Aurelia was inside, and the witches had those red vines of magic wrapped around her entire body as she thrashed against them. She let out an inhumane growl and tried to jerk herself free, but each time she did, sparks went flying.

But she didn't care. She kept fighting them.

She's hurting herself.

I rushed in, Cedar close behind me. She was trying to stop me. Trying to reach for me, but I was right outside her grasp.

"Listen, there has to be some mistake," I said as I entered, careful not to step in the blood. I put my hands up to show them that I posed no threat.

My heart was pounding in my chest. I could *feel* her pain through the bond.

Do something. I need to do something.

"She wouldn't just randomly do thi—"

I was cut off by a robed man—White Lotus, I guessed—coming into the cabin. The witches holding Aurelia stiffened, and Cedar tilted her body to the side, allowing him to step past her.

I gave her a questioning look.

"He's the high priest's right hand," she explained. "Does the heavy lifting."

"Let's hear it, vampire," he ordered. "Why did you kill one of our witches? And remember, I will know if you lie to me."

She spat at his feet.

"Who the fuck are you to order me around? Your fucking people can't keep me chained up here like some fucking anim—"

One of the witches pulled at the red vines. She let out a pained moan. Before I could register it, I was lurching forward.

Cedar was fast; her arms circled me and pulled me flush against her.

"Calm," she whispered on a breath, hot against my ear. I shivered against her. But whatever she was making me feel was minuscule in comparison to my anger and need to save Aurelia.

Fuck this.

"Don't fucking hurt her," I warned the witch.

"She's acting out," he said. "But she obviously won't get away with killing one of our own."

"I'll teach her," Cedar said quickly. "I'll punish her myself, don't worr—"

The random witch raised his hand. When he looked at me, I noticed that one of his eyes was the same icy blue as the high priest's.

"I'll handle it," he said. "For both of you."

I narrowed my gaze at him. Who the fuck did he think he was? How dare he treat Aurelia this way? She was a goddamned princess, for fuck's sake!

"Both of us?" I asked angrily. "What did I do—"

"Not you," Cedar interrupted, her voice hollow. "Me."

My heart dropped into my stomach.

What?

I looked between the two witches, but neither gave me an explanation.

"Always so clever, little one," the witch replied. "The hunter can scrub the floorboards. You and the vampire are coming with me."

Cedar

Is my little infatuation worth all this?

I bit back a groan as hostile magic burned up my back, tracing the scars that had been there for what felt like a lifetime. My body convulsed, desperately trying to get away from the pain, but even if I had enough energy to get up and make a break for it, the magic would follow.

It was the high priest's special punishment.

We all got them. *Lashings.* When we finally disobeyed or fucked up enough to warrant a punishment. It was inevitable. There was no perfect witch in the White Lotus.

After all, if there had been... How would he be able to control us?

He started with the whip. Long, braided, humming with dark, old magic that was probably older than the coven itself.

The whip itself left scars, but the magic intertwined with it made the wounds heal slower, leaving large scars that would plague us for the rest of our lives. Scars that could be tapped into with his magic even years after they healed.

He left a part of himself in us. It strengthened us. Made our magic extraordinary. Made us the White Lotus—perfectly honed little soldiers ready to do his bidding.

And gave us a *reminder*. One so painful and mind-numbing that even the thought of disobeying him would bring painful flashbacks.

I had watched other witches go crazy at the threat of the magic. They would do anything to escape this punishment.

Even turn on each other.

My hands dug into the cool concrete, my nails bleeding from the force. The cathedral basement was the venue of choice. Magical candles lit the way, the only other light source the magical vines coming from the priest and the runes beneath our feet, both a warning not to move an inch or risk something even worse than my punishment.

Bear it. Bear it for just a few moments—

The next blast sent dark spots across my vision.

"I thought Levana was my babysitter," Aurelia said, her usually snappy tone sounding a bit more troubled than usual.

Like she fucking cares.

"I am merely a worker bee," Levana said, her voice grating on my nerves. I never really had many issues with her—at least not until now.

She was the perfect little brainwashed underling. Sweet and caring, but so afraid to break the rules and receive her own punishment that she didn't even dare try to step out of line.

"And what?" Aurelia asked. "Cedar's like the boss or something?"

No one said anything, and the silence told her she was right.

At the end of the day, this was my assignment, and when she couldn't be a good little vampire, I would be the one getting in trouble.

All I wanted to do was save the fucking hunter.

I let out a groan as his magic ran through me again. I didn't know how much more I could take without blacking out.

"Watch her, vampire," the high priest commanded. "Don't avert your gaze when it's *your* actions that caused this."

"It seems to me that *you're* the one causing this," she said, her voice filled with venom. "No good leader would like to bring pain to their people."

"Like your father?" Levana asked with just as much hostility in her voice.

"*Exactly,*" Aurelia replied, "Your cult-like leader wannabe is reminding me a little bit too much of the place I come from. I thought this was supposed to be a safe haven."

Instead of answering, the high priest pulled his magic from me. I inhaled sharply, sweet air filling my lungs, and gasped, trying to keep up with the demand for it.

It's like I couldn't get enough. I hadn't realized I had stopped breathing.

My mind swam, my body shook. *Get up.* But it was difficult. He had wanted to make me an example. After a few moments, I managed to stand up to meet Aurelia's gaze.

She was worried about me. *I guess I should be sort of happy?*

But I really wasn't. Not when my entire body reeked of his magic.

It was humiliating and violating. Everything it was supposed to be.

"Now the vampire."

Aurelia shot the high priest a look, and I held up a shaky hand.

"She's been stuck in that house for over *five months,*" I said. "I don't condone killing anyone, but we haven't exactly been fair to her."

"She's let out with the hunter all the time," Levana argued. Now that he wasn't torturing me anymore, I could make out the worry etched on her face.

I wished it felt good to realize that my fellow coven members actually cared and didn't want to see me hurt, but I was honestly more disappointed in her and the others than anything else.

How did we let this happen? How could we stand by and watch other coven members be tortured?

But that was the world the high priest had built. It's what was ingrained in us.

I had been the same. I had only started to change when I met Vesper.

"I can count on one hand the number of times I've left the cabin," Aurelia stressed. The tension between them was unbearable. Neither was looking away nor standing down. There was a silent conversation happening between them, one that scared the absolute shit out of me because I knew Aurelia was trying his patience.

"Five lashes," the high priest said. Fear clawed at my heart. Panic exploded through me so fast my head spun.

It would be the same magical lashing we all got. It would allow him to pump magic into her. *His magic.* It would also allow him to keep his magic in her for as long as he lived.

Not safe.

He was too fast for me to stop him. His red, magical vines lashed out and grabbed Aurelia by the wrist and ankles. She fought him, screaming and kicking, but it was no use. It never was. Not with a power like his.

The vines curled behind her, creating one thick arm before descending on her back. She threw her head back, her scream vibrating through the cathedral. She arched against the vines holding her in place as another lash came down.

Her face was twisted in pain. I'd seen nothing like that before. Not from her.

She was supposed to be the perfectly poised princess. Cruel and rotten to her core. Nothing, not even the most powerful magic, was supposed to faze her.

I was watching all of it crumble right before my eyes.

All of us were.

"I'll take it in her stead," I said quickly.

All eyes turned to me.

The lashings stopped. Aurelia was breathless as she looked at me. Sweat beaded across her forehead, her eyes were bloodred, and her expression showed more pain than I'd ever seen before.

But there was something else in her eyes as well.

She was shocked and maybe a bit...hopeful?

The princess might be annoying and push her luck every chance she got, but I didn't like seeing her in pain. *How could anyone?* And I knew what it would do to Vesper. No matter how muted the bond was, she was likely feeling her pain at that very moment.

"More?" Levana asked, concern lacing her voice. "Are you suicidal?"

Evidently, I am.

My body was at its breaking point. I had never taken so many lashings before. Even when I was in my rebellious phase.

"As much as I appreciate the—"

"She's less affected by it," I said, cutting her off. "She grew up in the palace where pain is normal. This will mean nothing to her. If anything, she will use it as fuel. But if you do it to someone else in her stead..."

The high priest looked sharply at Aurelia and slowly lowered her to the ground. I caught the smile pulling at his lips in the darkness.

It had my skin crawling.

"I will allow it," he said.

I didn't have time to brace myself before his magic was pumped back into me, and I crumpled to the ground with pain.

Forcing my head up, I met the vampire's gaze.

For her, I whispered in my head. I knew from the look on her face I didn't have to say the words out loud.

Her troubled expression was the last thing I saw before I succumbed to the darkness.

"Don't you dare leave her," a voice hissed.

"I have to," a second one said, this one sounding regretful. "He ordered it. I have to. I'm sorry."

"Fucking hybrid bitch."

Heat. Warm tingles spread from my head to my toes, covering every inch of my body. *It feels so good.* When had I ever felt this good before?

It lulled me into a calm state. Made me forget entirely why my head had been buzzing in the first place.

I sank into it. Breathed out a sigh.

Through the haze, I could feel someone. They were at my side, their hands on my arms. Holding me down?

It didn't matter. Not when it felt this good.

But then it got hotter. And hotter. And hotter until all the heat was traveling to my core. It swirled in my belly and expanded outward.

I let out a whimper.

Oh fuck.

Sweat started to coat my skin. The hands I could feel on me were the only thing quenching the insane fire building up inside me.

I need more of it.

I arched into the person, my own whines sounding foreign to my ears.

"Witch."

I grabbed their hand and used it to find my way to their arm. Then up and up...

I was reaching for something. For them. I knew they would be the only person that could help me.

I *ached* for them.

Please. Please. Please. Please.

I hadn't realized I had been saying it all aloud until a hand covered my mouth. I was quick to grab it, bringing the person's wrist to my mouth before placing a kiss on their cool skin.

"Cedar." The voice was harsher this time.

I pushed myself off the ground and into them. *More. More. Please, more.* They smelled of fresh lilies. I groaned into where their shoulder and neck met, my mouth watering at the idea of biting into it.

I was so far gone, but I didn't care. The only thing running through my mind was how to get this person to touch me. To let me touch them.

I wanted to fuck. My cunt was already fluttering over nothing. But more importantly, I needed to fuck. I needed to make this person feel good. Needed to taste them.

I licked up their neck with a breathy moan. Their gasp spurred me on, and I sank my teeth into their sensitive flesh, my hands blindly grasping for them.

More. More. Mor—

A hand gripped me and forced me away. "Wake up!"

The scream had my eyes popping open. The voices were still chanting in my head, begging me to pick up where I'd left off. But the surprise of who was there in front of me had my mind clearing, if only for just a moment.

Aurelia's eyes narrowed at me.

"You're hurt," she said. "I had to give you venom to heal. A *lot* of it."

Venom?

At first, I didn't know what she was talking about. I was too shackled by the heat spreading through me.

I need her. Even worse than that time in the car, and for some reason it felt that if I didn't fuck her right then and there, I might just die.

My cunt clenched around nothing, pulling a whine from me.

And then it hit me.

"Why the fuck did you think that was a good idea?" I ground out. I blinked a few times, trying to clear my vision.

Aurelia's form was still blurry, but I could just make out her face. Her eyebrows were pulled together, and her lips were pulled into a deep frown.

If my mind had been any clearer, I might have wondered why the cruel princess was worried about me. But my hazed mind was focused on something else.

My hand reached out, fingers just barely brushing her lips. They were plump, soft, and still stained with some of the witch guard's blood.

I need to feel them.

Her breath hitched, but she didn't push me away.

"Sorry, witch. This is going to hurt."

And for a second time, I was forced into darkness.

Vesper

My skin reeked of blood.

It had taken over an hour to clean it up and then scrub the floorboards. Even so, the blood still stained the wood, leaving a very obvious print.

Looks like we'll never forget just how Aurelia fucked us with her little tantrum.

I wanted to be mad. To be honest, I was a little pissed off, but it was nothing in comparison to how worried I was.

What are they going to do to her?

Something about the coven felt off. The high priest's right hand was…weird. The way Cedar had bowed to him was even weirder.

When I had met her in the palace, I never would have thought she would cower in front of anyone.

Cower was not the right word. It was more like she had shrunk herself, trying her best not to get his attention. As soon as those blue eyes were on her, she flinched, and I could almost hear the chanting in her head.

Don't look at me. Don't look at me. Don't look at me.

The coven was hiding something. And not knowing what it was had my anxiety through the roof.

I paced, looking out the front door. I had kept it open so I could see them as soon as they got back.

There was a new guard out there, and he didn't look all that happy to be stationed at the previous one's grave.

It dawned on me then just how stuck we were.

And it's all my fault.

I was the one who forced Cedar's hand. It might be her coven, but I was using her to guarantee some sort of safety for the two of us.

I was wrong.

I'd gotten us trapped, and now I had to sit there and face the consequences of my actions.

It didn't help that I felt...*something*. I knew it was the bond, but it was much fainter than it had been. Like something was blocking it. Distance maybe? I made a mental note to tell Aurelia we needed to reignite it.

Something zapped through it. I *felt it* as she went through something. Something she didn't like. Something uncomfortable and likely painful.

But it was so faint I could barely make it out.

I had no idea what it could be. It came and went, and all I could do was wait. And wait. And wait.

The soles of my shoes slid across the cabin for the hundredth time as I circled the same path in the bloodied floorboards. My anxiety felt like a monster on my shoulders, its teeth scraping along the skin of my neck and whispering in my ear.

They're dead.

They've left you.

The high priest locked them up.

Your fault. Your fault. Your fault.

Then I saw them walking up to the cabin. Aurelia was carrying Cedar, her face still stained with blood. The witch was unconscious in her arms and paler than I'd ever seen her.

She looks dead.

I was at the threshold in seconds, staring as my bonded brought her in.

I cast my eyes to the guard at the door, who just stared at the bleeding witch with a disinterested stare like it was...normal? Expected?

How many times have their own people come home unconscious and bleeding for him to have that reaction?

"What happened—"

"Get the bed ready," Aurelia forced out. Her eyes were bright red, and she was breathing heavily.

Only when she got past the threshold did I see the blood on the back of her dress.

My heart stopped in my chest. Anger. Pain. Guilt. All of it hit me, but I pushed it away and focused on the limp Cedar in her arms.

Get your shit together. They need you.

I ran to the bedroom ahead of them, throwing open the door and watching as Aurelia placed the witch gently on the bed. I'd never seen Aurelia be this gentle with anyone before.

Not even me. *She never needed to.* We both enjoyed things a little rougher.

Seeing her treat Cedar with that type of care had the bond thrumming to life between us.

The princess was capable of gentleness when needed, and seeing her like this proved Cedar's words before.

She doesn't hate her. She treats her like something broken and weak. Something to protect. *Much like the bird back in the palace.*

Is that what she was to her?

Cedar's shirt was soaked with blood and there was magic rolling off her in waves. It felt...wrong. Left a sour taste in my mouth and had me sweating.

My heart broke in two at the state she was in.

I leaned over the bed, watching her.

"Was this your punishment?" I asked, unable to keep the anger out of my voice, then looked at Aurelia. She was in a better state than the witch, but obviously still hurt.

Aurelia nodded, her lips pursed.

"Tell me which one did it," I commanded.

"So you can do what exactly?" she asked. "You're stuck here just like I am."

"So I can plunge my sword into their chest. Tear their heart out. Make them beg for mercy."

Aurelia let out a scoff.

"Tell me who did this. The high priest? The White Lotus? Tell me." I reached out to brush my hand against her cheek. Her eyes flashed to mine. "You want their heart? I'll give it to you. Want to bathe in their blood? I'll make it happen."

I had never been so angry in my lifetime. My body was practically vibrating because of it.

"The high priest. Magical lashings. His stupid fucking robed people just stood there," she finally replied, her voice grim. "She took most of the punishment. Volunteered, I should say. She...*protected* me."

Cedar protected Aurelia?

A knot formed in my throat as my eyes burned and my stomach dropped. There were so many things running through my head, along with my own feelings and Aurelia's from the bond. But the anger was overpowering.

I wanted to kill that damned high priest. No, *I would.* How dare he do this to them?

"The robed people..." I tried to swallow my anger, but it was overtaking my entire being. "Are the White Lotus. Cedar is part of them. Their version of the organization or the vampire council."

"They left her," Aurelia said, the words getting stuck in her throat. "I tried to stop them. She was bleeding too much. I was...afraid I couldn't save her. I had no choice but to pump her with venom."

"I'm going to kill—"

Cedar's hand wrapping around my wrist had me pausing and looking down at the bed. Her eyes were hooded and her cheeks were starting to flush more and more the longer she looked at me.

I was glad to see some color coming back into her, but the suddenness of her change had me worried.

"Cedar," I breathed. "Are you okay? Let me look at you—"

She sat up abruptly and pulled me down to the bed so I was sitting on it. There was a hunger in her eyes that had my entire being on edge. Heat filled me as her eyes ravished my body.

Oh. I'd seen this before. Not just seen but felt it before as well.

"Venom," I whispered.

Aurelia sat behind me, her hand coming to move the hair from my neck.

"I gave her a lot," she whispered, her lips at my neck. "She will be...needy for a moment."

I swallowed thickly as Cedar leaned forward, her hands on either side of me.

"I can't wait," Aurelia said. Her hand pushed my shirt to the side before she sank her teeth into my shoulder. Pain shot through me. The gasp I let out was choked by Cedar's hand coming to grip my throat.

My heart all but stopped in my chest. A need like never before ran through me.

Her eyes were filled with desire. An image I'd never even let myself dream of before.

"I'm sorry you went through that for us," I whispered, unable to stop the guilt from overtaking me. "Thank you. For protecting us."

Her breathing was heavy, her gaze zeroed in on my lips. I couldn't help but lick them. I leaned back against Aurelia. The pain was somehow heightened, but so was the pleasure as the venom worked its way through my system.

"I want to kiss you," Cedar said. "Can I, Princess?"

She's not asking me. That made it just that much hotter. She already knew I'd be like putty in her hands.

Aurelia disengaged her fangs from my shoulder.

"Think of it as your gift," she replied. "Vesper won't mind being used by us for a second, will you?"

Delicious, sinful heat flared through my body, igniting everything in its path. My body jerked, and the brush of their hands against my skin caused me to whine.

I was so sensitive it hurt.

How did this happen? How did I go from worrying they might not live another hour to writhing under their gazes?

"You're not in your right mind. Let's wait until—"

"I know what I want," Cedar said in a low voice. "The venom may make my impulses easier to act on, but I've wanted to fuck you since I first laid eyes on you."

My breath caught. Aurelia's chuckle from behind me had me flushing. *Is this really happening?* Is this the same Cedar I met on the first day at the palace? The one who hid my tattoo and teased me?

The same one who had been sent to watch me? The one who lied to me?

It was hard to believe they were all the same.

Hard to believe I get to experience all of them.

"I fantasized about it," Cedar continued. "The noises you'd make. How prettily you'd beg."

Fuck. I could imagine it. The two of us. Her above me. Making me beg as she teased me with that wicked grin of hers. She would be relentless. Even if I begged, I doubted she'd let up. Something my body was all too excited for.

Wetness pooled in my underwear, my cunt pulsing with need.

"I don't beg," I forced out.

"Oh, but you do for me," Aurelia teased, her lips covering my wound and sucking the blood from it.

"And you'll do it for me, won't you, hunter?" Cedar asked, her other hand splayed across my stomach.

Aurelia was the one to loop her hand around me, pushing it into my pants, obviously frustrated with Cedar's slow pace.

I let out a guttural moan as her fingers circled my clit once before plunging inside me.

"Fuck," I groaned.

My mouth fell open as I panted. Being between the two of them was something else. Every touch. Every breath. Every moment felt heightened, and I was melting for them.

They were right. I would beg. They could degrade me. Hurt me.

Force me to come over and over again or not at all. I wanted to please them.

"You acted like such a tough hunter," Cedar said, her hand tightening on my neck. "But you're not, are you? You're willing to spread your legs without us even touching you."

Her thumb rubbed against my tattoo, an oddly comforting gesture as if she was telling me that she might be degrading me, but she still cared about me.

"Say it," Aurelia murmured against my shoulder, her tongue licking the wound. "Say you'll beg for us."

She curled her fingers inside me. A warning. I jerked against her, unable to keep still with the burst of pleasure that ran through me.

More. Please.

My mind was already begging, but I refused to let the words slip from my mouth.

"Never," I hissed. Blood ran down my shoulder,

Aurelia began rocking her fingers inside me. My hips ground against her hand as I found myself unable to stop chasing the heat.

"No?" Cedar teased. "How about we call you our dirty whore instead? Say you want to be used by us. Tell us how much you'd fucking love both of us ravishing your body."

"I—"

My protest was cut off by Cedar moving closer, her lips right at the side of my mouth as her hand left my throat.

"Too slow," she whispered against my skin before she tilted her head to the side.

Shock ran through me as Aurelia shifted and the sound of their lips locking hit me. Pleasure like never before rocked through me at hearing them. At feeling their bodies pressed against mine as they kissed.

It was too much.

"She's going to come," Aurelia said breathlessly.

Cedar pulled back. The sight of my blood on her mouth was a deliciously dangerous sight. It was wrong. Taboo. A witch should never look like that.

But she did, and the image was ours and ours alone.

I tangled my hand in her shirt and pulled her closer. She stopped just a few centimeters away from my lips.

"Say it," she ordered.

Fuck. Just her command alone was sending me hurling face-first into my orgasm.

"Never," I hissed again, the first wave running through me with a vengeance. "I'm not your to—"

Her mouth meeting mine was like two freight trains colliding. Volatile. Disastrous. And absolutely life-altering.

We melded together perfectly. Sweet yet metallic blood filled my mouth.

When Aurelia and I fucked, it was intense. We challenged each other. We clashed. We fought. We were like fire and ice.

But with Cedar, it was sweet as honey. She kissed in smooth, languid strokes, her tongue dancing with mine. There was no fight. She had me melting against her, submitting without so much as a second thought.

I came so hard I saw stars behind my eyes. Aurelia fucked me through it all, whispering dirty things in my ear as Cedar kissed me until my body went limp.

When Cedar pulled away, she looked conflicted; the venom was wearing off.

"Kiss me again, and I'll kill you," Aurelia warned her, and something flashed across Cedar's face before she hurried off the bed.

"Lying doesn't suit you, Brat," Cedar said over her shoulder, not even daring to look back at us as she fled. The room went silent, the only sound the slamming of the front door and my own rapidly beating heart.

Wow. I had no other words. My head still felt dizzy from the high.

Aurelia and I were silent for a few moments before we both had the strength to speak.

"That was—"

"I guess—"

We both paused, and I turned to look at her. She gave me a smirk.

Blood was smeared across her lips and cheeks, evidence of her kiss with Cedar.

"I guess you really like the witch, huh?" she asked.

"You do too," I shot back.

Aurelia actually looked a bit embarrassed at that.

"Just fulfilling my bonded's wish," she said. "It won't happen again."

But even as she said it, we both knew it was a lie.

Cedar

I sent magic flying at one of the trees. The red bursts cut the tree in thirds, sending its pieces flying. The sun had set long ago. Thank the gods, because if not, I was not sure I'd be able to show my face outside after what happened.

What the fuck did I just do?

I took a deep breath, trying to calm my racing heart. Ever since I'd left the cabin, it had been pounding nonstop. I tried to go back to my apartment. Tried to shower. Tried to drink. Tried everything.

The only thing that seemed to work was letting out all the magic that was buzzing under my skin after I'd been with them.

It was like I was filled with energy. Sex and vampire venom should have drained me, but I felt more energized than I had in months.

I had never meant to take it that far.

Nor did I think the vampire would be receptive to it.

She had a tight lock on the hunter since she'd claimed her with the bond. If anything, she should have been ready to rip my head off the moment I touched what was hers.

She wanted it too.

Kissing the princess with Vesper's blood still on her lips was the most erotic thing I'd ever done. When I was younger, I thought vampires were gross for drinking blood. But here I was, joyfully sucking face with one that had it all over her mouth.

I ran the back of my hand across my lips, remembering the taste of it.

I lost my damned mind.

It wasn't supposed to be this way. Thankfully, it had been Aurelia who made her come.

I might have failed one mission, but to get with the one I was supposed to guide through the prophecy?

That was tempting fate.

If she didn't see the prophecy through...

One thing witches were taught when it came to prophecies was that if even one didn't come true, the balance of the world would be at stake. Even the simplest one could have catastrophic consequences if it was not realized.

And I'm messing it all up.

Because of me, the world might never be the same again.

But what would it mean?

Would the Castle family someday take over all other vampire families? Would they kill off the coven? Would they start a war and kill off hundreds of thousands of humans?

It had to be horrible. That's why the prophecies were taken so seriously. One wrong move and it could upset the balance of the entire world. Why else would so many parties be so involved in it?

The coven had had their eyes set on the Castle family for a millennium. As far back as the vampires went, so did the witches.

The vampire hunters were another complication. They had sent so many of their own to the palace only to be murdered in broad daylight.

They likely weren't going to sit still for long either.

What the fuck am I supposed to do?

A snapping of branches had me whirling to look at the intruder.

My shoulders sank when I realized it was Levana. I really didn't want to talk to her. Couldn't she just let me lick my wounds in peace?

Her eyes glowed just slightly in the dark forest, the only sign that she was a hybrid.

"You made it out," she said, giving me a forced smile.

"Thank the vampire," I snapped and winced at how it came out.

I didn't mean to sound ungrateful. I had been bleeding out, and Aurelia saved me even though she had no reason to. She had done way more than Levana. I should be genuinely thanking her for it.

You also finally got to touch Vesper because of it.

My skin flushed at that.

"I'm sorry," she said, her eyes cast to the ground. "I felt you out here, so I wanted to make sure..."

I turned my head to the side.

"What are you sorry for?" I asked.

It's not like she had been the one who gave me the lashings.

"We all left you," she answered, cringing as I stared at her. "He ordered it. Aurelia fought us. Begged us to help, but—"

"She *begged?*" I asked, my voice raising an octave.

The spoiled princess? Begging?

I want to hear that. Just as much as I want to hear Vesper begging.

Which of them will sound sweeter?

I immediately kicked myself for that thought. There was no way she would beg, and for me? It was hard to believe.

"Well, more like threatened," she admitted. That was more believable. It had the same effect, though. It warmed my heart and almost put a smile on my face. "But yes, and we just...left." She paused, looking around. "I should go, but I'm glad you're safe."

I could do nothing else but nod.

I stood there, silent as she left.

I had no words. The knowledge that the princess had been begging or threatening anyone to save the likes of me weighed heavy on my head.

I ran a hand over my face, the tiredness of the day finally catching up to me. My back was a bit sore, the venom having finally worn off.

There would be no going back after this. At least before I could pretend like Vesper wasn't my darkest obsession.

But now she knew.
They both did.
And somehow Aurelia had wormed her way inside me, right next to her.
What have we done?

Aurelia

"I've thought it over and have come to a conclusion. We need to kill them all," I said, my mind running over the images of Cedar being whipped. I hadn't stopped thinking about it since. I knew something needed to be done. That we needed to leave or get back at them or *something*. I just couldn't sit there and do nothing anymore.

"You know we can't do that," Vesper answered with a sigh and ran a hand through her silver hair. Over the last few days, the bags under her eyes had gotten more pronounced, her skin paler.

Humans were already weak creatures and easily made weaker with lack of sleep and proper sustenance. It made my chest ache for her.

"Says who?" I growled, throwing my hands up in the air. "We go in, kill that freaky priest bastard, take out the witches, bring the redhead with us, and leave. Easy."

Vesper gave me a long look.

"I know it hurts to see Cedar like that, but we are outnumbered and underpowered—"

"Hurt? It doesn't *hurt*," I said with a scoff. *I hurt for no one but myself...and maybe Vesper on occasion.* Vesper's expression didn't change and only had my skin heating more. But Cedar? A witch?

Impossible.

"They whipped me too," I hissed. "I want to get back at them for it."

Vesper closed the space between us, her hand coming to cup my cheek. Warmth from her skin sunk into me and I found myself leaning into her touch.

Beyond the annoyance, my body still craved her. Our bond. It's why I'd been so hesitant to be bonded by anyone. My *soul* wanted to be with her. Be close.

And I wouldn't feel at ease until we were.

It's why it was worse whenever she went out and we were apart for so long.

I knew she must have felt it too. The call between us.

"And that's why you chose to save her instead of lashing out at them when you could?" she asked, causing my mood to sour even further. "That's why you brought her back, covered in her own blood, and pumped her full of venom? Is that also why you let us fu—"

My hand was around her throat in seconds, and I twisted us so that I could pin her to the wall. Her eyes widened for a second before the telltale sign of desire filled them.

I let out a growl.

"Don't want to face it?" she continued. "You like her more than you want to admit. You think I can't see it?"

I got closer, our lips centimeters away. "I think you're projecting."

Her hands found my hips. I let her pull our bodies flush. Just like every other time, we melded together perfectly, though it felt like there was someone missing.

A certain witch whose hands had a mind of their own.

"Then I'll bring her back," she said. "So we can go again. This time without venom. And then you can sit there, watching as she touches your bonded and hating every moment of it."

I gritted my teeth, trying to fight the mental image she was painting. I wanted nothing more than to see them together again. I had only gotten a small glimpse of what it could be—who knew it would ignite such a craving for it?

For *them*?

I should have pushed the witch away. Should have bitten off her hand for even attempting to touch my bonded.

Vesper was *mine*, after all. But when we were together... It didn't feel like I was *losing* her; it felt like we were *gaining* the witch.

Like we were adding her to *us*.

"I would *loathe* it."

Vesper brushed her lips against mine, just the barest hint of a kiss.

"*Liar.*"

I let her push me away.

"If you don't want to admit it, fine," she said and straightened her clothes. "But I'm done trying to deny this any longer."

And with one last look, she walked right out of the house.

I attempted to follow her but paused when the guard at the threshold gave me a look.

I turned back, pacing in the living room.

Fucking hunter. Thinking she can read my mind. She doesn't know shit.

In the privacy of the cabin, I allowed myself to fantasize about it. About them. Maybe even finding them in the house alone, in the middle of fucking, and using it as a perfect excuse to force Vesper to submit to the two of us.

Shaking the image out of my mind, I stomped back toward the guard.

"Hey you," I said to get the attention of the new witch guard outside the cabin. He looked at me with suspicion. "Go get the pink-haired one."

He gave me a look.

"I'm not your errand boy."

Not true. Anyone becomes an errand boy when power is at play.

I sent him a smile, showing my fangs. Unluckily for him, fear was the pillar of all Castle power.

"Did you hear what happened to the last guard who pissed me off?"

That got him moving, and I watched as he scurried away. I let out a chuckle at his actions. Interestingly, the only one in the coven who had any sort of backbone was the high priest.

And Cedar. The witch got *whipped* on my behalf. Not many people wou—

Stop it.

I forced all thoughts of the witch from my mind. I shouldn't even be thinking about her as much as I was.

I was still beyond infuriated at the weak coven leader. He hid behind his magic. Tried to beat compliance into me.

He wasn't the first. But I wouldn't let it happen again. If that meant biding my time until I saw a chance to kill him, then so be it.

I hadn't fully thought it through, but I'd known I'd either leave this place or kill him at some point.

If Vesper and her witch could stop distracting me, that would be great.

But what a pleasant distraction that was.

Vesper had never come that fast or that hard when it was just the two of us. Which should annoy me...but didn't.

She really enjoyed being used, and I was all too eager to fulfill her fantasies.

But it can't happen again.

At least that's what I was telling myself. I wouldn't let them catch me off guard like that again. Take control of me like that. I should have pushed the witch away, but her lips had tasted so sweet.

And Vesper's reaction had been even sweeter. I could still feel her cunt pulsing around my fingers as she ca—

A frowning Levana was walking through the tree line, cutting off my daydream. The guard was also back and refusing to look at me as he took his post once more.

"Can I help you?" she asked, though it lacked her usual bite.

"What's this?" I asked, letting out a small chuckle. "Feeling bad about leaving your friend to die?"

She avoided my gaze, telling me all I needed to know. And I was going to use it to get what I wanted.

I had spent enough time in the cabin, sulking. The coven was old, maybe as old as vampire families themselves. There had to be something here that could tell me about *her*.

I was done acting like a locked-up maiden, waiting to be saved.

"We're going out," I told her, walking past the threshold, almost expecting it to stop me. But it let me through with ease, magic washing over me.

"To do what?" Levana asked, suspicion in her tone.

I shrugged.

"Get you an ice cream cone or something? Fuck if I know. Just get me out of this house before I snap this fucker's neck." I stuck my thumb out, motioning to the guard, who until then was stick-straight and silent.

His gulp was audible. Levana shook her head, but there was a small smile on her face.

"Let's go."

"So it tastes fine to you?" I asked and grimaced as I took another small bite of the ice cream.

It tasted like dirt and sent a chill shooting through my head. *Why do humans even like this?* Maybe it was like cigarettes—a disgusting habit horrible for their health—and would just as likely lead to the destruction of their bodies.

"You're supposed to lick it," she said, barely concealing her laughter.

I sent her a look. *Laughing at me? The nerve.*

"You know I almost killed you for flirting with Vesper."

She froze and turned to me slowly.

"At the market," I added.

"I know," she admitted, her eyes shifting to the town center in front of us.

It was the middle of the day and mostly empty save for a few passersby. An obvious and pitiful excuse for a distraction.

I raised a brow at her. "Then what's with the silence?"

She ran her tongue over her teeth.

"Harmless," she said. "I mostly just wanted to piss you off. I won't do it again."

Satisfied with her answer, I nodded. We stayed in silence until she finished her cone. I handed her mine, and she took it hesitantly.

"I need you to do some digging on my mother's bloodline."

She choked on her ice cream, the suddenness of the movement causing a huge blob to fall on the ground.

Gross. I couldn't keep the frown off my face.

When she pulled herself together, she cleared her throat.

"I know a little," she said. "She was sold to your father to birth you. Apparently, she was a hot commodity."

I narrowed my eyes at her slight.

"Sorry," she mumbled quickly, sensing my anger. "I just mean that a lot of vampire families wanted her."

"Do you know why?" I probed.

Memories of being in my father's office swam through my head. He had insinuated she had been promised to another. Something I took as meaning that he had probably stolen her.

And Icas had hinted at it being a bloodline thing. But he hadn't given me anything concrete either.

I needed to find out what they meant before it ate me alive, but I had no one to ask. No one to trust.

I had seen something when I saw Cedar getting whipped. Memories of my mother dying on the cold ground. And of the lady I couldn't recognize. I had so many memories of pain, of death.

But I never knew *why*.

Those memories had been one good thing that came out of the beating, I guess. They pushed me to find out more.

Levana was definitely not my first choice to help me find out this information, but no one would ever guess that I reached out to her for this. She hesitated when the high priest was done with Cedar and me.

Everyone else had left, but she still lingered, like she wanted to be sure I would save her friend.

I knew I could use that. Use her. Even if her abandonment irked me.

Though it shouldn't since I don't like the witch. Right?

I tried not to give my thoughts away as she shook her head at my question.

"There's something about her ancestry," I explained. "Her bloodline. It caused people to love us. To fight for us. To want to breed us. I need to know *why*. Can you help me?"

She swallowed harshly, looking at the melting ice cream on the ground, and for a moment I was afraid she'd say no.

"Are you sure you can trust me with this?" she asked.

"Not at all," I admitted.

She met me with a true grin, her hand coming to clasp mine.

"I'll see what I can do as a thanks for helping Cedar."

Just the mention of the witch had my skin heating, bringing back moments of our heated exchange. I wouldn't demean myself by regretting it.

I didn't regret any of my choices.

But fuck, it's going to be hard not to do that again.

But I couldn't trust any of them. Not even her.

It was my turn to clear my throat. I snapped my hand away from hers and stood. We weren't buddy-buddy enough to be touching like that.

"Your reasons are your own," I said and turned away from her. "Your fun time is over. Take me home."

She scrambled to follow me but caught up after a few seconds of light running.

"Does this mean we're friends now?" she asked from behind me.

Embarrassment traveled up the back of my neck.

"No!" I hissed harshly.

Her laugh had my skin heating even more.

Vesper

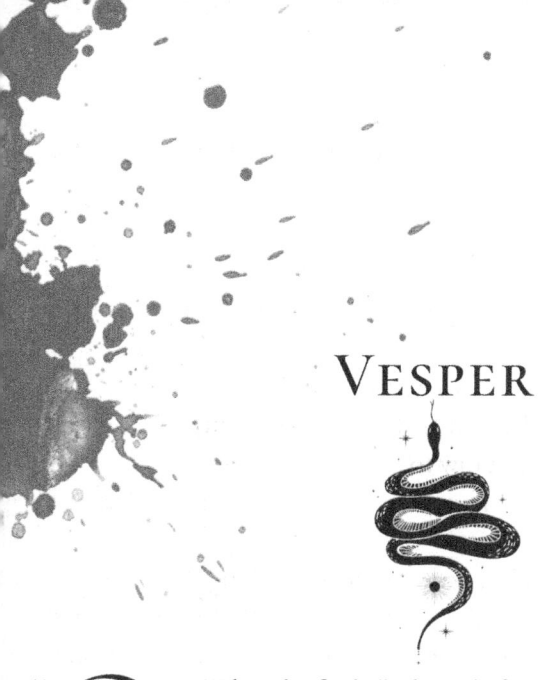

"Ow! What the fuck?" I hissed after I was kicked in the leg.

I looked down to see Tate with a frown on his face.

"Either someone died, or your vampire girlfriend is ignoring you," he said. "Which one is it? Because I'd really like to enjoy our time together. Even if it's stupid shit like *this*."

He emphasized the word by shoving a book into its place on the shelf.

Another day, another task from the coven.

Today, it was helping the local bookstore restock. Many of the books weren't in English and were hard to sort. We had already been chided by the elderly storekeeper for missorting them more than once.

I looked back at the book in my hands, my lips pressed into a thin line.

My mind was a mess after what had happened between the three of us. On one hand, I felt like I had severely taken advantage of Cedar when she was under the influence of Aurelia's venom.

I'd never seen someone take so much of it before. Nor did I think Aurelia would even try to save her. If anything, I thought maybe she'd take her chance to run.

But the more I thought about it, the more I remembered that Aurelia never wanted to harm anyone in the first place. She had a cold, cruel exterior, but she cared about her people. And she was never one of those vampires who abused the human feeders.

Fuck, even when I had been trying to kill her, she had still made sure I was comfortable with everything we were doing.

She was actually a good vampire. Sometimes misguided...but her heart was in the right place.

Apparently good enough to share you with the witch.

That was something else that had taken me by surprise. I didn't know what to think about it. How to *feel*.

I wanted her. No matter how annoying she was or how pissed I was at her for lying to me.

I wanted *them*. I just didn't want to ruin everything.

On the other hand, there was the issue with the high priest because I wanted to fucking kill him. How dare he hurt them like that? I had barely been able to contain my rage. If Cedar and Aurelia hadn't distracted me, I might have done something that would get us all killed.

I'd never felt that type of anger before. So violent and all-consuming.

And I kept reminding myself I was the reason we were stuck in this weird coven in the first place.

"Sorry," I murmured and put my book back into its place. At least I thought it was the right place. Honestly, I was probably doing more harm than good when it came to this task. "I appreciate you coming along and helping with this."

Tate grumbled something under his breath.

"What was that?"

"Like I have any fucking choice if I want to spend time with you." He slammed the next book a little too hard on the shelf, earning us a shout from the storekeeper.

"Sorry!" I yelled back, wincing as he muttered something that sounded strongly similar to *damned vampire hunter*.

I paused, my hand on the next book. Feeling a bit spiteful, I purposely put it on the wrong shelf.

No one yells at my brother.

"They don't appreciate you," he said, giving me a sidelong glance. "We'd be better off leaving this place."

They didn't appreciate that the vampire I brought was killing their people. So they gave me meaningless jobs. The things they didn't want to do. All while they hid in their ranks, talking shit about us.

And I would take it. So at least that way we could try to fall back into their good graces.

If Aurelia doesn't kill anyone else, that is. I almost smiled at my own thought. Aurelia sure had an almost...violent way of showing her love, but I'd take the messy, brutal version of her any day of the week.

But this was the second time Tate was mentioning running away with him. If I was being honest, it broke my heart.

I wanted nothing more than to do that. But it would put him in even more danger than he already was.

Every time I looked at him, I remembered how our parents made him whip me and cut open my skin with a magical knife that left lingering burns while I was held in our basement as punishment. He had never cried harder or apologized that sincerely. When it was over, he was more hurt by what he had done than what our parents made him do.

I never want him to feel that way again.

"I get why," he said. "They hate you guys, so you think this is the only way they'll even put up with you being here."

"Tate..." I warned.

He leaned against the bookshelf and gave me a hard look. He looked so much older in that moment. Gone was the pouting teen; in front of me was a young adult. One who'd seen the world. Who didn't take any shit from anybody.

It hadn't been long since the start of my mission, but looking at him, it felt like a lifetime had passed.

But he isn't the only one who's changed.

I couldn't even claim to be the same person anymore. I had turned my back on everything I knew.

"It was the high priest who allowed you in. You don't need to do any of this shit. No one will dare defy him."

I paused. What the hell did he know about the high priest?
Fucking Gabriel.

"Why is Gabriel telling you this?" I asked, trying desperately to keep the anger from my tone.

Tate avoided my gaze and began putting books back at a hurried pace.

"He feels bad, you know?" he whispered. "And I just want the two of you to make up. It's better if we are all together."

My heart continued to crack in my chest. I'd worked so hard all my life to make it impenetrable, but between Tate and Aurelia, it was almost impossible to keep up the wall.

"I thought you didn't like him," I commented with a raised brow.

"I like *you* better, but it's becoming clear to me that you're willing to let these witches walk all over you. I thought you'd make the move to leave, but I was wrong." He was silent for a moment. "Think about talking to him. He'll wait for you after this."

"I have to help another shop—"

Tate pushed a paper into my hand, silencing me.

"Think about it."

Stupid. Stupid decision.

I shouldn't have let Tate sway me. The paper had a time and location for us to meet. Nothing else. I flushed it down the nearest toilet as soon as I had a chance.

I should have trusted my gut and stayed away.

I didn't want to talk to Gabriel. Didn't want to face him. I was still angry at him and didn't know if I could forgive him.

Cedar and Levana might have lied as well, but they were not blood. How could my own brother...

Tate tugged at my arm, forcing me to look down at him. He had a real smile on his face. Another thing I couldn't forgive him for.

Tate should have been far away from this mess. Far away from any witch or vampire. I wasn't even sure Aurelia and I could leave when the time came, let alone Tate.

"This better be worth it," I said. "I'm putting a lot of trust in you."

"Trust that will be rewarded," he said with a wicked grin.

He pulled me along to the outer borders of town, stopping right before the barrier.

To anyone else, there were just trees ahead, but after going through it myself, I knew there was an invisible wall of magic surrounding the place, and behind it, guards.

If we're caught sneaking out...

I looked over my shoulder to see if anyone had followed us. There was not a witch in sight. But it didn't cause any of the tension in my shoulders to ease. Not one bit.

We were being watched. I could feel the heaviness.

Just as I was about to pull Tate away from the border, a hand reached past it and pulled both of us through it.

I opened my mouth to protest but shut it quickly when I saw Gabriel's smiling face. He motioned for me to be quiet.

In the years he'd been gone, he'd gotten much older-looking. Smile lines. Crow's feet. He wasn't that much older than me, but he had left the family way earlier than I had. Done more than I had.

It almost made me wonder exactly what he'd been up to all these years.

I was tired of people lying to me, and I couldn't just keep forgiving them like it was nothing. Especially when...

My eyes shifted to the space behind him. Two witch guards were waiting, their eyes on me and Tate. I maneuvered so I was in front of him.

"Be back in forty," one of them said before looking me up and down with a frown. "I can't promise anything after that."

"What he means is that's when our shift ends," the other added. "If you're not here by then, you're on your own."

"Pleasure doing business with you," Gabriel said before handing the two a glowing purple bag. Even as a human, I could feel the magic pulsating from it.

Curiosity ate at me. Whatever was in there was powerful. Once upon a time, I had stolen magical artifacts whenever I had a chance to bargain with Levana, but something about whatever was in that bag made the hair on the back of my neck raise.

One of them pocketed it and jerked his head behind him.

"Quickly."

Gabriel started further into the forest, not waiting for us to follow. Tate took the initiative, turning to send me a smile when he realized I wasn't following.

With a sigh, I did.

Vampire hunters.

At least a good twenty of them.

I hadn't been around this many since the boarding school my parents forced me to attend, and suddenly being thrust back into the world I'd left had me overly anxious.

For most of my time at Prince Icas's house and the Castle family's residence, I had been the lone vampire hunter. It had been like coming from a different world and trying to blend in when feeling like a beacon.

Now I felt like a beacon for a whole different reason.

The small camp Gabriel had set up was far from the witches' town and had its own magical barrier surrounding it. I relaxed just slightly inside.

At least we're not out in the open.

It was better than I originally imagined, with trailers instead of tents, but it was still a bit lacking.

Especially for a kid like Tate.

The hunters paused as we entered, two running to us almost immediately.

"We're ready to set out, boss," the one with a scar cutting through his face said. But that wasn't the thing that made me pause.

It was the red eyes.

Vampire? No, the man seemed too human for that. He was missing their fluid movements. The sharp features all vampires seemed to have.

Vampire hybrid, then. I had thought Levana was unique, but maybe not.

"Are you going somewhere?" I asked, unable to take my eyes off him. There was something dangerous about him.

Levana was carefree for the most part—when she wasn't picking a fight with Aurelia. But this one was looking at me, assessing me, the same way I was him. His body was taut, his jaw locked.

He doesn't like me.

"We only stay near the coven for a few days at a time whenever I have business," Gabriel said.

"Or when I want to see you," Tate added with a smile.

I wanted to tell him to stop warming my heart with those words, but I kept my mouth shut. I could be selfish with the feeling for just a moment.

"That too." Gabriel smiled back. "We have a base in the city nearby. We stay there from time to time."

"Or go where we are needed," the one with the scar said. "Which doesn't seem like a lot these days since we're stuck with the coven."

It was obvious his comment was meant for me. I guessed if he could be blunt, so could I.

"I thought you were vampire hunters," I told him. "It's a bit weird for you to employ vampires, isn't it? Do you like killing your own kind?"

Gabriel took in a sharp breath, but the man with the scar just smiled.

"You don't know, do you?" he asked with a scoff, looking me up and down.

My hair raised, my whole body suddenly on edge. I looked down at Tate and then Gabriel, both trying to keep their expressions unreadable.

But Tate was failing. He looked a bit guilty, his eyebrows pushed together and a frown on his face.

What does he know?

"He's only a quarter," Gabriel replied. "It's common in the...*organization*."

I looked back at the vampire hybrid. Was it, really? I didn't remember seeing any of them when I went to school. Though if I was being honest, I had kept to myself, merely communicating with students out of necessity or to catalog them in my mind for whenever I'd need it.

"Well, Vesper wouldn't be bothered by it anyway," Tate said with a nervous laugh. "I mean, you got that princess of yours, right?"

"Right," I murmured, looking around. I felt like there was something they were still hiding. *Is it really safe to leave him here?*

"Anyway, I just wanted to introduce you. Maybe talk?" Gabriel asked, his tone helpful. "Then you can go right back to your princess."

And the redheaded witch, the small voice in my head supplied. I tried not to let my skin heat at the thought.

I gave him a stiff nod.

"Tate, you know the drill," Gabriel told the boy, pushing him toward the vampire. "Help pack up while we talk."

Tate sent me a small smile before following the vampire, who was still looking at me with that smirk.

"What's his deal?" I asked. Gabriel led me to a small campfire area and handed me a canned beer. I held it in my hand but didn't open it.

"He can hear you, you know," Gabriel warned.

"I don't care," I said, holding his gaze. "I also don't actually really care for the answer, actually. What I really want to know is why I'm here."

"You should ask yourself that. You could've rejected my offer."

The fuck I could.

"You know I can't say no to Tate."

"I do know that." He gave me a small smile. "I used that fact selfishly."

"Why?" Anger boiled under my skin. He was supposed to be mending bridges, not burning them even more. I wouldn't be surprised if, by the time I left, I'd want to cut him out of my life completely.

Gabriel had never been the type to apologize. My parents never raised him to. But they also raised me not to take shit from anyone.

"Because I want to take you with us," he said, his voice turning serious. "Actually, I should add that I'm taking you out of this coven whether you like it or not."

I gave him a deadpan stare. One, two, three, then five seconds passed by in silence.

He held up his hands.

"Bad joke, sorry."

Not fucking funny.

I looked around at the vampire hunters. They were wary of me. A lot of them still watching as Gabriel and I talked. The only people who weren't watching were Tate and the vampire, talking animatedly as they packed up some of the outside equipment.

They were in a rush from the looks of it. Everyone was helping load their stuff into the trailers. The little nagging voice at the back of my head started to get louder.

Ask him. The signs are all here. Ask.

"Which one is it?" I asked and then turned to him. "The organization or the council?"

His gaze hardened.

"Why would the council be after us?" he asked.

There it is.

In all honesty, I didn't know why the voice in my head told me to ask him about the council. They shouldn't interfere with vampire hunters. They were separate entities, and while they hated each other, they respected each other's rules.

And it's not like they didn't benefit from killing misbehaving rogues. They cared too much about their reputation.

The organization was more likely, given how Gabriel worked outside their bounds. I wouldn't put it past him to report back to them through messenger maybe once or twice a year, but as long as he didn't fuck up in some serious kind of way...

"I can't imagine they'd be happy with you killing their people and all that." It was a weak argument. Gabriel could sense it too, but he didn't call me out on it.

He kept my gaze for a moment longer before his eyes shifted to the rest of the hunters.

"Only the bad ones," he said.

"Aren't they all, as far as you're concerned?"

He raised a brow at me. "You used to think so too once upon a time."

I had. Back when I was still listening to my parents. Back when I truly saw their punishments as a way of teaching me instead of abusing me. When I was very happy to be used as a tool.

I'm not like that anymore. Not after Aurelia.

"The organization got a tip," he said. "They know you're here, and they know the prophecy wasn't fulfilled."

I stiffened.

So he wants to give me a warning that our little hideaway in the forest is going to get a little crowded soon.

"Are you afraid the coven cannot protect us?"

He let out a snort. "Protect? They don't *protect* anyone. That was a little illusion they used to keep you here until you finish the prophecy."

I ground my teeth together to stop whatever awful words were brewing inside me from coming out.

He was right, though. The veil had lifted. Especially after what they had done to Aurelia and Cedar, it became clear to me that we were walking on thin ice and the threat of what they might do to us was hanging over us.

"Then why are you working with them?" I asked, my tone hard.

"This is separate. I'm trying to be a good brother and protect you."

I let out a bitter laugh. *Separate.* Of course, just like everything in his life. There was the organization. The killing of vampires. And then there was the family he left behind.

One obviously more important than the others. Gabriel didn't care if his deal with the coven made life harder for me. He didn't care that it made me rethink every single interaction I'd ever had in my life.

He only cared about his work.

"Protect?" I asked. "You've never protected me in your life. Why would you want to start now?"

"Yes..."

His tone told me not to mention it. He would say the same thing. That he hadn't been able to help. That as much as he had wanted to take both of us, he couldn't. That our parents wouldn't have allowed it, or he just hadn't been equipped to handle two minors tagging along and killing vampires.

But I wasn't taking that anymore.

"Thank you for the warning," I said, and got up, placing the beer can where I'd been sitting. "I don't wanna see you again. Don't you dare try and use Tate again. If you do, you'll regret it."

I turned around, ready to say goodbye to Tate, when Gabriel let out a laugh.

"Do you think your threat scares me?"

Anger boiled underneath my skin.

He says he wants to be a good brother, but at the end of the day, he's still the same old Gabriel.

The one who helped plant people in my life. The one I thought I could trust until he showed up at the coven with our younger brother, who he was supposed to be keeping safe.

A lot of the things he did when I was younger, I could forgive. Because in my mind, he was still the big brother I could rely on if I needed to.

But I'd seen the true him now.

"I'm leaving, Tate," I called across the space. Tate's head lifted toward me, and just as he was turning to walk over, I felt Gabriel's hands on my shoulders.

"Listen to me, you little shit! You may still be pissed at me, but trust me when I say I'm trying to protect you!" He was unabashedly loud. "The coven will give you up to them! Don't you see? If you're with us, I—"

I shoved his hands off me.

Who the fuck does he think he is, after all these years, telling me what to do when I survived perfectly fine by myself?

Tate ran to me, his hands clasping around my middle, and it felt like it was the only thing keeping my shaking body together.

"I'm done talking about this," I said. "Get to a safe place with Tate. At some point, when it's clear, I'll meet him. But don't you dare use him again."

I met his gaze, making sure he understood every single word that came out of my mouth.

I'm tired of being stepped on.

I turned to look down at Tate, who had a frown on his face. I ruffled his hair.

"I'll see you soon, okay? Just stay safe."

He unwrapped himself from me. "I don't wanna leave you. Sorry for making you come here. It was my fault."

Damn it. I didn't want him taking the blame for something Gabriel made him do. Guilt ate at me.

I didn't want to say goodbye either. Seeing him had been a highlight while being stuck in the coven. And even though I never said it... he meant a lot to me.

"It's not your fault," I said. "But I have to go or I'll get in trouble. I love you, little man."

His eyes started to water.

"I'll miss you," he said, his voice thick. "And I... I love you too. Be safe, okay?"

"Always," I said, ruffling his hair one more time.

When I see him next time, how much more of a man will he have become? Will I even recognize him anymore?

Just as I was ready to walk away without saying goodbye to Gabriel, his voice rang across the clearing.

"Yeah, go on, Ves. Go back and kneel for that vampire princess of yours. Like we could expect anything from you. You were too cowardly to kill her, and now she has you pussy whipp—"

It happened so fast, my mind didn't have time to catch up. One moment I was near Tate, the next I was closing in on Gabriel like my mind shut off and let my body take the lead.

I rammed my fist into his face, sending him flying to the ground. I'm pretty sure the loud crack that sounded after my fist connected meant something had been broken.

"Take care of Tate. That's your last warning."

And then I left.

Cedar

I knew Vesper would find me after what happened between the three of us. After all, how could she not? It didn't seem like her to fuck and just get over it the next day.

Things between us felt much more serious. Life altering. Which had been another reason why I'd been so worried to even start something.

I'm scared.

I'd never imagined that one day, I would want to be with someone bad enough that I'd be willing to turn my back on the coven. That I'd be willing to put the state of the world at risk.

All I knew was the coven. I barely had a concept of the world outside its walls. I had only been outside on missions, and even then, the infiltration of the Castle palace had been one of the longest I'd been on.

Yet as soon as I saw her—felt her—I was an absolute goner.

I wished that she would leave me for longer to rot in my pit of embarrassment. At least then I could have some time to recover before facing her. I wasn't embarrassed about what I'd done, or how it felt. I loved every moment of it.

I loved her moans. Loved the look on her face as I watched her come apart. It was everything I'd dreamed about.

I'm embarrassed because of how much of a fuckup I am.

I had one job. I'd even criticized Vesper for fucking the princess and ruining the one job she had but then I went and did the same.

The high priest would figure it out at some point. But I didn't know if he would punish me or just let it go because maybe he still had faith that I'd help Vesper see the prophecy through.

I'd never failed him before Vesper and Aurelia showed up, so I hoped that he would overlook it.

But if Vesper keeps tempting me, there will be less and less room for him to forgive me.

Once was a mistake; everything after that was a choice.

My heart skipped a beat in my chest as she entered the bar. Her face was stone cold, showing not even a hint of the woman who had been between Aurelia and me.

When her eyes met mine, all the breath was stolen from my lungs.

How about we call you our dirty whore instead? Say you want to be used by us. Tell us how much you'd fucking love both of us ravishing your body.

My command to her sounded loud and clear in my mind, and for a second, I was worried she'd know what I was thinking. But she gave no indication either way. Her face was stone cold, her body tense. She was watching everything and everyone.

She wasn't the same distressed human I had brought to the safe house nor the version who loved to be used by the princess and me.

She was something completely different.

This is a hunter with a plan.

"Can we talk?" she asked, not bothering to sit down at my table.

Fuck. Being alone with her probably wasn't a good idea. But I threw my magical beer back and went with her anyway.

"You can lock up without me," I shouted to Mage, the barkeep, as I made my way out. She would often keep it open late for me to get a drink after my shift. Oftentimes, she would join me as well and complain about the state of the coven.

But she was more than a simple barkeep. She was the only person in this place that resembled something even remotely similar to a family.

The only person who cares.

Her warm eyes watched us carefully.

"You let me know, young one," she said, her eyes lingering on Vesper.

I nodded and left the bar with Vesper in tow.

"So what happened?" I asked, shifting on my feet.

The forest was darkening even though the moon peeked through the clouds and shone down on us.

It was a clear night. Perfect for stargazing.

Because of how far away we were from the city, millions of them lit up the sky.

I looked up at them, trying to calm my racing heart.

The barrier protecting the coven was next to us. So close I could feel it vibrating against my skin. It grounded me.

"How about you start telling me the truth about what happened with your punishment?"

Her gaze was sharp, her words sharper.

I didn't know which Vesper I liked better—the one who gave no shits or the one who writhed in pleasure as Aurelia sank her fangs into her. Both were satisfying for different reasons.

The harsher side of her invoked some type of challenge in me, while the submissive side brought forth the more animalistic side of me.

"Aurelia told you," I said, remembering their conversation when I first came to. It was hazy and lust-filled, but she distinctly told her I'd taken most of the lashings. "There's not much else to say."

She took a step forward, invading my space. Her scent was strong, familiar. I ached to lean into it, but I stood straight, looking down on her.

"Let's stop with the games." Her voice was low and dangerous. It sent a thrill up my spine. "You could have thrown her under the bus. But you didn't. Why did you take the punishment for her?"

"Lashes embedded with his magic live within us. Even if he dies, or I do, some of it will always be inside me. At times, it can help make my magic more powerful, but the caveat is the control he has over you," I explained. "He managed to get two, and I'm not sure how much magic is still in Aurelia, but more than that would've been detrimental to any type of plan you may have."

Her facial expression gave nothing away.

"How often are you lashed on our behalf?"

Her question shocked me. I didn't really think she would care.

"This is the first time since you guys arrived, but it is not the first time I have gotten a warning," I replied honestly.

Her jaw clenched, the only sign that she was unhappy.

"And after?" she asked. "Between—" She cleared her throat. "I wanted to apologize. Aurelia and I took advantage of you."

I raised a brow at her. All embarrassment left me to be replaced by a shocked burst of amusement.

"Took advantage of *me*?" I echoed. "I'm pretty sure *you* were the one who was taken advantage of. Have you forgotten how Aurelia sank her fangs into you and fucked you in front—"

"Okay!" she said hastily, her hands up in the air and reaching toward me like she wanted to stop me.

I couldn't help it. The need for her was too strong.

I gripped her chin with one hand, the other wrapping around her waist. An electric current went through me as our skins touched.

Her breathing hitched and her eyes widened, and a burst of confidence ran through me. Before I could talk myself out of it, the words were slipping from my mouth.

"Is this what you wanted to talk to me about, hunter?" I asked. "You wanted to make sure I loved seeing you get fucked by your vampire as much as you loved me watching?"

She swallowed thickly but gave me no response. Her tongue darted out to lick her lips.

Fuck. I found myself leaning forward without meaning to.

"Gabriel tried to get me to leave," she said, causing me to freeze.

My back straightened, panic rising in me. *Already?* I knew it was an option—probably the best one—but I hadn't expected it to happen so soon.

It hurt to think of this place without them. To be abandoned by them.

If I said anything, I'd be risking what I had with the coven. I had fucked up my job already, but helping them flee when the high priest was so adamant about finishing the prophecy?

There would be nothing left for me here. Nothing to save me. It didn't matter how proficient a White Lotus member I was—he would end me for interfering.

Leaving was the best-case scenario for them. Something I had thought long and hard about. Something that became clear after the punishment.

I originally thought that his interest in the prophecy would protect them, but it seemed to be putting them more in danger than anything else.

The priest has an ulterior motive, and I didn't know how to decipher it.

His interest in them scared me, and it wasn't just him. It was all the White Lotus members.

They wanted them dead. The only reason they had agreed to take them in was the prophecy. We had more to gain than to lose if it was realized. But that didn't mean the coven liked outsiders. Especially ones they couldn't control.

"Since you're still here, I'm guessing you said no."

Regretfully, I forced myself to step away from her. The sudden lack of warmth had my body aching for it, so I gave in to the desire and let my fingers brush her wrist and hold it. She didn't pull away.

Part of me was relieved that she didn't just take off in the middle of the night, leaving me.

It fed my delusion. Told me that if she was thinking of running away, she was waiting for me. That maybe she had brought me out here to tell me she was taking me with her.

"He also said the organization is coming," she said. "Apparently, they had a tip that not only was I hiding in a coven, but Aurelia was still alive, and my prophecy was unfulfilled."

My heart stopped. *This really can't get any worse, can it?*

There was no choice. Not anymore. But could I really do it? Could I really just throw away the ties of an entire life dedicated to the coven?

Vesper was supposed to be my big break. The one that would finally prove my abilities to the rest of the coven.

I had been blind before meeting her. Meeting them.

"So... Do you have a backup plan?" I asked, my eyes digging into hers.

Her cold mask broke. She raised a brow at me.

"I come to you when I know I shouldn't because I can't trust you, and that's all you have to ask? If *I* have a backup plan?"

I reeled back from her hostility. *What the fuck?*

"I think it's a perfectly valid question. Your fucked-up hunter organization is no joke, but neither is the coven. You think they're done with you? This is just the beginning."

"What is it then? What else can the coven possibly do?" she asked, taking another step closer.

Fuck. Even in the middle of an argument, I couldn't deny the way she made me feel. I wanted to look away. Needed to. But I couldn't.

My throat dried.

"Won't say, huh? You and your secretive shit. I thought we were past that. I'm here because I have no other choice, Cedar. Do I have to spell it out? I'm asking for *help*. Now, are you going to help me or what?"

I didn't know what to say. She was wrong; it wasn't that. I wanted to put my hands on either side of her face and kiss her. Every moment with her felt like we were on borrowed time, every second just ticking closer and closer to the bomb that loomed over us both.

I needed to make a decision. I couldn't keep going back and forth between wanting to save them and wanting to maintain my life in the coven.

But what else is out there for me?

Vesper was tied to Aurelia. Blood bond or not, they were a pair.

I am the outsider.

"Listen, I know you don't trust me anymore...but my hands are tied. I got you here, and I can try to cover if you want to leave, but—"

"Trust?" she asked with a laugh. "You've lied. Continuously. You knew my brother all along and lied about it. You were sent to spy on me and never even gave me a heads-up about the danger I was in."

She wasn't just asking for help. She was letting out all the frustration I had caused up until this point. The anger and stress of the situation were too much for her. And she was taking it out on me.

It's not fair, a voice in my head yelled. *It's not like I wanted any of this! I was born into it just like you!*

"I tried to warn you!" I growled, frustration now seeping into my voice too.

I hadn't chosen to be bound to this job. If I had, I would have gladly been more truthful with Vesper. But my hands had been tied.

Unless you fully cut ties, the voice said again.

Damn it.

"There you go with the cryptic bullshit," she hissed. "Just tell me what else I need to prepare for. It's the least you can do. I'm so tired of all this. Tired of the secrets. Tired of people walking all over me. All I want is help, and I just keep getting the short end of the stick."

"You being here is me helping you," I reminded. "If I hadn't brought you here, the Castle family would have skinned you alive long ago."

"Your coven is fucked up," she said. "Don't think I can't see it. Fuck! I knew I should have come here or asked you for anything. Not like you've ever fucking help—"

The hand holding her wrist tightened while the other went to her throat and forced her lips to mine.

We clashed—lips, teeth, and tongue. She kissed me like she hated me, and the only way to relieve her anger was through cold, hard fucking.

But I could give her so much more than that.

I pushed her against the tree, barricading her against it so she couldn't fight me. The little grunt she let out went straight to my head. Her hand curled in my hair, the other ran down my chest. Her movements were rough, hurried. I wanted more. *Needed it.* I wanted her anger. Her hurt. Her pain. I wanted to feel it all.

Her hand slipped into my pants, and her finger went through my wet folds, going right past my clit and plunging two fingers inside me. No warning. No foreplay. Straight to the point.

I don't know when I'd become a wet mess for her. Maybe it was when her eyes lit with fire and she started yelling at me. Maybe it was when I had my hand on her throat.

Fuck, maybe it was when she walked into the bar in the first place.

I was woefully and completely enamored with her. She might not have realized it, but I would do anything for her.

Give her the air I breathe. Take lashings for her bonded. Leave my coven for her.

I was going to completely change my life for her, and she didn't even know it. From the moment she walked into the palace, my future was promised to her.

I moaned into her mouth and jerked my hips against her hand. The hand I placed on her hips moved inside her pants so I could fuck her exactly the way she was fucking me.

I broke our kiss and pressed my forehead against hers, both of us panting. The cold night air had heated up around us considerably.

"You came here just to provoke me, didn't you?" I asked. "You *wanted* me to fuck you like this, didn't you?"

My voice was breathless as she hurled me closer and closer to an orgasm, her fingers moving at an unbelievable pace. It was almost too much. Never in my life had I come so quickly, but with Vesper? I wouldn't be able to hold back.

"You're so full of yourself," she said with a groan just as her head fell back against the tree as I curled my fingers inside her.

She was so sinfully wet, but so was I. The sound of our fingers fucking each other's wet cunts paired with our groans cut through the night air in an obscene symphony.

"I think I'm pretty full of you right now," I shot back.

"Your cunt's eating me up," she said. "You can take more."

She forced a third finger into me and curled it. My eyes rolled into the back of my head.

I love the little bite she still had in her. I let my head fall into the crook of her neck. My teeth grazed where Aurelia would normally sink her fangs into her.

She let out a shaky moan.

"Come for me, Vesper." My whispered command got overshadowed by the sounds coming from us, but she obeyed nonetheless.

I wasn't far behind. My body had a mind of its own and forced me to come alongside her.

Light flashed behind my eyes as they closed. Everything was heightened. I could feel her breath. Hear the sounds of us. Every time our skin brushed, a tremor would run through me.

Slowly, we removed our hands. When I opened my eyes again, hers were trained on me. I pulled back to get a better look at them. There were so many things left unsaid between us.

What does this mean?

What about Aurelia?

Is this even okay?

But we breached none of those topics and instead focused on the issue at hand. Just as life-changing, but not as vulnerable.

"I don't trust the high priest," I said after a long pause. "He wants the prophecy completed. I don't know how he's going to do it, but I have a feeling that it's not going to go well. On top of that, now that we know your people are coming for you, it doesn't look good. You won't be protected here. So I need *you* to have a backup plan. And unfortunately, I don't know how much I can help. I'm pretty useless here."

Her eyes fell to the ground and she bit her swollen bottom lip.

"What about you?" she asked, the anger in her tone disappearing.

"Obviously you don't like what's happening. So let's say Aurelia and I leave. What will you do?"

I paused. *What will I do?*

The high priest would blame me, no doubt. I had been assigned to them. I was the one supposed to watch them and make sure everything went smoothly.

What would happen to me?

I knew too much to be cast aside. And as a member of the White Lotus, I wouldn't escape punishment.

Would I die like the others? Burned alive in a fiery burst of magic while I screamed for help?

But they would be gone. Not safe, but at least with a fighting chance.

My resolve hardened.

"You don't need to worry about me," I said quickly. "Is that what you want? To escape? Be on the run from both the coven and the hunters? You know it will never stop after that, right? It won't stop until she's *dead*."

She paused before searching the area around us. There was nothing besides the racing of our own hearts in the silent night.

When she looked back at me, her expression had changed. Slowly, a soft smile was spreading across her face, all the anger disappearing.

"So that's it?" she asked. "You're going to sacrifice yourself so we can escape?'

I jerked back.

"I never said—"

"You didn't have to," she said with a sigh. She ran a hand through her silver locks. My eyes fell to the dark tattoo on her neck. "I should have known when Aurelia said you took that punishment for her."

I couldn't look her in the eyes.

"Vesper..."

"Not hearing it," she said, hand raised. "Should have known you're a suicidal idiot."

Suicidal idiot? My jaw dropped.

"Hang on a sec; you're giving me whiplash. First, I'm not a

suicidal idiot. Second, this is about you and Aurelia getting out of here before all hell breaks loo—"

She reached into her pocket, digging out something I couldn't make out in the darkness.

"Not just me and Aurelia. You're coming with us too." My heart stopped at that. "I don't know why you're so hesitant to help, but I'll get us all out of here."

My heart burst to life in my chest and my skin heated.

What?

"Wait—"

"Nope," she said. "I realize now I should have taken this into my own hands. I've put you in a difficult position. Don't worry. I'll work on it for the three of us."

For the three of us.

She wasn't going to leave me.

For the first time in my life, I wasn't going to be left behind.

I didn't remember my parents. The coven had been my family, and the high priest was somewhat of a father to me. I never had one to show me what a real one should have been like, but I'd guessed it would be like him.

It's why it felt so wrong to betray him like this.

Can I actually leave?

Can I pick up and leave everything I've ever known for these two?

You know it's always gonna be the two of them and the two of them only, a cruel voice said in the back of my head, showing me pictures of them together while I waited on the sidelines.

They will leave you behind one day. Vesper will get bored of you.

I swallowed the knot in my throat.

"Let's rethink—"

Vesper cut me off with a look, telling me that she really wasn't going to be taking no for an answer.

My stomach flipped.

And here I thought I liked the submissive version of her more.

"I don't really know how to use this, but I'm guessing you rub the—"

Old magic burst through the air. It was potent and so strong I could smell it. Invisible wisps of it brushed across my body before shooting past me.

Whatever warm feelings I'd had vanished into thin air to be replaced with ice-cold fear.

I lunged forward, closing the space between me and Vesper and forcing her hand open so I could take a look.

In the middle was a large medallion. Pitch black and with a family crest on it that I had only seen in our old history books.

Trouble. She's gonna get us killed.

"Where did you—"

"About time, hunter," a disembodied voice floated up from the coin. It sounded as if the person was standing right next to us. "Hello, witch."

I jerked back. *Can they sense me?*

"We need a way out. For three," Vesper said. "I've called to discuss."

"Not here," the voice said quickly. "I'll meet you in three days. Same location."

"You're coming here?" Vesper asked, her eyebrows rising. She met my eyes, but I had nothing to tell her. For the first time, I was totally out of the loop.

"Obviously, hunter. How else are we going to do this? I have some news. Be useful and protect Aurelia until then, will you?"

A crackling sounded from her hand, and with that, the magic from the coin disappeared in a smoky wave.

"Who the hell was that?" I asked.

Vesper grimaced.

"A vampire named Atlas," she said, then turned to me with a smile. "Oh yeah, and I need just one tiny favor."

I couldn't hold back my groan because she knew that no matter what she'd ask, I'd likely try to accommodate it.

Let's just hope it doesn't kill me.

Aurelia

"Get the fuck out of here," I said, glaring at the intruder sitting on my windowsill. "How'd you even find me anyway?"

It chirped at me, indignation in its tone.

The same beady black eyes somehow held far too much attitude for a little common bird its size.

"Was I not clear, *pipsqueak*?" I said, my hands on my hips. "Vesper might have kidnapped you and forced you upon me as a gift, but I let you go."

And yet, here I am, giving the damned thing a name.

How the mighty have fallen.

It let out another chirp and tilted its head sideways at me.

"Don't you get it? I'm fucking royalty. I don't need a *common* bird like you."

But Pipsqueak still wouldn't move.

I sat down, my back against the wall right under the window. Pipsqueak annoyingly flew down onto the ground and kept eye contact with me.

I was getting more annoyed by the minute. And not because of the stupid bird.

Because my silver-haired hunter decided she was going to leave me cooped up in the cabin alone. All fucking day. The sun had set hours ago, and there was still no fucking sign of her.

Doesn't she realize that was what got us into this mess in the first fucking place?

Her sneaking out had been the entire reason Cedar and I had gotten punished to begin with.

Maybe one time wasn't warning enough.

Or maybe she liked it, a wicked voice said in my head. *Or maybe she's out with the witch. Maybe she's planning on leaving you.*

I clenched my fists, nails biting into my palms.

"I'm not usually this pathetic," I explained to Pipsqueak. "I usually rule with an iron fist. I was known to be cruel."

It tilted its head, looking as if it was listening intently.

"Now *this* is fucking pathetic," I said to myself. "Talking to a fucking bird is…"

Lonely.

Something I hadn't felt since my time in the palace because that had all but disappeared when Vesper showed up.

It reminded me of the times I would curl up into a ball in my room after my mother died, crying as if it could bring her back.

My hand dropped to the necklace still around my ankle. Somehow, after all of it, I still cared…

Fuck.

I still…*loved her.*

I loved the goddamned hunter. I hated to admit it, but it was there, plain as day, bond or no bond.

At one point, it had become all I wanted. All I dreamed about. She was far from the person I had in mind, but there was no going back.

She had brought color into my life when the world had been painted gray. She had saved me over and over again.

Her methods might have been…unorthodox, but she was trying her best.

It was the most hopeful I'd felt since my mother died.

And that's the difference between now and my time back in the palace.

I had *hope.* Enough hope to feel. To get angry. To get sad. To get jealous.

I had no room for it before, but after running away with Vesper...

The bird chirped again as if it could read my thoughts.

"Shut up," I whispered.

It chirped again and did a little hop forward.

"*No,*" I hissed. It hopped forward two more times, its tiny feet brushing against my dress.

Another chirp.

"*Krae,*" I breathed and reached my hand out, palm open. It flapped its wings, sending itself just high enough to land on my palm before it essentially snuggled into my palm.

Tears pricked my eyes.

I'm so tired of being alone. Of being kept locked up when in reality I should be out there ruling.

I want out.

It wasn't a want. It was a *need.* I had had a chance when I killed that stupid fucking witch guard.

I could have left.

But I hadn't.

Because Vesper's face flashed through my mind. Her smell. The taste of her blood. The feeling of her skin against mine. The undeniable yet pathetic love I felt for her.

And now there was another, unexpected image.

Cedar. Her face twisted in pain as the priest pumped magic into her with a wicked grin. He thought I couldn't see it. But I did. I saw right through that fucker.

And Cedar had been right. I fucking hated them. The witches. But it had felt shittier watching her go through all that pain for me.

Because of me.

I let out a sigh.

Another image flew through my mind.

Cedar in front of Vesper, her mouth stained with the little mouse's blood.

She hadn't backed away when she turned to kiss me. She didn't balk at the blood. I had thought she only wanted Vesper, but there was something in that kiss that told me she wanted me as well.

What have I gotten myself into? I let out a groan.

I missed my palace. My people. I hit my head against the wall behind me, letting a stray tear go.

Since the moment Vesper stabbed me in the heart, I hadn't had time to mourn my previous life. Hadn't had time to mourn *us*.

I wanted to run away with her. I was ready to. I knew we weren't supposed to be together, but I wanted it more than anything.

Even if she had been fated to kill me.

How fucked up was that?

All my life, all I ever wanted was attention from my cruel father. I had wanted his acceptance. His love. And then he had let my mother die and had sold me off at the earliest opportunity.

The only reason he was sending men after us was to cover up what happened, lest he look weak in the eyes of the public.

Have the people mourned me? Do they miss me?

I hated it. Hated the life I was forced to live.

"Fuck!" I growled, startling the bird.

I forced myself up, angrily wiping my bloodred tears. The bird flapped its wings hard, flying over to the bed.

I'm not this fucking weak. Not this fucking pathetic.

"Don't come back here, you little shit. I don't need these feelings!"

I stormed out of the bedroom with a growl, looking for everything and anything I could smash.

This is not what my life is going to be about!

I grabbed the coffee table, slamming it against the wall. It hit it hard, splintering. I grabbed a chair next—

I paused when I felt something scorching through the bond.

My stomach dropped and my breath caught. Heat coiled in my belly and—

I grabbed the pillows from the couch, tearing them open, feathers flying everywhere.

Fuck this life. Fuck the witches.

Whenever Vesper got back from wherever the fuck she was, I was going to make her pay.

She thinks she can ignore me? Go out and get fucked without me?

It was not just that she was ignoring me. She was definitely with the redheaded witch, and the bond left no doubt as to what they were doing.

The same witch who had taken my punishment. The same one I had stupidly saved. The same one I—

"Damn it!"

Not only could I feel what they were doing, but I could *see* it. The bond, it was feeding me such clear emotions, I could tell exactly how the witch was touching her.

Lips dancing across her skin. Featherlight touches from her fingers as they crossed her skin.

I paused and let out an exhale as I took it in.

The heat of the pleasure she was feeling started from my chest before spreading out.

Warmth. Satisfaction. There was a bit of something else there. *Longing?*

I wanted to scoff. *What could she be longing for? Her annoying vampire bonded she abandoned at the cabin?*

I balled my hands into fists, my nails digging into my skin.

Was that all I was to her? An annoyance?

Even as their pleasure washed through me and had my pussy clenching, tears pricked my eyes.

They were a sight together. Even more so now that I could feel how Vesper felt about it. I *wanted* to watch them. Wanted to hear them. See the way the blood under their skin rushed to the surface with every heated touch.

But I was stuck. Slowly, the feelings got fainter and fainter.

I paced around the room, waiting. But the bond had gone quiet.

They were obviously finished. I could feel Vesper's inner conflict.

She wanted me, something that should make me ecstatic, but it only made me feel even lonelier.

I was *right here;* yet somehow she felt so far away. Was it...me? Because I wouldn't admit that I wanted the witch too?

She made it clear what she wanted, called me out on my own desire too. It made me all the angrier...because she had been right.

Was this what I got for not being truthful with her?

Where is she?

Then I heard it. The sound of footsteps. They walked toward the door with ease, stopping just outside.

Vesper. Her scent wafted through the closed door. The bond tugged, begging me to get closer.

She was hesitant. Worried. She didn't want to open it. She was nervous.

As she fucking should be.

She had been gone all fucking day. She'd said she needed to go help out at some random bookstore with Tate.

And then she went out and fucked the witch.

Are you bothered that she did it or that she did it without you?

This fucking voice is really getting on my nerves today.

I heard her sigh just before her hands twisted the knob and pushed the door open. Her heart raced, her breathing quickened. She knew I was there. Waiting.

My movements were quick. I grabbed the only surviving pillow and threw it at her head.

She dodged it. It slammed into the wall behind her with a thud, the force of my throw causing feathers to explode and coat the floor right where the blood of the last witch guard had stained it.

"Can you not throw things? I'm human, remember? I can die easily."

Sometimes I thought she was more of a demon than a human. A demon specifically sent to bring havoc to my world.

"Where were you?" I hissed. "And why couldn't I come with you? Hours! It's been hours, Vesper! Do you remember what happened the last time you were gone this long?"

"I was just doing something for the coven," she said and rolled her neck. "And you can't come because they don't trust you out. Maybe I need to remind *you* of the tantrum you threw last time? At least this time it was a pillow and not some witch's neck."

There was something flowing through the bond. Emotions. They were quick as she tried to calm herself, but I caught them.

You think you can fool me?

She was trying to hide what happened. Something important enough to make her panic at the thought of my tantrum.

I closed the space between us. Our faces were inches apart, our chests brushing together.

"I think you're lying," I whispered. "You forget the bond is a two-way thing? You think I can't feel your panic? Your hesitancy? You think I didn't feel you come on the witch's hand?"

Her face paled.

"Look, I panicked because you tried to tear my head off with a pillow," she muttered, ignoring that last bit.

"It's *soft*."

"Not at thirty miles per hour."

I paused and let my eyes roam her body. Her clothes gave nothing away. Neither did her scent. She smelled of the forest and fresh air.

"So are you going to admit it? Even when we said we'd never do it again?"

I knew what I felt through the bond, but I wanted her to admit it. Even if I also dreaded it.

But then amusement flashed in her eyes and a smirk tugged at her lips.

"Are you jealous, sweet Princess?"

Fuck. I hated what that nickname did to my belly. Hated what it made me want to do to her.

And *yes*, I was fucking jealous.

Her hand brushed across my cheek before she pushed my hair back. Her fingers trailed down the side of my neck, causing my breath to hitch.

She's doing it on purpose. Trying to distract me. Probably because she didn't want me asking those questions, but in the moment, I forgot to care. I wanted more. I wanted *her*. I wanted to one-up the witch. I wanted *my* scent to be the one on her. I needed to taste her. Needed to feel her as her cunt fluttered around my fingers and as her mouth told me dirty lies.

And if she was giving me the opportunity, I would fucking take it.

"This is going to hurt," I warned, baring my teeth at her.

But it didn't scare her. Instead, she met me with a dangerous smile that only spurred me further.

"I hope so."

This is the Vesper I want. The one who played well. The one who fought me when no one else would.

The Vesper I lov—

I grabbed her by the hair and forced her neck to my mouth. She didn't fight me. Not even as my fangs sank into her skin.

The taste of her sweet blood burst across my tongue, sending heat straight to my core. *As delicious as always.* The bond made it so much sweeter.

I could feel her pain. Feel her want. Feel her *need*.

She moaned against me as I took gulp after gulp. Her hands were already winding around my waist and pulling me to her before I could prompt her.

She walked us back until my back hit a wall.

I was taking it out on her.

My loneliness. My anger. My helplessness. And she let me. She was eager.

Just as I was about to unlatch my fangs from her to meet her mouth, she stopped me with a command.

"Don't stop," she whispered, her voice harsh. "Drink your fill, Aurelia. Use my body how you see fit. Let me make it up to you."

Make it up to me?

But that was the thing; I didn't want that. All that involved was poorly patching things up between us only for it to tear at the seams the moment it got tough.

I wanted things to change. I didn't want to be there anymore. I didn't want to be at the coven's beck and call. I didn't want to sit in a room for hours staring at nothing. I didn't want to be punished by the high priest, nor did it excite me to see Cedar in pain. I didn't want to be indebted to her because she took the beating in my place.

I was a fucking princess of the Castle family and next in line to take the throne. I had a whole fucking family of vampires that had been counting on me to ascend.

I deserve more respect than this.

So the words just made me angrier. Just made me bite into her harder. Had me digging my claws into her shoulder as she hiked up one of my legs so the other could slip right in under my nightdress and—

I let out a moan as her fingers slipped against my folds. *Perfect.* She had always felt so perfect against me.

She wasn't playing. I knew it was a distraction, but I couldn't help myself.

I dislodged my fangs and licked the length of the holes left in her neck.

"Tell me you thought of me while she fucked you, Little Mouse."

She pulled back so she could meet my eyes. They were hooded, arousal clear in them even if I couldn't smell just how turned on she was. Her fingers began rubbing circles on my clit. Hard, punishing movements that reminded me that even though I was commanding her, she was the one in charge of my pleasure. She watched my expression change as heat built up from my belly and flowed through me. My mouth dropped open, ready for her.

But she didn't kiss me. She just continued to watch.

"Tell me," I ordered again. This time, my hand brushed against her wound, hard enough for her to flinch. I smeared the blood up her throat and over the bottom half of her face, covering her mouth. She licked her lips, tasting her own blood.

She looks so fucking hot.

There was something so feral, so wrong, about a human tasting their own blood. I wanted more. I wanted to see her degrade herself in ways she never imagined.

I wished the witch was there so she could see it as well. I wanted to taste her again. Feel her lips against mine.

What would she say? The sound of her chuckle echoed through my head.

I jerked against Vesper's hand as she slipped her fingers down and into my entrance. She slid into me with ease, pumping them in and out of me at a pace that had my hips bucking against her, begging for her to go faster. To give me more.

The sigh that left my mouth had her smirking, and the side of me that wanted to wipe it off her face reveled in the confidence of it.

My Vesper.

I leaned forward and licked the blood from her lips.

"I wish you had been there with us, my sweet princess," she said. "I wanted both of you on either side of me again. I wanted your teeth in me while she fucked me."

"It will always be me," I whispered. "I don't care what happens with her. *I* was first."

"Always," she breathed, her voice dropping to a whisper so low no other human would be able to hear. Like it was a secret just between the two of us. "You mean everything to me."

A dirty secret. A forbidden one.

We weren't supposed to end up like this. Not together. Not in the coven.

We had been destined to end each other. If not her sword piercing my chest, then my fangs in her neck, draining her until her heart stopped.

But I never wanted that. I wanted *her*. I hated that after everything, I still yearned for more.

"You're mine," I whispered against her lips, the strength of my declaration emphasized by the moan she pulled out of me. "I might not be able to leave. Might not have the power I once did. But don't forget who you belong to. We're tied. *Forever.*"

"I'm yours," she said breathlessly. This time, I covered her mouth with my own, allowing her tongue inside.

"And the next time *we* want to fuck the witch, I'll show her exactly who's in charge."

I ripped her shirt open. My bloodied palms ran across her chest, leaving a trail. She kissed me back ferociously. I met her with just as much passion.

I need her.

She gasped when my fingers found her nipples. I pinched them, twisted them. Mixing her pleasure with pain.

She pushed me harder up against the wall, the pumping of her fingers inside me becoming harder. The heel of her palm was slamming into my clit, sending zaps of pleasure through me each time.

We were so fucking good together. Fed each other's desires perfectly. Our bodies were made to be like this, tangled in each other, seeking the other's pleasure.

My hand trailed down her exposed torso until it got to her pants. I pulled away so I could take in her expression—blood smeared across her face, eyes lit with a hunger I hadn't seen in months, chest rising and falling rapidly with each breath.

Her mouth fell open just slightly as my fingers passed her mound and found her clit. Her underwear was a mess with her own desire.

The smell of it was overpowering and had my mouth watering for a taste.

"Tell me what she did to you, Little Mouse."

"She fucked me against a tree after I yelled at her," she said with a groan as I played with her, the movement between my legs stalling as she was overtaken by her own pleasure.

"Keep going like a good little toy, and I'll continue," I ordered. "You stop, I stop."

She picked it back up immediately, and I matched her pace, circling her clit until she was shaking against me. *So easy to play with, yet so rewarding.* There was nothing more addicting than seeing the all-powerful hunter, the same one who was supposed to kill me, the one that had upended my life, be brought to her knees by my hands.

Turning her into a writhing, groaning mess was becoming the highlight of my life. The bond only made it more satisfying as I could not only see it happening but feel it slowly chipping away at her as well.

"That's right," I cooed as she brought me closer and closer to orgasm.

I took it first, selfishly, before asking my question. I let myself fall into the waves of pleasure, leaning into my hunter with the taste of her blood still on my lips.

And then, just as she was about to come, I paused.

"Were you a good little *whore* for her?"

The question took her enough by surprise that she tried to jerk back. I had her in my grip. Just a single hand on her shoulder was enough to keep her there.

I played with her, teasing her clit as her mind floundered for a response.

She opened her mouth, but only moans came out. I applied more pressure, wanting to see her crack.

"Fuck! I—"

"Yes or no, Little Mouse?" I asked with a sickly sweet smile. "Tell me the truth."

She cursed again under her breath. Her orgasm was so close, I could feel the beginning of it through the bond.

She pressed her forehead to mine, all fight leaving her. It was so intimate, it had my heart seizing. So soft. Nothing like the passion and hatred that once raged through us.

In my mind, I wanted to attribute it to the bond, but I knew better. I knew this was all Vesper.

"Tell me the truth, or I'll leave you hanging."

She took in a sudden inhale of breath, and the whine she let out was the most magnificent sound on the planet.

Maybe I should have waited. Given her at least one orgasm.

But there was no fun—or revenge—in that.

"Or maybe..." I whispered and leaned forward to lick the wounds on her neck. "Maybe if you beg me, I'll let you off easy. You looked so *decadent* last time."

"You're not being fair," she forced out through gritted teeth.

"Beg or tell me how much of a good little whore you were."

She was silent for a moment, the shaking in her body getting more intense.

"*Please*, Aurelia," she groaned. "Please don't leave me like this."

Disappointment washed through me.

"Don't leave you like what?" I asked, slowing my movements.

"Please let me come, my princess," she begged. The desperation in her voice was sweet, scratching an itch I didn't know I had.

But it simply wasn't enough. She'd angered me. Left me in the cabin to get fucked.

She needed to learn a lesson.

"Do you even deserve it?" I asked. "A little hunter who got cocky. Stabbed me and now thinks she can run off wherever? I think you're forgetting who you belong to."

Her face twisted. Guilt zapped through the bond so strongly, it almost made me pause.

Almost.

"To you," she whined. "I belong to you. Please. I don't deserve it, but I can't take it. Please let me come."

I smiled against her skin and licked up a drop of blood that had fallen from her wounds.

She's right. She doesn't.

"No," I whispered and pushed her away.

She stumbled back with a shocked expression.

"What? You really think I'd let you off that easily?" I asked and popped my fingers into my mouth. Her wetness was almost as sweet as her blood.

"*Aurelia.*"

"*Vesper*," I said back with a smile. "Have a good night."

And with that, I went to my room, locking it behind me.

Vesper

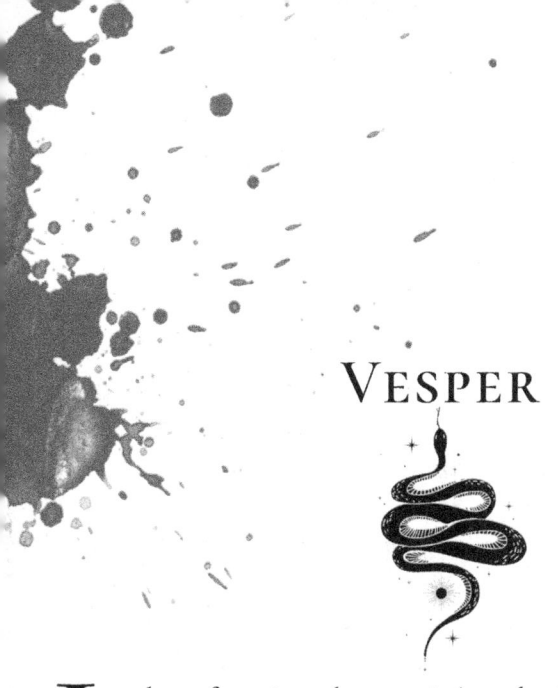

I sank my fangs into the vampire's neck, ripping out his throat as I pulled away.

The anger never subsided. I didn't mind her being with the witch. I fucking loved seeing them together.

I minded that Vesper had refused to submit.

Warm, thick blood splattered across my face and chest. It was disgusting. I hated the smell of vampire blood. Hated the way it felt. And absolutely despised the way it tasted.

It wasn't sweet like a human.

It tasted dirty. *Wrong.* Maybe it was our biological way of keeping us from drinking each other's blood for anything other than a bond.

But I wanted a mess. I wanted to walk back into the confines of the coven and have them take a look at what a *real* monster looked like.

They thought what they did last time had been punishment enough?

It hurt like a bitch, but Cedar had been right about one thing—that pain had been fucking child's play and had only fueled my anger.

On the rare occasion I was let out, they acted like we were monsters. I had grown tired of their whispers. Grown tired of how differently they treated Vesper and me.

They gave her endless jobs. Stupid little insults. All their dirty work because they knew she was desperate to get their acceptance.

They were fucking laughing at her. And she didn't seem to care one bit!

Another vampire was coming from behind, the pounding of his footsteps against the dirt alerting me of his presence.

The anger still raged inside me. Every little comment the witches made swirling through my mind

Disgusting. Look at how arrogant she is.

Almost like the princess never left the castle.

Did she really think she could come here and keep her stuck-up ways?

I twisted just as the vampire's arms threatened to circle my waist. They stopped short, not fully able to close around me as my entire hand went through their chest.

Weak for rogues.

There had been four of them holed up in the woods outside the coven's border. They knew nothing of the coven and the witches were willing to let them stay in the area...until they got too messy with the humans they took.

As we came upon them, there had been a pile of bodies rotting in the corner of their campsite.

They hadn't even had the decency to get rid of them.

The vampire's eyes widened, and he had just one split second to look down at my arm in his chest before his body shut down, dropping forward.

With a disgusted noise, I pushed him off, wiping his blood on my already ruined clothes.

"Well, look who decided to show up for work today," Cedar commented.

She stood a few feet away with her arms crossed. Unlike our first mission, she wasn't getting involved. She let Vesper and me do the whole thing while she watched.

Easy for her. I gave her a fake smile even as my chest warmed at her comment.

"Wish I could say the same to you," I snarked. "Do they really pay you that much just to babysit?"

Vesper had been a bit awkward, but Cedar and I were unfazed. I knew they had fucked, and apparently she knew I knew.

"I doubt they pay her at all," Vesper said. She too had been standing there watching as I took down vampire after vampire. She had been unhappy with me for most of the day after I left her hanging the night before.

It was amusing to see her so obviously frustrated.

It felt good to get back at her. But another part of me wanted to scratch my itch for her. Wanted her to beg for me again. Wanted to make Cedar watch and wish she could get involved.

It was so delicious to hear Vesper give up control.

But right now, Cedar's silence spoke a thousand words.

If they don't pay her, why is she here? Does she have some sort of fucked-up family obligation?

It was one of the only things Vesper and I had in common—fucked-up families demanding we did fucked-up things.

It made me wonder about Cedar's tie to the coven. I hadn't seen anyone who looked remotely similar to the witch, nor had she mentioned anything about her family.

Maybe she was more similar to us than I had originally thought.

"I do it for the fun of it, Princess," Cedar said with a grin.

"Ah yes, and because you want to fuck Vesper again," I shot back.

Cedar raised a brow at me.

"No need to be jealous, Brat. As much as I *love* spending time with a vampire hunter, the fun lies with you. Annoying you is the highlight of my day."

My face flamed. *There it is again.* It was not a nickname many had dared to call me before. I hated it even more than *princess*.

"I'm not a hunter," Vesper murmured.

We both gave her a look, and she raised her hands.

"Okay, *okay*."

"Job is done," Cedar said and turned back toward the pile of bodies. "Cleanup will be here soon, so we can leave."

I followed her, almost walking past Vesper until her hand shot out to grab mine. The brush of her skin against mine had electricity shooting through me. My first instinct was to lean into it. Into *her*. Continue what I had started the night before.

"You did good, Princess." The praise rolled smoothly off her tongue. The genuine smile that spread across her lips was threatening to have my heart explode.

Shit, what can I do to hear those words again?

But instead of letting me go, she pulled me to her. I expected a hug or something, but when she turned me so I was facing Cedar, I was taken aback.

What is she—

Quick hands ran through my hair, separating the strings and crossing them.

My entire body threatened to explode with heat when I realized what she was doing.

She's braiding my hair.

I couldn't look Cedar in the eye for fear that she would see exactly what the act did to me. It brought back images of me at my vanity, my mom running her hands through my hair.

My eyes stung. My chest tightened. My vision started to redden due to the tears building up.

She's being kind again.

Back in the palace, when my bird was murdered, it had been the first time anyone had ever been that kind to me. I thought it had been the last. But there she was, doing it again.

"Shit... um..."

Cedar let out a sigh and closed the space between us. Her hand shot up, threading through my hair. I swallowed my shocked gasp.

No one in the palace dared touch me like that without permission.

I was a fucking princess, for Krae's sake; she should respect it.

But even so... I couldn't ignore the burst of heat it sent exploding to my core.

No one had dared to treat me this way before. Not before Vesper. And now the witch?

I didn't know how to feel about it.

"If you didn't know how to braid, why'd you even try?" she grumbled.

"Because she said she got blood in her hair last time!"

I couldn't help but smile at Vesper's response.

"Then you should have done it *before* the mission," Cedar shot back.

She moved around me, her hands undoing Vesper's work and quickly redoing it.

"She was mad at me," Vesper muttered.

"How do you know I'm not anymore?"

Vesper was in front of me in a second, her eyes on mine.

My breath caught. Cedar was so incredibly close behind me, her hands in my hair sending shivers down my spine. Her nails ran across my scalp. I fought tooth and nail to keep from leaning back into her, but I couldn't stifle my sigh.

Vesper's lips twitched, understanding passing through her eyes.

I swear to Krae, if she says anything—

She didn't. But she looked back up over my head and nodded at Cedar, like she was giving her...*permission*? And then her nails were at it again, over and over, until I couldn't help but fall back against her, my back against her front. Closer than we'd ever been, and I was keenly aware of every single movement, every single breath.

Fuck. Not her too. I can handle the hunter pampering me, but the witch?

Vesper stepped closer, her scent infiltrating my senses. I couldn't help my quick inhale. She was still looking at Cedar, a silent conversation happening between them as if...

Shit, it's two against one.

The entire time we'd been with the coven, it had felt like it was the two of them and lonely ol' me off to the side, forgotten. Who knew that when I allowed it, they'd *both* try and overtake me?

Cedar finished the braid, but then in a move that shocked me to my core, grabbed it and yanked it hard enough that my throat was exposed. The witch looked down on me, a playfulness in her eyes.

My breath caught. My skin heated. She was so close. My eyes fell to her plump lips. I licked mine, unable to stop thinking about how she absolutely ravaged my mouth the first time.

My mouth fell open when Vesper leaned forward, leaving a hot, open-mouthed kiss on my neck before sucking on the sensitive flesh. Her teeth dug into my skin hard.

Even if it would just stay for a moment, she was still marking me, and with Cedar's gaze on mine and her hand in my hair, the meaning was loud and clear.

They are in control.

"How'd you know how to do that?" I asked, my voice sounding embarrassingly hoarse.

"A secret." Cedar's chuckle had heat swirling in my belly. She loosened her grip, and I forced myself to break our hypnotic eye contact to look at Vesper as she pulled away from me.

Her lips morphed into a sinful smirk. Only then did I realize that she had been feeling me through our bond.

She brought the tail of the braid up to her lips and placed a kiss on it.

"I guess I'll just have to work harder to please you, Princess. Or maybe... *we* can work on that." Her eyes shifted to Cedar again, whose hands ran up the sides of my arms.

I had never been more willing to sink to my knees for two individuals in my life.

In the matter of moments, I was rendered useless by both of them.

Damn. This game is getting harder to play.

Vesper

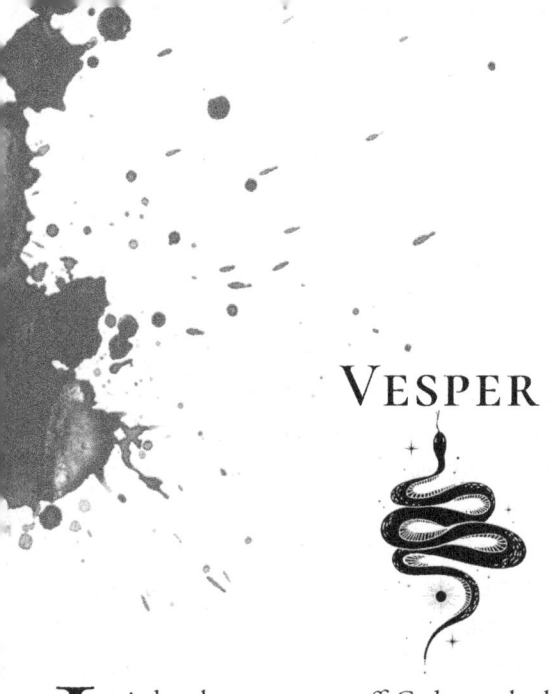

I tried to keep my eyes off Cedar as the high priest stood in front of us. He was too observant. One wrong look, and he would know everything we'd been trying to keep from him.

And the number of times we fucked.

I could almost hear her voice in my head.

Keep calm. Don't look at me. Just keep your eyes ahead.

I was stuck between not wanting to look at the priest and not being able to look away.

Images of Aurelia's and Cedar's bloodied bodies filled my mind and caused my anger to soar. Behind him, lurking in the shadows, was the witch who had taken them on the day Aurelia killed our guard.

My hand itched to grab the nearest weapon and shove it straight into his chest.

Keep calm, I told myself. *Don't ruin this more than you already have.*

Aurelia was at my side, her anger palpable through the bond and also quickly filling the room. But it wasn't directed at the priest. It was directed at Cedar.

"It's too dangerous," Cedar said, though her head was still bowed to him.

"What's another rogue?" Aurelia asked. "Isn't this what you guys wanted all along? I don't see why all of a sudden you don't want us to go."

"Maybe there's a good reason," I whispered to her. Aurelia shot me a glare.

"Taking the witch's side, huh? Where was this attitude when you were skinning those rabbits for the clan? How is this any worse than continuing to degrade yourself by doing their dirty work?"

I flinched at the harshness of her words. I'd fucked up, *again*. Because not only was she pissed...she was hurt too. I could feel it through the bond.

"My *Aurelia*." The priest's voice was whimsical and slightly amused. "You've finally decided to work with us now, is that it? I heard you did well on the last mission we assigned you."

Aurelia didn't inflate at his words like he might have expected; instead, she frowned at his obvious attempt to flatter her.

"I don't know, maybe whipping us was the key," the sarcasm was heavy in her tone. The priest let out an amused huff.

"It's never failed me before," he said.

His words hung over each one of us, the unspoken ones loud and clear.

And it's unlikely it ever will.

"How much more dangerous are we talking about?" I asked Cedar.

More dangerous than I am willing to risk.

I already knew it, but it was important for Aurelia to hear it. And even more important to keep up appearances for the priest.

"This isn't a normal rogue," Cedar said. "And it's not just one. It's possibly a whole clan in the making. Going after them will put a target on you guys. Bring Gabriel in, High Priest; he will agree with me that the best course of action is—"

"I don't care," he interrupted with a sickly sweet smile. "I am assigning this mission to them—*and you*. I will even give you a few more witches to tag along. But there is no room for pushback. You should know that, Young One."

Young One. The nickname came out sweet, but the meaning

behind it was degrading. Like he was reminding Cedar that she had no clue what she was talking about.

I swallowed thickly. She wouldn't be able to protect us anymore. Aurelia and I were in danger again.

But fighting with the priest would only make it worse.

"I want to do it," Aurelia declared. Cedar shifted beside me, ready to fight.

"Did you consider my request?" I asked, quickly trying to change the subject before Cedar got in trouble.

The priest's eyes were on Cedar, challenging her to say another word, but as soon as I spoke, his eyes shifted to me.

"It's approved," he said.

I couldn't hide the shock from my face.

When I had asked Cedar for a favor, I totally thought it would be denied. The coven leader was putting everything on the line.

"What request?" Aurelia hissed under her breath.

"I'm going to meet a seer," I breathed. Aurelia met my gaze for a moment, her eyes narrowing, before looking at the ground.

"I'll fix this," I vowed. Her eyes slowly met mine again. "I'll change the prophecy."

A seer. A real-life seer. The same type of person who solidified my future. Who ruined it and any other chance I had at living a normal life.

There was a mysticality to them. No one had the privilege to meet them. To know them. They were kept a secret for fear that they could be used and abused.

But they were the only forces in this world that could tip the scales.

I expected an old woman in a cloak. One whose eyes would roll back in her head as she was telling the future.

So when I was led up into a small back room inside the cathedral, I didn't expect to see a child.

A prisoner child.

The room itself was dark save for a few magically lit candles. Their red flames cast shadows on the stone walls.

The child had been playing in the shadows when we arrived, making hand puppets. When he turned, the rattling of a chain sounded, but I couldn't make it out in the darkness. He was small, hunched over. But there was a power to him.

It filled the room and threatened to suffocate me.

"You have three minutes." The priest said and exited, locking the door behind him.

I was so surprised by it that I snapped around to look at the door.

That was a mistake.

I heard the rattling before I felt the warmth of magic surround me.

My head swiveled back to the kid, but instead of sitting in the middle of the dark room, he was right in front of me.

I jerked back, my heart racing in my chest.

"You're here to ask about your family's prophecy," he commented, his voice sounding hollow.

My chest ached. No matter how freaky the situation was, or the kid seemed, this was no way to treat him. I imagined Tate in the same situation.

How could they?

The coven was far more fucked up than I originally believed.

"Why are you—"

"I'm not going to answer silly questions like that," he said with a frown. "Don't waste your three minutes."

I was stunned. I had planned to come in and demand to hear about the prophecy straight from the horse's mouth, but after seeing the child, my mind was very far from that.

"I'm sorry; I just—"

The kid let out a sigh, his gaze turning hard.

"A day will come when the singular Castle bloodline comes to maturity, and a child born with poison for blood will usher forth an end to their rule."

Word for word, he repeated the same prophecy I had heard my entire life.

"I don't want to kill her," I whispered. "Is there another way?"

I felt the magic swirling in the air as soon as I asked the question.

"*You* don't have to kill *her*," he said.

"I don't want her to die," I clarified.

"She doesn't have to. You have to *usher forth* an end to their rule. There are many ways to do that."

I cleared my throat.

"Can I have a hint at one of the ways?" The squeak of my voice was utterly pathetic.

He narrowed his eyes at me. He was a child, but I somehow felt like I was the one being scolded.

"Well, *not* stabbing the Castle family princess in the heart and making her hate you would have been a good place to start."

I swallowed the lump in my throat as guilt washed over me.

"She doesn't hate me," I murmured.

This got a wicked grin from him.

"No, she doesn't," he said. "But your actions set you back. They saved you both for a bit, but the prophecy remains the same."

"What if I...don't see it through?" I asked.

"The state of the world hangs in the balance." He shrugged like it was just a minor inconvenience. The weight on my shoulders felt heavier. "And the three of you will never know happiness."

"Three?" I echoed.

He merely gave me a deadpan stare. *Does he mean Cedar, Aurelia, and me?* The knowledge that Cedar was here to stay made my stomach flip.

"Okay. So back to it. How do I complete the prophecy—"

"Time's up."

I panicked, my head snapping to the door. *No! This is my only chance!*

The priest was back in, this time with a witch by his side. The witch grabbed my wrist and began to pull me out.

"How do I save her?" I asked, pulling against the witch's hold. My voice was panicked, loud. It echoed through the room.

"Don't make me hurt you," he threatened.

"That wasn't three minutes," the seer commented. The hate for the priest was clear in his stare. He was challenging him in a way he knew he'd get away with it.

"It was enough."

The seer gave him a sinister smile and whispered so only I would hear.

"Your other questions. Max. Since I was born. Because they can. And you're thinking too hard. If you do everything right, she can save herself. It will become clear soon."

I was dragged out of the room too fast to even digest what he was telling me.

If I do everything right? It will become clear soon? What will become clear soon?

But the words that really echoed through my head were, *Because they can.*

Why do they keep you here? That was the question I was going to ask when I saw a child in the middle of the room, alone and chained to the wall.

Because they can.

If they could do *that* just because they wanted to...what did that mean for Aurelia and me?

Or...for the three of us?

Aurelia

Vesper pulled me behind the door to our room, her eyes searching to make sure we were alone.

Then, when she was sure, her hands cupped my cheeks, and she brought her lips down on mine.

Shocked by the action, I froze. A part of me wanted to push her away, but the need for her had grown. It was like the bond between us was growing stronger and stronger every day. Bringing the witch in seemed to solidify it even more.

My hands grabbed her hips, pulling our bodies together.

"Good news, I take it?" I whispered against her lips.

She pulled away, her eyes searching mine.

"Confusing news," she said. "But hopeful. I just need to figure some things out."

"Like what?" I asked.

Meeting with a seer was no small feat. I was surprised the coven even let her given how much they seem to hate our presence.

"The prophecy," she replied. "We thought I'd have to kill you, but...he said you *don't* have to die."

My heart felt like it could start again.

"What do we need to do then?" I asked, my nails digging into her.

Can we really get past the prophecy? And if we can complete it... what will happen after?

There'd be no more running. No more fighting.

I could go back to the way things were...

But it's different now. The life I once had was no longer viable, and if I was being honest, I didn't want it anymore.

"That's what I need to figure out," she said. "He gave me some hints, but the priest interrupted us. Either way, I promise you, Aurelia. My princess. I will take you back to your palace, and this time, no one will dare hurt you or lock you up anymore. Just trust me, please?"

Tears pricked my eyes.

Would she really do it? Could she?

"I trust you," I whispered. "But promise me one more thing."

Her thumbs rubbed across my cheeks. "Anything, Princess."

I swallowed the emotions clogging my throat.

"That you won't leave me. You're coming back with me." Something flashed across her face that had me panicking. "I don't know what a vampire hunter will do within the walls of the palace, or if the family will even accept you, but I want—" I cleared my throat. "I want you there."

And maybe the redhead too. But I left that part out. Understanding flashed across her face, and I was met with a rare, soft smile that had me swooning.

It looked so out of place on her hardened, scarred face, but it made me love it even more.

"They could lock me up. Kill me. Condemn my soul to hell. None of it would keep me from coming back to you. My place is at your side. Forever. I *promise*."

My hands trailed up to her face, cupping her just like she was mine.

"My perfect little mouse," I whispered. "Thank you."

I stood on my tiptoes to press my lips against hers.

Hope, that dangerous emotion, sprouted in my chest again.

Cedar

"He said she can save herself."

I gave Vesper a look.

"Aurelia?"

From the annoyed look on her face, the disbelief in my tone might have been a bit too thick.

We were back in the forest, hopefully for the last time since this was the night we'd finally meet the vampire Atlas. I didn't trust the idea of having to meet a random vampire, but I was getting antsy after the meeting with the seer.

Not only were they going to send us out against a rogue who would undoubtedly kill us, but something ticked off the high priest when Vesper was talking to the seer.

He was angry. The type of anger I hadn't seen for a long time, reserved for betrayal. For something way more serious than Vesper and the seer.

Vesper learned something dangerous.

"He also said I didn't have to kill her; just usher forth an end to their rule. I didn't tell her that part yet, I... I don't want to get her hopes up. Because honestly, I don't know what it means."

The things she was telling me didn't seem big enough to warrant that reaction.

"But..." I bit my tongue, unsure how to say what I was thinking without tearing down this newfound hope of hers. "She's the next in line. No matter what you do, she will be head of the family, and it will live on."

She was silent for a long time.

"I'll think of something. Tell me about the rogue instead."

I didn't immediately answer her, choosing to turn around, my mind still reeling from everything that happened. I didn't know what to tell her. What would scare her. Was any of it worth sharing if we were all just going to die because of it?

"Don't hide it from me," Vesper hissed, her hand wrapping around my wrist and yanking me back to her.

The breeze whistling through the trees was cold against my skin, but it wasn't enough to lower the heat that spread across my skin at her touch.

Her eyes burned into mine every bit as intensely as they had the first moment she saw me in the room that first night. Just like then, it caused my heart to beat faster. But instead of excitement filling me, this time it was fear.

The high priest had been hinting at what he was going to do since the last White Lotus meeting. I just never imagined he would be going for it this fast.

"What's the deal with this rogue?" she asked. "Will it kill her?"

Her? She's thinking about Aurelia?

Flashbacks of the meeting hit me like a truck.

We all know the hunter should have died anyway. She's a liability. If you ask me, we should just send them. Tie up loose ends.

I didn't want to think about it. Didn't want to entertain the idea that the reason they were doing this was not to get rid of the vampire alone. I jerked my hand from her grasp.

"Can you think about yourself too for once?" I hissed. "Did you ever stop to think that maybe your life is in danger too?"

She moved even closer.

"That's why you better stop with this secretive shit and tell me," she said in a low voice. "My life has been on the line since the moment I stepped into the palace. The only reason I'm still breathing is because of your help covering my tattoo. But back then I knew nothing. I relied on you. Don't let me stay in the dark any longer."

My face pinched. "Isn't it okay to rely on me now?" I asked, grabbing her arm. "Even just for a moment? Until I figure things out myself?"

"Tell me more about this rogue," she deadpanned after a moment.

My heart sank in my chest.

"Ooh, the little hunter has a suicide mission, does she? How *cute*."

I jerked around to see Atlas waiting for us in the darkness. Her pitch-black hair blended into the shadows; the only things visible were her red eyes and the twinkle of the various jewels she had sewn into her coat.

This wasn't the first time I was risking my life. It would be the second time.

For Vesper.

The vampire screamed danger. There was an aura about her, old and powerful. If I had come across her in the wild, I would have steered clear. My guess was that she was at least a few hundred years old. Maybe a thousand.

She stared at us with an amused smile on her face, but her eyes were narrowed.

She doesn't like the hunter.

The way she looked her over had my hair standing on edge.

I shifted toward her, covering her body with mine. The action had the vampire raising her brow.

"If I wanted to kill your hunter, I would have done so a long time ago," she commented, her eyes roaming my face. She tilted her head back, sniffing the night air. "You're more powerful than I thought. Hunter, what are you doing with this one? If she so much as touches a hair on Aurelia's head, I'll tear both your throats out."

Vesper moved from behind me, her face cold.

"She's trustworthy," she said. Her declaration had my heart skipping a beat in my chest. Something the vampire no doubt heard with the way her eyes shifted back to me for a brief moment. "We thought we were safe here—"

"With witches?' Atlas let out a harsh laugh that bounced off the trees around us. "The witches are brutal. Vampires at least are honest about their nature, but witches? You won't know how fucked you are until those burning tendrils of theirs are wrapped around your neck. I thought you were smarter than this, hunter."

"Stop calling me that," Vesper hissed through gritted teeth. "We need your help. I want to get Aurelia out of here. Secure her place in your clan—"

"Whoa, whoa, whoa," Atlas cut her off, raising her hands and stepping toward Vesper. Her movements were unhurried, one long leg gracefully stretching out before the other. "Didn't you hear me before? The council is watching. Not just me, but everyone in the area. My guess is the rogue they're sending you after is the same one causing us problems. Either way, we can't accept anyone new."

Her mention of the rogue caught my attention.

"Not just one rogue," I said. Her eyes shifted to me, and the smile finally dropped from her face.

"No, it's likely it's multiple. But that's not my problem, nor do I recommend sending the hunter and Aurelia after them. The council has tried to intervene, but every party they've sent has magically disappeared."

The vampire council's people are disappearing?

They were known for being ruthless. For doing the cleanup no one dared to do. And they were...missing?

"Can you get them to a clan across the border?" I asked. "Or maybe something underground?"

Atlas ignored me completely, focusing on Vesper.

"I can take Aurelia, but that's it. I can't have her in my clan, but I can help her travel between a few in the north."

No. Fear gripped my throat. "Vesper and Aurelia are a package deal. They are bond—"

"Okay," Vesper interrupted, her hand coming to my shoulder. "Take her. Before the mission."

"Which is?" It took me a moment to realize Atlas was directing the question at me.

"I don't know," I whispered. "We have some information on their movements, but not a lot. My guess is it'll take another week or two unless we're tipped as to where they will hit next."

She gave me a tight nod. "A week from today. Meet me here with Aurelia at the same time. I don't think you're stupid enough for me to have to warn you not to tell anyone, hunter."

"I am not," Vesper said, though this time she had a small smile on her face. "Thanks for your help, Atlas."

The vampire's eyes lingered on Vesper before turning away. "I'm not doing this for you; it's for her."

"Still, thank you," she said.

Atlas looked back, a frown on her face.

"Don't feed the bond, hunter. If you do it, it will be painful for her to leave, and when we meet again, I'll be taking her. By force if necessary."

"Taking her by force? Sounds more like we're facilitating a kidnapping than a rescue mission," I blurted out.

Atlas's lips pulled upward.

"She's a dear friend, and sometimes she doesn't know what's good for her. I'd rather have her mad at me for a short time than risk her life. Don't do anything stupid while we wait, hunter."

And with that, she disappeared into the darkness. As soon as she was gone, I grabbed Vesper and forced her to look at me.

"You're going with them," I said. "You can't stay here. If Aurelia leaves, they won't be happy. They would—"

"Kill me?" she asked with a raised brow. "Lock me up like the child seer they have in the cathedral?"

"Yes," I replied, desperation leaking into my voice. "They are no better than the vampires out there. No better than your family. They will hurt you. Do you know what self-preservation is?"

Vesper gave me a sad smile.

"I just want her to live," she said.

"And me?" I asked. "Do you care that your actions aren't just going to doom yourself but me as well?"

For the first time since coming to the coven, I saw Vesper's resolve crack.

"If I could take both of you far away," she said, her voice dropping, "I would."

I found myself wishing for a chance to make that dream of hers come true, no matter how unrealistic.

When I went to bed, I drained my magic praying to Helma.

But not for me.

For *her*. For *them*.

Wishing one day, they could get the life they wanted, before it was too late.

Aurelia

I'm *going to fucking kill Levana.*
I thought the ice cream would be enough to ensure secrecy, but apparently not.

Cedar stood in front of me, Vesper at my side.

We were due to go out and ambush the rogue soon, and she had just come in with a folder and a smirk.

"You could have asked me, you know?" she said, throwing the folder on my lap. "Levana is good at some things, but familial history is not one of them."

"What did you ask her?" Vesper's breath was hot on my neck.

I gritted my teeth. I didn't want to call attention to it. *To me.* What if I opened the folder and it was a disaster?

"She wanted to know why her mother was so important to her father and other families," Cedar replied. "Are you okay if I give you a summary or would you rather have us leave so you can read it?"

The offer for privacy took me aback. *No one has ever given me the option before.*

But... I gripped Vesper's hand in mine, seeking out comfort.

"Tell me," I said, my eyes meeting Cedar's green ones.

Something akin to pride flashed through them.

"Your mother's female bloodline was rumored to be direct descendants from Krae," she started. "Many royal families searched for your mother's family for decades, but her mother and her mother's mother all took great care in hiding that fact."

My breath caught.

Descendants from Krae? She was supposedly the start of vampires, but...

"She's real?" I breathed, unable to wrap my mind around it.

I thought the goddess had abandoned me, but maybe I was closer to her than I'd ever realized.

"Rumored," Cedar said.

"But believable enough that people went after your mother's family," Vesper added.

"How did they find her?"

Cedar grimaced.

"This is the not-so-nice part of the story..." After a moment of silence, I realized she was waiting for my okay to continue. I gave her a nod. "Her father sold her to the highest bidder. The Solei, actually. I am not sure what happened between Solei and Castle for your mother to end up with your father, but all records point to her having been sold to him."

My jaw clenched so hard it began to ache.

"But why?" Vesper asked. "Shouldn't she have been revered instead of sold? The same happened to Aurelia—she was going to be married off to produce heirs."

"They loved my mother," I forced out. "Where Krae is, so are the people. It's a control factor."

And another reminder no one actually loved me. It was a bitter pill to swallow.

"How did you find this out?" I asked.

"Magical records. Witches track these things. Know thy enemy and all that." She waved her hand as if it was no big deal that she could just search my entire family lineage.

"Then why couldn't Levana find it?" Vesper asked.

"She's not allowed in the archives anymore," Cedar answered with a grimace. "Sometimes hybrid magic goes haywire, and she—well, let's just be glad the archives weren't burned to a crisp."

I stood and closed the space between us. Cedar didn't move, instead giving me a look of suspicion.

"I never thought I'd figure it out," I admitted. "It stings, but now at least I know why my mother was so wanted."

"And why *you* are so powerful," Cedar said, the praise rolling smoothly off her tongue.

I stood on my tiptoes, wrapped an arm around her neck, and gave her a deep kiss. She hesitated for a moment before returning it.

Vesper's gasp behind me had me pulling away and smiling at Cedar.

"Your reward," I said with a small grin.

"Does this mean you accept me?" she asked with a twinkle in her eyes.

Accept didn't even come close to what was happening between the three of us. But I needed to take it slow.

"Let's just say you're now in trial run territory."

The laugh she let out warmed my chest.

"I didn't want to say anything because I wasn't sure..."

We both turned to Vesper, whose hands were gripping her pants nervously.

"Vesper..." Cedar whispered.

Vesper glanced at Cedar, then back at me.

My heart sank. *Is there something they're hiding from me?*

"The seer said you didn't have to die," Vesper said. "That if everything went right, *you* could save yourself."

I can save myself?

Hope like never before sprung to life inside my chest. Could it really be true? Could I save myself and end this prophecy forever?

We could be free. All of us. I wouldn't have to run. Vesper wouldn't have to risk her life. *We would be left alone. Just us.*

For the first time since coming to the coven, I raised my head high.

"Let's go get that rogue."

I was on a high after what had happened in the cabin.

Suddenly, everything was clear. *And having the witch on my arm was a bonus.*

I couldn't wait to finish the job so I could have both of them in my bed.

The coven was a complication, but that felt much more manageable now that I had people by my side and answers to the questions that had been bothering me for a lifetime.

"When we get home, you're eating her out after this," I whispered to Cedar, making sure Vesper couldn't hear. She was a few paces in front of us, scanning the area.

Cedar let out a chuckle.

"Right... Who put you in charge, *Brat*?"

I gave her a look but didn't dignify her with a response. At least that's what I told myself, and it was not at all because the nickname had my stomach flipping.

"I've been dying to taste her for a while," she replied in a low voice. "Her blood was positively delicious coming from your mouth. I can't wait to find out what the two of you taste like together."

My skin heated. I looked up to see Cedar's green eyes burrowing into mine.

"I didn't want to do this at first," I admitted. "I told Vesper it wouldn't happen again."

Cedar raised a brow at me.

"That's not what she implied after I fucked her against a tre—"

"Am I going to have to separate you two?" Vesper asked with a bit of annoyance in her tone.

"Under what authority?" I asked with a scoff.

"Yeah, hunter," Cedar said with a grin. "Not like you can do anything about it."

Vesper's chest puffed out at her comment.

"We have a job and you two are over there—"

"Discussing the best ways to fuck you?" Cedar supplied.

"Tied up for sure," I added.

"Definitely. On the bed. Ass up. Taking a strap while her mouth is on your cun—"

"Enough!" Vesper growled, her pale face turning impossibly red. She turned around and stomped a few paces forward.

Cute. The little mouse is embarrassed. But I didn't miss the hint of arousal coming from her as well.

"Hurt her and I'll kill you," I warned.

Cedar pushed me forward, the heat of her hand on me sending butterflies flying in my stomach.

"What makes you think I'll hurt *her* and not *you*?"

I sent her a smirk.

"My heart's made of ice," I said.

Cedar made a disbelieving sound but said nothing else.

The air was quiet, the cars from a nearby highway so distant that it was but an afterthought. The sky was changing. Beautiful hues of pinks and yellows washing away the light blue from the day.

I let Cedar go ahead of me to catch up with Vesper, who was decidedly trying to ignore her.

Rocks crunched underneath our shoes as we got closer and closer to the meeting point. I slowed down, and both of them turned to look at me.

I heard the witches before I saw them. But something felt...off.

I couldn't put my finger on it, but I felt as though we were being watched.

"Cedar, taking the scenic route, are we?" A familiar voice called.

And there she is.

Levana stepped out from the tree line while two witches I hadn't seen before appeared in the path ahead of us.

"Three of them?" I hissed under my breath. "Your high priest has *that* little faith in us?"

Cedar let out a huff of a laugh.

"If they weren't here, Brat, you'd be likely to die. You should be thanking them."

There it is. Brat again.

Cedar brushed past me, not at all bothering to apologize when her arm hit mine. I stormed up to Vesper.

"This wasn't the pl—"

"We are not privy to the plan. Just go with it," Vesper whispered.

I turned to the pink-haired witch. She sent me a smile.

Oh god, she thinks we're friends.

She took a few steps forward.

"Sorry about your *project*. I wanted to help, but I'm not allowed in the archives anymore. I hope Cedar found what you were looking for."

I gave her a small smile. Even if she wasn't the one to finish it, she kickstarted the investigation, so I should be thankful.

Descendants of Krae.

It made me giddy.

"It's okay," I said. "Thank you for hel—"

It happened too fast for even my vampire sight to catch up.

One minute there were six of us standing on the path, then nine.

They found us.

Three vampires stood behind the newest witches, their hands on them. One arm wrapped around their fronts with the hand clutching their shoulders, the other on their heads.

Levana's eyes widened. But it was too late. Her hands clutched the vampire's, but he had her in an iron grip.

I was frozen, unable to help her even as the scene unfolded right in front of my eyes.

No.

All three vampires ripped their heads from their shoulders in one swift movement.

Time slowed. I watched as Cedar's magic flared to life. As Vesper stopped dead in her tracks.

Please no.

We had never been friends. But if that were true, why did such horror fill me at the sight of her headless body?

Why did it feel like a knife was ripping my chest open?

The breath was stolen from me.

I had heard about the same reaction happening in humans. Laughed at how, in the face of death, everything would slow for them. I never thought it would happen to me. Never thought I would feel like that on the brink of death.

I was horrified at Levana's death, but something even stronger ran through my mind.

Fear.

I am going to die here.

It felt like ice-cold fear had been injected straight into my veins, and my feet moved faster than my mind. While my brain was forcing me to relive flashbacks of my and Vesper's time together, my body already knew what I had to do.

I pushed Vesper back, shielding her with my body, and in the next blink, I was at Cedar's side, baring my teeth at the vampires.

Am I actually going to fight them?

My body already knew the answer my brain was afraid to admit. The bond opened up at that moment, Vesper's panic seeping through it.

"Take Vesper and run," Cedar commanded. "You can't win here."

Her command caught me off guard. *Shouldn't she want to protect herself?* As a witch, she might be able to protect herself long enough until help came or even find a way to escape.

But she wasn't thinking about herself at all.

Just like me, her body had moved to protect the silver-haired vampire, but it was her brain that caught up first.

She was going to sacrifice herself. *I can't let that happen.*

"*Go,*" she hissed.

I gritted my teeth.

"You better win this," I warned. "We have plans."

I turned back to Vesper, ready to grab her and run, but my view was obstructed by another vampire. This one was more powerful than the others and stood at least a foot taller than me.

He had dark brown hair, scars running across his face, and familiar piercing blue eyes that I had only seen on two other people in this world.

A feral smile pulled at his lips.

Danger. Run. But my feet were planted on the ground.

"Well, I'd never." His tone was laced with amusement. "To think the coven was nice enough to send you straight to me. I was wondering why Daddy had been so quiet about your disappearance."

My mind screeched to a halt.

"Who are you?"

He leaned down, getting eye level with me. I flinched.

His eyes...

They were cold. Desolate.

They look like...

"I guess you can call me your little brother."

Vesper

The *prophecy.*
 The thing that had been controlling my life. Had made it a living hell. Had sent me to the palace. Had given me Aurelia...

It's falling apart before my very eyes.

The vampire had his back to me, but I heard his declaration loud and clear.

Baby brother.

Castle bloodline.

Meaning... Was this what the seer meant?

The seer's words flared through my mind.

You don't have to kill her.

I don't want her to die.

She doesn't have to.

He had given me the answer, but I hadn't realized it.

It's her brother.

I didn't care to think about the details. Something told me that the only way out was to kill the vampire right in front of me.

It will become clear soon.

Yes. It was clear. I knew what I had to do.

For the first time in years, my body thrummed with the need to kill. Hope and desperation mixed violently in my chest. Not only was there still a chance for me to complete the prophecy...but I didn't have to kill Aurelia.

The singular *Castle bloodline.*

I didn't care to think what it meant for Aurelia. I'd figure it out later.

My hand reached behind me with a mind of its own, before my consciousness caught up to what it was doing.

I may die here.

The difference between our group and theirs was staggering. They killed three witches before we even knew what was happening.

They killed Levana.

Guilt and grief pierced my chest, but it was nothing compared to the new burst of hope that spread throughout. They might have killed her, but it brought me a chance to do something I never thought possible.

The vampires behind Aurelia had their eyes locked on me. They saw what I was doing but made no move to stop me.

I hadn't even realized my feet were taking me to him until Cedar was by my side, grabbing my hand.

"Don't be suicidal," she hissed.

"Oh no, *please* be suicidal," he said, his head moving so his gaze could meet mine.

Fear. It shot through me as soon as I got a look at the cruelty behind the famous Castle blue eyes.

His are nothing like Aurelia's.

Aurelia had humanity, even if she seemed cruel at times. She had feelings. Hope and dreams.

I lowered my sword. The action had the smile plastered on his face widening.

I wouldn't stand a chance.

He was what I assumed was a spitting image of Aurelia's father when he was younger. The haircut. His eyes. Everything except the scars that littered his face.

Scars that look a lot like mine.

"Does your daddy know about you?" I asked, raising my voice.

He let out a bark of a laugh.

"Know about me?" His laughter was weaved into his words. "He's the one who made me like this. He *killed* my mother. Tried to kill me in the womb until *hers* stepped up for me."

"Mine?" Aurelia asked.

He turned back to her.

"Your mother was the perfect wife. The perfect queen. She saved me only to throw me away to some random orphanage. Hiding the true heir to the throne so her own daughter could have a chance at it. She was stupid."

Aurelia's face twisted.

"She would never," she hissed. "She loved children. If she had known about you..."

"She did know. She visited me frequently as well, until her own death. Something no doubt had to do with her harboring the king's dirty little secret."

The air was tense. I'd never seen Aurelia so speechless.

"Did you find this in your records?" I asked Cedar.

"No," she said through gritted teeth. "I think she had a handmaiden who disappeared, but—"

"Ding, ding, ding," he said, waving his hand in the air as if ringing a bell. "Correct! Father was fucking his wife's handmaiden."

"Is that why you're killing people? Vampires?" Aurelia asked. "You're sending him a message?"

Her voice was steady, but I could feel the fear through the bond.

"That's right," he said and rolled his shoulders, standing up to his full height. He towered over her. "For Daddy dearest. A better message would be to kill you, though."

The only thing that stopped me from charging at him was Cedar's grip on me.

"You *do not* fight him," she ordered.

You can't boss me around, was what I wanted to spit back, but my throat was too tight.

"You won't, though," Aurelia told him.

He let out another laugh.

"What makes you think that?"

"Payment," she said. "For my mother saving your life."

"She's the fucking reason I ended up this way," he spat. "If anything, I wish she was still alive just so I could kill her myself."

The jab didn't visually seem to upset Aurelia, but I could feel her anger through the bond.

She's close to killing him.

"You loved her, I can feel it. Everyone did."

The man froze.

"It doesn't mean anything now."

"Doesn't it, though?" she asked, her eyes trailing his form. "You're a rogue now. Killing to get attention after *Daddy* banished you. Wishing you were me. *I* lived in luxury. *I* was the one he introduced to the world as his daughter. And you were...left outside in the cold. Abandoned like...a puppy. Until your mother's employer took pity on you. *Pathetic.*"

I couldn't see his face, but his fists clenched, and the vampires behind Aurelia looked just as scared as I felt.

"Are you really trying to make me angry, sister?" he asked, circling her. His hand trailed her shoulder. Once behind her, he leaned down and whispered in her ear. His eyes were on me and there was a smile on his face.

I couldn't make out whatever he was saying, but it certainly had an effect on Aurelia. Her entire body stiffened. Her eyes went hard. Her teeth bit into her bottom lip hard enough to draw blood.

"The family is rightfully mine," she growled, her head snapping to him. I didn't see her make a move to swipe at him, but saw her frozen as he moved.

In a blink, he was back with his gang of vampires, trampling all over the witches' dead bodies.

"I'm the heir," he said. "Even if Daddy doesn't want to admit it. The only reason he kept you and not me was because you're a better pawn. You'd never be able to take over; your whole life, you've been groomed to be wed to some other family. You never had a chance. But I will take back what's mine."

"You don't know what you're—"

"Goodbye, big sister," he said and turned away, his arm coming up in a nonchalant wave. "If you know what's good for you, you'll stay away from this area and from the family. If not... I'll kill you."

The way he threatened her with such an easy, happy tone had my skin crawling.

And then he was gone, just as fast as he'd shown up.

My gaze shot to Cedar.

"Did you know?" I asked, my voice hoarse.

Her jaw ticked.

"It wasn't in the archives," she said. "I didn't really believe you when you said she didn't have to die, but maybe..."

She didn't have to finish. This was both the best and worst possible scenario.

Levana was dead, but in her place sprouted something that could change the world as we knew it.

Aurelia

Little brother. The words echoed through my head over and over as we waited for backup to arrive.

It shouldn't be possible.

I didn't remember Mother ever having a handmaiden. I searched my memories for one, but came up blank—

The nightmare.

My thoughts came to a screeching halt. I did remember her. Maybe not consciously, but subconsciously I'd committed her to memory.

How could Father...

I was the one who was supposed to take over the family. *I* was the princess. If there was another—*a boy*—born into the family...

Even if Daddy doesn't want to admit it. The only reason he kept you and not me was because you're a better pawn.

His words hurt because I knew they were true. I didn't even need to look at all the scars on his body to see what Father had tried to do to him. No doubt after Mother died, he sent people to try and deal with his mistake.

But he lived.

It was a miracle he was alive, and maybe, in some other life, I would have been happy to have a brother. At least then I would have someone who could relate to the craziness of the king.

Maybe we would have been friends. Would have loved each other the way families were supposed to instead of trying to hurt each other.

He let me live.

Even though he threatened to kill me if I got involved, he still let me live.

A kindness I wouldn't repay if the roles were reversed.

If I had to grow up from afar, watching as a spoiled brat got to live it up in the palace, taking what was rightfully mine while I was shunned, tossed to the curb, and given no other choice but to become a rogue... I would have taken them out as soon as I got a chance.

Was this why my mother died?

Images of her dying, black-veined face filled my mind. I didn't want to believe it.

"All this time..." I murmured, wrapping my arms around my torso.

Vesper shifted next to me, her hand coming to brush across my upper arm.

"Your father is a master manipulator," she said. "If your father had accepted your brother, he likely would have had to give the family to him at some point as male heir. If he didn't, your brother would probably kill him. You, on the other hand..."

"Acted like a good broodmare while he had no intention to ever let me be head of the family. My mother... They loved her. The family looked up to her, but me... How could I have been so blind?"

I should have known. He was younger than me. Why couldn't I remember anything? Why was there no trace?

Father covered his tracks.

Cedar stepped in front of me, her hand clamping down on my shoulder.

"You don't have time to feel sorry for yourself," she said, her voice hard. "We need to discuss our story. If the rest of the White Lotus finds out there was another Castle—"

"What makes you think they don't know?" I asked, slapping her hand off my shoulder. "It's pretty damn hard to hide the existence of a family heir from a seer."

Anger pinched her face.

"Listen, I'm trying to help you. If the others find out they don't need *you*, what do you think happens to Vesper? They are going to push the high priest to send her after him. She has no fucking chance against—"

"Krae," I breathed. "Vesper this, Vesper that. What about me? I just learned my father kept this from me and was probably the reason my mother died. What about you? Levana dying doesn't mean anything to you? It's not just *Vesper* we have to worry about. We have real fucking problems here. Like my brother possibly going after Father and taking over the family. And all you can think of is her?"

"I care about her," Cedar replied with a frown. "So I want to protect her. *Both of you.* I'm telling you the White Lotus will put all our lives in danger. The witches in there are selfish, all of them just trying to get credit for ending this thing. If Vesper decides that she doesn't want to cooperate, they'll just get another hunter in her family to take over."

Another hunter?

"Gabriel would never—"

"Not Gabriel, Vesper."

Cedar's eyes dug into the silver-haired hunter, and a heavy silence fell over the three of us. Understanding followed.

"He's just a boy," Vesper whispered.

Tate? They would send the kid if Vesper refused?

The witches and their cult-like coven were fucked, but surely they wouldn't go that far to fulfill the prophecy, right?

"So we need to get our fucking story straight," Cedar hissed. Her gaze was on me. "The rogue was strong. He had dark hair and blue eyes. He did not talk to us other than to give us a warning. Is that clear? Let me figure out how to explain it to the high priest, but until then, go with this story. Trust me."

Her voice cracked at the end. Only then did I realize how

panicked she was. Sweat rolled down her pale face. Her breathing was hard. Her hands were shaking.

She is scared. For us.

I looked at Vesper, who was still frozen. No doubt shocked at the idea that the coven could use her little brother in such a cruel way. If I was being honest, it tugged at my chest as well. The kid was annoying, but he was innocent. He didn't deserve all his family or the coven would ask of him.

"Okay," I said after a pause. "I'll let you do the talking."

And for the first time, the tension between us seemed to lessen ever so slightly.

"I'll try my best to stop them from bringing Tate into this," Cedar vowed.

Vesper gave her a forced smile. On the outside, she didn't show just how much those words affected her, but through the bond, I could feel her panic lessen.

It wasn't long until the White Lotus came—three of them who immediately took in their comrades' dead bodies. You would think they would show some type of emotion when coming face to face with the gruesome sight. Their heads had been torn off, for Krae's sake.

Nothing.

They merely looked them over, took note of everything they had on them, and then used their magic to light their corpses on fire.

Even crueler than the vampires.

It wasn't until their bodies were fully burned to ash that they even acknowledged we were there.

Their leader was another man I hadn't seen around before.

Almost like they're purposely hiding these people away.

Cedar walked toward them, and they met her halfway.

"I don't see any vampire corpses," he said, his voice deadpan.

The way his eyes rolled over Vesper had me inching closer to her.

"They killed them too fast. When they saw us, they took off."

The man raised an eyebrow at us.

"And spared you?" he asked. This time his eyes went to me. "I thought the princess was foaming at the mouth for this chance. What happened?"

"They ran," I added before Cedar could. "We would be dead if they hadn't. He was too strong."

"*He*? Did you meet the rogue?"

Damn it. Cedar's quick look told me to shut my mouth.

"He let his minions do the work, but he was watching. We were right. He's been recruiting—"

"Did you talk to him?"

This time the question was directed at me.

"No; like Cedar said, he was just watching, and then they left."

"Now why would they spare you three then?" one of the others asked. "He hasn't been known to leave behind any survivors. I find it hard to believe they let even one of you live."

"If you find it hard to believe, get the priest. Better yet, pay a visit to the seer. They will tell you all you need to know."

Cedar's voice was confident, the bluff almost undetectable.

Something akin to pride swelled in my chest.

She passed the trial run.

Vesper

"I thought the whole plan was *not* to tell them?" I asked, unable to stop pacing a hole in the floor of the cathedral room we'd been locked in.

It wasn't a surprise that they wanted us isolated. We'd failed a mission. Three of their witches were dead. And we had said nothing about the rogue, even though it was obvious from Aurelia's slipup that we had, in fact, met him.

It would have been best if we had told them we'd never seen the leader. That instead he had sent his goons to come get us.

But that was in the past, and there was no changing it.

I wasn't mad at her. I was still trying to wrap my head around the fact that I *wouldn't* have to kill Aurelia.

Is it wrong to be so happy even if three people are dead? Even after losing someone I thought was a friend at one point?

Levana's smiling face flashed through my mind. It hurt like a punch to the gut, but there was a weight lifted from my shoulders too.

I couldn't help it. All the burden and fear that had been keeping me up at night were significantly lessened. For Aurelia, I *wanted* to complete the prophecy. I wanted to free her from the hell her life had been.

Killing is what I've been raised to do.

Specifically, this very job, which now seemed more within my reach than ever before. It didn't matter how strong he was. Or just how unlikely it was that I'd win against him and his army.

But I had hope. Because it wasn't Aurelia anymore.

For her. For them.

The three of us could make it out. Together.

Aurelia crossed her legs and leaned back on the rickety wooden bench. Cedar was at her side, her legs spread wide and her gaze on me.

She was with us now. There was no stopping it.

We were inevitable.

"The princess already let it slip," Cedar said with a shrug. "And my plan was always to tell them, just not *them*. If the group knew beforehand, who knows what they'd do? It's safer to tell them all together, along with the high priest."

"Not trusting your own coven, huh?" Aurelia asked.

Cedar's eyes cut to her, and she gave the princess a smirk.

"Did you trust your own family?"

"*Touché.*" Aurelia smiled back at her.

Them getting along was something else.

"Chances are, if they find out there is another Castle, they will try to go off on their own. This group, while loyal to the high priest, will find any way they can to make themselves more important."

"So we tell them as a group, have the high priest give the orders on what to do next, and hopefully... *What*?" I asked.

"Try not to get killed off by random White Lotus witches, Vesper," Aurelia said. "I thought you were smarter than this."

My jaw clenched at her slight.

"They won't need us anymore," Cedar explained. "We need to make ourselves important before rogue witches decide we need to be killed off."

I opened my mouth to say something snarky about their oh-so-sudden friendship, but I was cut off by the door opening.

"The high priest will see you now."

Max was standing in the middle of the circle we had formed, the magical chains on him fastened to the floor. The rest of the White Lotus members were with us in the circle, Gabriel standing right across from me.

The high priest was standing on the raised altar, his gaze sharp as he took us all in.

It was just as shocking seeing the kid a second time. But this time he wasn't looking at me. His eyes were trained on Aurelia.

"What's so interesting, boy?"

The boy's lips quirked.

"Seeing you in the flesh is just...interesting."

A frown tugged at Aurelia's lips.

"So how does this work? Do you, like, dream about my future or something?"

The high priest cleared his throat, calling all of our attention to him.

"Enough chatting," he ordered. Magic swirled around us, licking at my skin and causing a burning sensation to run up my spine. "Cedar."

"We met the rogue," she said, her voice spreading through the chamber. All eyes were on her. The hostility of her comrades' gaze was palpable. "Levana's group was ahead of us. Three of his group got to them before we could. It happened so fast, we couldn't even react. Then he appeared."

"What did he look like?" the high priest asked.

"Dark hair, blue eyes, scars," Cedar replied. "He saw Aurelia and stopped them from killing us."

"Suspicious, if you ask me," the man who'd met us at the site said, his eyes narrowed on the princess.

"So he just left you alive..." the high priest wondered. "Did you communicate in any way?"

Cedar looked at Aurelia, who puffed up as her turn came up.

"He recognized me," she said. "Had some long-winded speech that really just meant Daddy wasn't as faithful to my mom as the world thought, and he now has a bastard out there running wild."

The silence was deafening.

All the witches looked to the high priest while Gabriel stared at me.

No one spoke; they just let Aurelia's words sink in.

"Meaning the prophecy—"

"Can be fulfilled with his death," the boy in the middle said. "The Castle in the prophecy has always been her brother."

"But the prophecy didn't say *last*," the high priest said, his voice echoing. "It said *singular*."

All eyes were on Aurelia. She had been the one to grow up in the palace. She had been the one groomed with the cruelty from the Castle bloodline.

"Aurelia has...another future," the boy said.

They were all trying to wrap their heads around it, suspicion clear in his eyes.

What if she isn't a Castle at all? I could hear the question running around their heads.

If the prophecy was true, either the man was lying or...

"My parentage is not the issue. He is my father. What we know is that the rogue is *also* my father's dirty little secret, and he poses a risk to us all, prophecy or not."

"How do we know you're not just saying this to get out of the prophecy?" One of the White Lotus members asked.

"Ma—The seer just said so," I said quickly, catching my slip of his name. "The Castle in the prophecy was always her brother, not her."

"Then you're a bastard," another member said.

"She's not a bastard; she is unfortunately of Castle lineage," the seer explained.

I could feel a sharp burst of curiosity running through Aurelia.

"You're sure I can save myself, boy?" she asked, her voice harsh.

"If anyone can, it's you," Max said. "Trust your gut."

Aurelia took a step toward him.

"Tell me what you mean already. I'm tired of guessing."

"I can't hold your hand through it. The choice is yours and yours alone." He paused, looking every last one of us in the eye. "But what's most important is that all of you need to figure out how to kill the real bastard. The one who threatens to crumble everything in his path. Including us."

His words silenced everyone. Even my heart stuttered for a moment.

"I will be the one to kill him," I vowed, taking a step forward. I wanted more than anything to get answers for Aurelia, but at that moment we needed to convince them. "That part of the prophecy hasn't changed. I will be the one to do it."

"It took us months to even narrow down the list of places he could be," one of the White Lotus members said. "We don't have time to waste on tracking him down again."

"I know where he is," Aurelia told them, a frown on her face. "It's a place only I can enter. I want your word that the White Lotus members won't interfere. That this mission is ours and ours alone. The White Lotus will only be there as backup for me. Under my command."

Laughter rang out through the group, though Gabriel was suspiciously silent.

"Tell us where he is, dear princess," the high priest purred.

"We need a vow first," Cedar said. "From you, High Priest."

The amusement was sucked out of the room, taking all the oxygen with it.

For a moment, the high priest seemed to consider it. But only for a moment.

"I don't make vows. If you won't tell me, you'll face the consequences. Take them."

Red vine-like magic shot up from the floor, coming at us faster than I could blink. They snuck up my arms, my legs, their magic burning into my skin.

"Don't you fucking touch me!" Aurelia screamed.

Magic can hurt vampires. My eyes were trained on her, watching as she tried to flinch away from the ropes. The burning of her flesh sounded throughout the room.

"Stop!"

"Don't," Cedar and I yelled at the same time. But while I was darting for the princess, she was darting to me. Everyone moved at once, trying to reach us, many with bloodthirsty smiles on their faces.

"*Stop!*"

The high priest's voice sounded animal-like as he commanded the entire world to stop.

More red magic vines wrapped around every single member, except for Gabriel, who hadn't once moved from his spot.

I looked at him, but my gaze was quickly drawn to the boy in the middle. Magic buzzed around him as his eyes clouded over. His mouth was moving, forming words that were progressively getting louder and louder.

"Fire. Run. Crown. Run. Fight. Save them. Run. *Please. Get away from here. Fire. It burns. It BURNS.*"

Over and over again, the words repeated until I couldn't take it anymore. I moved toward him, the red vines falling away.

"Don't interfere, hunter," the high priest warned as his magic tried to reach out to me again. But the vines wouldn't come.

The boy is calling me.

I don't know how I knew it; I just did. He wanted me to come to him.

The magic around him pricked my skin, but it was nothing compared to the quick spiral into madness the poor kid was facing. It zapped up through my palm when I placed it on his shoulder. He fell into me, his entire body going slack.

"Only the three can defeat the rogue," the seer said, his voice muffled against my chest. "If not, the coven *burns.*"

Aurelia

"There's no going back after this," I said and slipped into bed behind Vesper.

Her skin was cold to the touch. I pushed my body against hers and buried my head in the back of her neck, inhaling deeply.

My mind was still whirling from the knowledge of my brother's existence. From what the seer said.

It was all more than I'd signed up for.

"What are you planning to do?" she asked, her voice low.

Cedar was in the living room, asleep on the couch. She refused to leave us after our meeting with the coven but was so exhausted that the moment she sat down on the couch, she knocked out.

"I'm still thinking it through," I admitted, my hands running up her sides. "But whatever it is, we'll bring the witch."

Vesper turned in my hold until her golden eyes came face to face with mine.

"She's really starting to grow on you, isn't she?" Vesper asked, causing my heart to skip a beat.

"Maybe I just don't want her to die." The excuse sounded weak.

A smile pulled at Vesper's lips. Her eyes had bags under them. Her skin was looking paler than usual.

It's been a lot for her.

Running around the coven. Trying to make them like us. The missions. Ever since she'd entered the palace, it had been nonstop.

"It's okay to admit you like her too; my feelings won't be hurt," she said, flirtation woven into her tone.

"And you?" I asked.

Vesper licked her lips. "I think you already know the answer to that."

"I do," I said, letting a smile pull at my lips. "Listen, I never thought I'd—"

A tapping at the window had me sitting up. Heat ran through me when I saw what was outside.

"What is that—"

I pushed Vesper down, giving her a forced smile.

"It's nothing, don't worry—"

The fucker rammed its beak into the window three more times.

Vesper's head turned to the side. "Is that the bird I gave you? I thought you killed it?" There was a laugh in her voice.

I climbed out of bed and smacked the window, sending the bird flying.

"I told Pipsqueak to stay away," I grumbled under my breath.

I heard the rustling of the bed before Vesper's arms wrapped around my body. She placed her chin on my shoulder, her breath hot on my neck.

"I knew it was just a mask," she whispered. "The cruelty. The anger."

"I don't know what you're talking about," I huffed.

She placed a kiss against my neck.

"You're sweet, caring, and not at all like the cruel princess your father brought you up to be," she said. "I see you, Aurelia. And I'm... sorry for hurting you."

I stiffened at her words.

No one had ever said anything like this to me.

I was not sweet. I was prickly and ready to draw blood from whoever got close. It wasn't in my nature to be caring.

My mother, maybe, but I wasn't her.

Stay fierce. It was the last thing she told me and something I lived by. Maybe a bit too much.

"I knew you were trying to save us," I told her softly. "I just... When I was younger, I used to believe that blood-bonding was the ultimate gift to those in love. I wanted to wait until I knew I was truly in love."

She swallowed thickly.

"I'm sorry I took that choice from you."

"I would have chosen you anyway," I said, turning to look at her. "If you continued to be a good little mouse."

Her gaze met mine, and slowly she leaned forward until our lips met.

It was the sweetest kiss she'd ever given me. Save for that time she shoved a sword through my heart.

When she pulled away, her face was hard.

"Aurelia, there's something I need to—"

My vision went black. My ears rang so loud it hurt. One minute, I was standing next to Vesper, and the next I was suspended in darkness.

An image exploded in front of me. Fire towered over me. Heat licked at my skin. I turned, trying to get away from it, but there was no escape.

I froze when I saw the same little seer boy standing in the middle.

"Run!"

His voice broke through the ringing, and I was forced back into the void.

Images passed through my mind. Me. My brother. My father. The throne. Vampires I'd never seen before, then some I had.

I was dancing with someone.

Then I heard the bells. The same ones that played when I was marrying Prince Icas.

"Aurelia? Aurelia? Aurelia!"

Vesper's shaking had me thrown back into my body.

I blinked a few times to get rid of the lingering images. Her worried gaze was the first thing I saw.

"We have to go. I saw—"

"*Fire*," I breathed.

It was a warning. A crystal-clear one at that.

Run or die.

Cedar

I stood behind the high priest, his white robes just centimeters from my face.

What's happening?

One minute I was in Cedar and Aurelia's cabin, and the next I was back in the basement of the cathedral.

But everything seemed so different. Taller.

I had to look up to the high priest.

Is this a memory?

It was fuzzy, but I was pretty sure I recognized the old White Lotus members standing in a circle I would later come to occupy. I had long forgotten their names, but that wasn't important. What was important were the people huddled in the middle of the circle.

I know them.

Familiarity teased the edges of my mind.

Red hair. Blue eyes. Black hair. Green eyes. Freckles.

I couldn't move. I wanted to run to them, but I couldn't.

"Again," the high priest commanded.

A magical whip was brought down on the couple. Their screams of pain echoed through the room. I tried to look away, but the high priest was there, his hand on my head, forcing me to watch.

No. This hadn't happened. I didn't remember this. It had to be fake. A vision planted in my mind—

"You monster!"

Green eyes met mine. Red hair, so much like my own, shone in the darkness.

"This mistake was your last," the high priest said. I looked up at him; there was a smile spreading across his face. "We don't collude with royal vampire families."

"Please, we didn't—"

"For Cedar, please. She's still so young—"

They were both silenced by a burst of the high priest's magic exploding all around them.

"Finish them," he ordered.

A scream was lodged in my throat.

This can't be right. My parents, they abandoned me in the coven. They left. They didn't die here.

But even as I tried to convince myself what I was seeing was wrong, there was something heavy weighing in my gut.

The high priest placed his hand on my shoulder.

"Your turn, Cedar."

Horror painted my insides as small me raised my hand. Red sparks burst from my palm, and then fire engulfed the entire room.

The heat of it licked my skin, punishing me for the most forbidden act there was.

No wonder the gods never listened to my prayers. They heard them, but they purposely didn't answer.

They had been punishing me.

Fire exploded around us, and just as I was ready for it to take me with them, the ceiling opened up like a book, showing me the night sky.

I looked up at the millions of stars above as the redness from the flames started to bleed into the blackness. The walls of the cathedral collapsed around us, and slowly, one by one, all the bodies around me disappeared into black smoke.

The trees surrounding the cathedral, which had once been vibrant and full of life, were now black and twisted, branches falling off as they no longer had the strength to hold on.

Fire licked at the dark sky. Even as the ceiling opened up, the heat in the air was still so striking it had me choking on it.

I looked down, back at the circle where my parents used to be, and while the runes were still there, someone else was in their place.

In the middle of the circle was the small boy they kept locked up in chains underground.

My first instinct was to run to him. To save him from the fire. But when he turned around, there was a twisted smile on his face. So much like the high priest's.

"Don't forget who they are," he warned, his voice hoarse. "This time, make sure you protect the ones you love, hm? Let's end the cycle here."

Images of Aurelia and Vesper ran through my mind.

"I would never—"

"You don't have much time now, Cedar." His entire upper half snapped back, his eyes still holding my gaze. The smile only widened. The voice that came from him didn't sound at all like it belonged to that of a little boy. It sounded like a demon's.

"What's happe—"

"*RUN.*"

I sat upright, gasping for air. The darkness of the living room in their cabin came into view, but it did nothing to stop my panic. It had been a dream. It had to have been a dream.

But it felt so real.

The smoke that had been filling the basement had infiltrated my lungs. I could still feel the fire licking at my skin as it closed in on us.

And that vision with my parents? What the fuck was that?

The weight of eyes on me had my head snapping to the corner. Aurelia was there in Vesper's T-shirt, nothing else underneath. Her eyes were glowing red in the darkness.

"I guess witches have nightmares too," she said, her voice low.

It was more than a nightmare, it felt—

"I think it was a vision," I whispered so low, I doubted even vampire hearing could pick it up. But she did.

"The fire?"

My eyebrows shot up to my hairline.

"How did you—"

Vesper walked out of the room, her footsteps light. There was a sullen air about her.

"We got it too," she said, her eyes flashing to Aurelia.

A human and a vampire got a vision? It was unheard of.

"I think the kid sent it to me," Aurelia said. "With a message."

His messed-up smile and contorted body flashed through my mind and sent a chill through me.

I'm scared.

But that was obviously the point. He'd shown me something that would make me flee. Something that would cut all my ties to the coven. But had that really happened with my parents?

The high priest had told me so many times I'd been abandoned and never gave me a reason to doubt him.

"Run?" I asked and shakily got up from the couch. All the pressure from the coven, the visions, and the rogue-turned-prince was getting to be too much for me.

This time, make sure you protect the ones you love.

Yes. This time, I had to. There was a future here, between the three of us. It was unfurling as we stood there in the eye of the storm.

We had a choice—go down with it or make a break for it.

Staying in the coven might have the illusion of safety, but it was just that—an illusion.

Running would put us right in the path of it. Dangerous, but if we were smart, we just might have the chance to outrun it.

I didn't know what it would look like or how it would end, but I wanted to be with them. Wanted to see this through. Even if it meant leaving behind everything I knew.

"And then some," she said and jerked her head to the side. I followed her movements to a pile of bags already waiting for me near the door. "Get ready, witch. I know how to complete the prophecy."

Vesper

The night air was completely silent. Heavy. Like there was something surrounding us. Even as we walked out into the open, it felt more enclosed than the cabin ever did.

It makes me want to turn back.

That was my first indication that something was wrong. Cedar, Aurelia, and I snuck out of the house and through the forest. There were no guards around us.

Just like the day we snuck out of the palace. Back then, just like now, we had been running from something.

At least this time, Aurelia didn't have a hole in her chest, but we had no place to go.

Cedar wasn't our knight in shining armor coming to save the day anymore. She was a traitor, leaving her coven with two people who had the ability to change the balance of the world.

We couldn't trust anyone.

Not vampires—at least not the ones in the general vicinity, who would kill us and take Aurelia back to her palace. Not the organization—they'd kill Aurelia before we'd even have a chance to fight them off. And the witches already proved that they were their own brand of crazy, and there was no telling what they'd do.

"They would never have left us alone," Cedar said, her voice a whisper. We crept through the trees until we got to the edge of the barrier where the guards were supposed to be.

Not a single one in sight. I couldn't even feel them. Cedar and Aurelia were silent as we searched the area.

Where did they all go? It wasn't like the coven to leave us unattended. I shared a look with Cedar. Her furrowed eyebrows and frown told me she thought the same.

"I can't smell anything," Aurelia murmured.

She can't smell anything. There was a creepy crawling feeling on the back of my neck.

"Get down!"

Aurelia was quick to grab both me and Cedar and push us to the ground just as arrows flew at us.

The organization found us.

They were the only people who still used bows and arrows. They would hide, ambush, then take their targets out.

A loud boom echoed through the forest. Heat crawled up my back, and all of us turned in time to see fire looming over the tree line, its orange and red tendrils reaching for the sky.

It's coming from our cabin.

The vision wasn't about the vampire. It was a warning that the organization would kill us if we stayed in the cabin any longer.

Run. Run! RUN!

The voice that had been a whisper in my dream was now yelling inside my head. I pushed myself up and took both their hands in mine, pulling us through the forest.

I could hear the footsteps of the various hunters running after us even if they made little noise. Which meant these weren't just any hunters.

My entire body was doused in a fear so potent all I could think of was getting us out.

They'll kill us. Gabriel warned me. The boy warned me.

I didn't take it as seriously as I should have, and now we're fucked—

Cedar paused and looked behind her, her magic lighting up her fingertips. She waved her hands around, and red vines shot out around her. They weaved together, creating a barrier between us and the incoming threat.

I couldn't see the people beyond the shadows of the forest, but I could feel their eyes. They were crawling over me, assessing every single one of my weaknesses.

They recognize the traitor I am, and they're out for blood.

"Don't just fucking stand there," Aurelia hissed and brought our attention back to her. Neither Cedar nor I argued with her as she led us through the forest.

Think. Think. Think.

My heart was pounding in my chest. My breathing was quick. Everything that I had been taught during my time with the organization filtered through my head.

They moved in groups, one large and coming from behind with arrows. They would ambush in groups. If the first could kill the target, good; if not, the second group would take over.

They won't be coming from behind.

"Watch out," Cedar warned.

Her magic flashed in the air before the arrows descended, but it wasn't enough to hold them back. One of them slipped through and embedded itself in my shoulder.

I let out a groan. My knees were weak, and I was about to fold to the floor if not for Aurelia's strong grip.

Cedar's hand was on my shoulder, steadying me, but I pushed her off.

"Later!"

I mustered whatever strength I had left and ran after Aurelia as she led the way. Every so often, she would pause, lift her chin, then turn in another direction.

It didn't take me long to figure out that she was smelling our attackers.

"You hunters hide your scent well," she murmured as we came to a halt at a gap in the forest.

There was a long road spanning between us and the next cover. If we crossed it, we'd be out in the open. They would attack us.

Two groups had already shown themselves, but what about the others?

"You two go, I can cover you," Cedar said, her arms already up and readying her magic. I grabbed one, forcing it down.

"We go together," I hissed. "Stop trying to sacrifice yourself."

Her eyes widened and her lips pressed together in a thin line, vulnerability in her expression.

Even without vampiric hearing, I could feel the hunters surrounding us, readying their bows.

We are going to die here.

I should have gotten us out earlier. I had been too hesitant. Too cowardly. Too trusting that we were safe in the coven, no matter how mad they had been.

"I'm sorry," I whispered and squared my shoulders. I would protect them. Even with my last breath.

"No time for th—*What the fuck?*"

I turned to watch what Aurelia was looking at.

At least five cars were speeding down the highway. All of them black SUVs.

We stumbled back as they came to a halt in front of us. Vampires piled out of the ones in the front and back, none of them looking at us as they darted to the tree line. I couldn't even make out any of their faces.

Her dad. They found us!

I pushed Aurelia behind me. Cedar seemingly had the same idea and stood next to me in a battle-ready stance.

Battle cries sounded from behind us as the vampires attacked the hunters. I gritted my teeth against the pain in my shoulder.

I'm fucking ready.

But when the door opened, it wasn't her dad at all.

Long black hair shone in the moonlight. Bright red eyes narrowed in on the princess behind us. Her long, regal coat glimmered so bright she might as well be a beacon.

Our salvation came in the form of a vampire with a superiority complex.

"It's your lucky day, hunter. Everyone, get in," Atlas commanded. We all funneled into the back of the SUV before Atlas slammed the door behind us and yelled for the driver to go. There were four seats inside, facing each other. Just enough for us all to fit. *Thank god. The witch gods. Krae. Whoever. I don't give a fuck.*

"Hold still."

It was all the warning I got before Aurelia wrapped her hand around the arrow and yanked it out with her vampire force.

The pain was so severe, the scream got caught in my throat. Cedar held me against the car seat. When I finally exhaled, a whine left my throat.

"I know," Cedar whispered and pulled me to her, letting me rest on her chest.

Pain shot up my entire body. I couldn't stop myself from shaking because of the force of it.

In and out. In and out. Cedar was breathing deeply beside me, urging me to copy her rhythm.

I did with great difficulty, my entire upper body aching with each inhale and shaking with the exhale.

"What are you doing here?" Aurelia asked pointedly.

Atlas gave her a smug smile.

"So your little pets didn't tell you they reached out to me?"

Aurelia's accusatory gaze met mine. *Shit.* I had just gotten on her good side again, and here I was, already fucking things up.

"No," she grumbled. "They've got a lot of explaining to do."

Atlas laughed.

"Well, they have time. It's going to take two hours to reach my compound."

I gave her a bewildered look.

"Thought you didn't want to attract the attention of the council?"

She shrugged. "Maybe I'm being merciful."

I didn't say anything, but there was one resounding thought in my mind over and over again the entire time we were in that car.

I highly fucking doubt that.

Aurelia

"She needs venom," Cedar said pointedly.

Vesper was leaning against her and looking paler by the minute. The arrow had been taken out, but she was losing blood quicker than I expected.

Humans and their slow healing.

"Really, hunter? A little wound like that will do you in?" Atlas taunted.

The old me might have laughed and joked along with Atlas, but I was unable to take my eyes off her. I knew what state she was in.

I wanted to be mad at her for not telling me about their plan...but I couldn't. I was even a bit...*grateful*. That feeling alone made me want to gag.

Aurelia Castle, vampire princess and heir to the Castle family throne, was never *grateful*. And to a vampire hunter no less.

But I was.

And I was almost positive I was in love with her.

And definitely not opposed to whatever was happening with the witch.

Fuck.

"How much longer?" I asked, getting antsier by the minute.

Atlas raised a brow at me. "We're here, darling."

I turned to look out the window, my jaw clenching at the sight.

I'd heard rumors of the extravagance that was Atlas's main residence, but seeing it in person was...eye-opening.

Atlas wasn't like the other royal vampires, but she sure did know how to put on a show like one.

Large walls surrounded a property with vampire lookouts, watching us as we came in.

Beyond the walls was a looming building. Unlike many of the vampire families who chose to live in manors and more modern structures, Atlas's home looked more like a goddamned castle.

Forest surrounded it, peeking out above it. The sun was setting, casting a reddish-orange glow over the structure. Black brick made the outside, which made the windows shine like crystals. At the front was a pitch-black double door with what looked like gold handles.

She is a ruler through and through.

Even though the two properties were different, it felt much like the palace. My heart clenched remembering the place that had been my home for my entire existence.

The car came to a halt, Atlas jumping out and holding out a hand to me.

I probably should have placed my hand in hers and let her lead me away from the bleeding hunter and her witch.

But I'm not the same vampire anymore.

It had taken being almost sold off and forced to marry, getting stabbed in the heart by my lover, and being magically tortured and locked in a cabin for months for me to realize it.

I stepped out on my own, Atlas's face dropping when I wouldn't take her hand. Cedar let out a scoff.

"Of course; go ahead and leave your bleeding bonded—"

I turned and offered my hand to Vesper. She was barely conscious, but enough that she still felt surprised at my actions. The feeling tickled the bond between us.

"Let's get you inside," I said, softening my voice. "When we get settled, I will attend to your wound—"

I felt a flutter of something through the bond. So light, almost nonexistent. But it told me I had done well. *Praised me.*

The feeling went straight to my head.

"We have nurses on staff who can help," Atlas said.

"No need. I will do it."

Respect flashed across Cedar's face, and she gave me a smile. A *true* smile. It had my heart speeding up in my chest.

I had wanted their anger. Hell, I purposely poked and prodded them to get it.

But their praise was so much sweeter.

Maybe soon I'd be like Vesper, on my knees and begging for my lover.

"If you're worried about your human, I can promise you everyone in my clan has the utmost con—"

"I *want* to do it," I emphasized, my eyes sliding to hers. I gave her a smile to soften the blow. "Let me heal my bonded."

She looked like she meant to say something but then just nodded.

Vesper's cold, clammy hand slipped into mine, and my head snapped back to her. She had a weak smile on her face that had my heart breaking.

"Come on, witch," I said as I helped Vesper out. I put one of her arms around my shoulders, trying to ignore the way her blood made my mouth water. "Take her other side."

"You're strong enough to carry her bridal-style if you wanted," she retorted, but still did as I said. "Had to admit it was a comfy ride when you did it with me."

"Why don't I get that treatment?'" Vesper grunted out

"Because *she* was unconscious." I pointed out, glaring at Cedar. "And I want to make sure you stay awake. So help me out. Unless you want me to add another to the list of reasons to hate you."

"Ouch, Brat. You have a whole list?" she asked, teasingly.

"She does," Vesper confirmed. "I wouldn't be surprised if it was half a mile long."

"True." I shot her a halfhearted smile. "But maybe proving your worth will shorten it."

Beyond the hesitancy in her gaze, her eyes lit up.

Atlas cleared her throat.

"Inside, please," she said. "Let's remember there *is* a vampire hunter organization after us."

None of us said anything as we followed her into the residence. Guards opened the doors for us, their eyes trained on Cedar.

Another surprise awaited us when we walked in, though.

There were vampires everywhere. In pairs, sometimes in threes. They were chatting, laughing, leaning against the walls, only to stop and look at us as we entered.

They bowed their heads to Atlas as she passed.

Unlike the cold hallways of my palace, where only guards and staff roamed, she allowed people in there as well.

"They all live with you," I said, my eyes darting to Atlas.

She gave me a grin.

"Some of them, sure. Easier to protect them this way." She shrugged. "I also have residences all over, and when I'm not there, I let the people take over."

I kept Vesper close, noting how her blood made other vampires' gazes linger.

Atlas noticed it and slipped her arm in mine, attempting to pull me away from Vesper. I gave Cedar a look, and she nodded and shifted so she could carry the rest of Vesper's weight.

I let Atlas pull me away.

"It's the *witch*," Atlas said in a loud whisper, obviously wanting Cedar to hear. "My people are no strangers to human blood. And like I *was going to say*, they have impeccable control. But a witch? There hasn't been one of those here, well, in forever."

"Yet you use ancient witch magic," Cedar shot back.

Atlas gave her a grin. "Just something I picked up along the way."

"Stole likely."

"Semantics."

Cedar looked like she wanted to fight the old vampire.

"That's the one," a whisper came from behind us.

"The dead princess!"

"Did you hear about her family? Apparently, it got taken over by—"

Atlas cleared her throat, stopping the whispers.

My family? Did something happen to Father?

The sound of my brother's threat ran through my mind as panic clawed at my throat. *Was I out of time?*

I looked to Atlas for an answer.

"Someone claiming to be your brother has taken over the palace," she said, her eyes narrowing at the gossiping vampires. "There is no word of your father. It's one of the reasons I came to get you."

If the rumors have spread this far…

My stomach dropped. None of this looked good.

"And the other?" Vesper asked, her voice getting weaker by the second.

Atlas's eyes glanced at them before coming back to me.

"I had a vision," she finally said. "An image of fire. And…a message. For the hunter."

The seer. That little kid is in charge of all this?

"A message?" I asked. Atlas's eyes cut to Vesper.

"He told me to say thank you. For *seeing* him."

Vesper swallowed thickly and nodded.

I had so many questions. So many things running through my mind. Decisions to make. People to protect.

But somehow…it was easier.

I had changed because of Vesper.

Because of *them*.

All I'd known before them was pain, and while there was still plenty of that to go around, I found myself happier than I'd ever been. *Driven.*

I had a goal. A purpose.

And I would stop at nothing to make sure I could keep them by my side.

Clarity hit me like a truck and an eerie calm spread over my entire body.

I can save myself.

I knew I could. There was only one way. And it was something only I could do.

"I told you we have things to talk about. Let the nurses take care of the human. I can fill you in—"

"Let's hurry," I said, pushing Atlas lightly. "*My* human cannot wait."

Vesper's blood was already dripping on the floor, and the sound of it hitting the hard marble beneath our feet had my anxiety rising with each drop.

Humans are fragile. Even ones as strong as Vesper.

"Right," Atlas whispered. "This way."

"Explain while I heal her," I ordered Cedar as I positioned myself on the bed, legs open and ready for the injured human.

Cedar carefully laid Vesper down between them, and she groaned as her back hit the soft bedding. My heart hurt for her.

If it had hit just a few inches to the left, would she have died?

It hurt to think of it.

"Relax," I whispered to her, my hands coming to caress her shoulders and chest.

Her skin was pale and clammy, her heart beating far faster than usual.

She's struggling. I have to hurry.

"Aren't you mad?" Vesper asked in a pant.

"Furious," I admitted. "After everything, you're still keeping secrets from me. I'm..." *I shouldn't say it.* I didn't like the vulnerability in the words bubbling up my throat. "I'm *hurt*."

Vesper's hand grabbed mine. The urge to pull away was strong, but I didn't.

I placed my mouth at her neck, my eyes going to Cedar with an unspoken command.

"Vesper's idea," she said. I sank my teeth into my bonded's neck. I tried—and failed—to ignore the heat that coursed through my veins as her blood entered my mouth. "Apparently, Atlas gave her a magical medallion and she decided to use it when things got—"

Vesper's groan interrupted her tale.

"I wanted an out, but I wasn't sure it would work," Vesper said in a low whisper, her voice strained as the venom worked its way through her system. "I didn't want to get your hopes up."

I was careful not to take any blood from her, simply giving her my venom slowly and steadily.

Her body was already reacting. The scent of her desire was strong in the air.

Cedar had her eyes on us, her facial expression unchanging, but her body was giving away what she was feeling.

The way these two smell together should be illegal.

It was mouthwatering.

Krae... Why are you doing this to me?

Not only was I bonded to a human who had tried to kill me, but now I had the witch to worry about as well?

It was all fun and games in the coven when there was still hope. But now I worried about both of them. And while I knew Vesper wanted her, I never thought the redheaded witch would make me feel anything other than frustration.

"Can I look?" Cedar asked, her voice hard. She reached out to Vesper's shirt, her hands on the collar.

"Is it okay?" Vesper asked, her voice weak.

It took me a moment to realize she was asking *me*.

I dislodged myself from Vesper's neck, blood running down my lips and neck. I licked my lips greedily, taking whatever blood I could.

"Have at it, witch."

In one fell swoop, she ripped the shirt from her, exposing her bloodied chest and breasts.

What I wouldn't do to lick it up. I stilled at the thought. *What am I saying?*

I could do anything I wanted.

And given their reaction, with Cedar's gaze becoming hooded as she looked over Vesper's naked body and the hunter's heart racing, I could probably get them to do whatever I wanted them to do as well.

"It's almost healed," Cedar said, her finger gentle as she traced the wound.

Vesper's breathing spiked.

For fuck's sake.

I was tired of the two pining after each other, so I grabbed Cedar's hand and trailed it lower and lower until her fingers brushed Vesper's nipple.

Their combined intake of breath was heavenly.

"My little mouse has been itching for more, hasn't she?" I asked Vesper, but my eyes were on Cedar as she absolutely devoured Vesper with her gaze. "And you, witch? Have you been dreaming about this?"

I moved her hand lower and lower until—

"All the time," Cedar said, her voice rough. "I can't tell you how many times I fucked myself to the two of you wet and ready for me."

Fuck. The image alone had my head swirling.

"You know what this means, right?" I asked. "I don't let just anyone touch my bonded."

The weight of my words settled over the three of us.

"I left my coven for you. That alone should tell you how I feel about the two of you."

"But I need you to say it."

"Aurelia..." Vesper warned.

"I care for the both of you," Cedar said. "I promise to never hurt or betray you. I respect your bond and want nothing more than to serve you both."

Serve me.

Images of her on her knees while I sat on my throne, her face between my legs, flashed before my eyes. The light in the witch's eyes told me she knew exactly what those words would do to me.

A smirk spread across my face.

"Then let's show her, hm?" I asked. "Let's show our little mouse how much she means to us."

Cedar

I *must be dreaming.*
   Surely the universe wouldn't have handed me something this perfect.

I had run from my own coven. Away from the control that had taken over my entire life. Something I had thought was out of reach.

I was so pitiful that I had never even dared dream of something bigger. I thought I'd live and die in the coven, working for the high priest.

And now, the powerful yet vulnerable vampire hunter I was in charge of wanted me to touch her? And her vampire bonded was allowing it?

Luck had never touched me with a ten-foot pole, and now suddenly everything I wanted was being handed to me on a silver platter.

There has to be a mistake. Something even bigger must be brewing.

Because there was no way I'd get every single thing I wanted.

I knew that there would be an even bigger uphill battle in front of us, but at least we were together now and somewhere safe.

Well, better than the coven for sure.

But for the first time, I pushed aside the anxiety-inducing thoughts and did something I never would have allowed myself to otherwise—I leaned forward and placed my lips on the side of her neck, on the opposite side of Aurelia's bite.

She shivered at the contact. All the while, my fingers were teasing the waistband of her pants, and her stomach trembling under my touch only ignited the flame inside me until it became strong enough that I couldn't fight it anymore.

"Is it okay for me to touch you?" I asked against her skin.

"*Yes,*" Vesper gasped and arched into me.

"Are you ready to beg, Little Mouse?" Aurelia asked. Her hands brushed across my chest as they came to pluck Vesper's nipples. "As it turns out, you like to be used, don't you? You're not the strong vampire hunter I once thought you to be."

Vesper gasped when I slipped my hands into her pants and cupped her over her underwear.

So perfect. So needy. So sensitive to my touch.

"No," I whispered and pulled away to look into Vesper's eyes. Her golden orbs were filled with a desire I'd never thought would be directed at me. "She doesn't want control. She never did. You want to be ravaged, don't you? You want to *submit.*"

Vesper let out a whine. Her hands came to grip my shirt as if she wanted to push me away, but she used it to pull me closer instead.

Blood dropped from the wound on her neck down her chest. I pushed her underwear aside, dipping two fingers inside to gather wetness. Her cunt was hot and ready to take me, but I pulled away and spread her wetness over the blood on her chest, trailing my fingers down to pinch her nipples. Aurelia's and my hands brushed for just a moment, but it had me aching for more.

Our gazes met, a silent conversation passing between us. She gave me a wicked grin and gently placed Vesper on her back while she slipped out from under her.

Her body pressed against mine while she leaned down and licked the trail I had left for her. Aurelia's delicate fingers were smearing Vesper's blood while I left hot kisses down her throat until I was able to take a nipple into my mouth.

Vesper let out a moan.

"Fuck," she cursed.

"You taste delicious, Little Mouse," Aurelia murmured. "Are you aching yet?"

Aurelia grabbed my hand and led it back to her pants. We pulled them down, and Vesper kicked them off, spreading her legs for us, and I couldn't help but pull away for a glance at her swollen pussy dripping for us.

I let out a chuckle.

"That needy, huh?" I asked.

"A *whore*," Aurelia corrected.

Vesper narrowed her eyes at her. I swooped in and placed a lingering kiss on her lips before pulling away and meeting her gaze.

"*Our* whore."

Her lips opened, but I didn't push my tongue in. I watched as Aurelia's and my hands slipped between her legs. My fingers filled her cunt while Aurelia started to rub circles on her clit.

"But a good whore has to work for her keep," I said. "You want to come, don't you?"

"Fuck," Vesper whined, her hands fisting the sheets on either side of her.

"Tell her, Little Mouse," Aurelia said as she pinched her clit. "Be good for your lovers. You want this, don't you?"

"I do," Vesper panted. Her response had my stomach flipping. I was already impossibly wet, but the sound of her breathy response had excitement zapping up my spine.

"Then you have to work for it," I said and turned to Aurelia. "Aurelia, baby, go take a seat on your throne."

Aurelia's eyes lit up, and she went to maneuver herself over Vesper's face, lifting up the skirt of her dress. My throat clearing had her pausing.

"All of it," I ordered.

For once, Aurelia listened to me. She pulled the dress over her head and threw it across the room, leaving her in only her underwear.

My eyes fell to the necklace around her ankle. The same one I helped Vesper make when she had lost her bird.

So the princess does have a heart.

Vesper was between her legs, eyeing her clothed cunt like a hungry wolf.

"Turning docile on me now?" I asked, eyeing Vesper's hands as they ran up Aurelia's thighs.

"Don't get used to it," she said. "*Baby* was a nice touch."

Vesper hooked Aurelia's underwear to the side as she descended.

"Lean forward," I said. "Just because she's tongue-fucking you doesn't mean you can back out."

Aurelia gasped when Vesper's lips connected with her cunt. The sight was intoxicating. Aurelia's eyes were hooded, her entire body bared to me. Vesper had her thighs in a death grip, forcing her pussy to her mouth as she ravished it like it was her last meal.

The noises Aurelia made were fitting of her title. Delicate, musical. Vesper's were straight-up deviant. Fucking, sucking, groaning. All of it had my core clamping down on nothing.

I rewarded the obedient whore by pumping my fingers in and out of her.

Aurelia leaned forward, bracing her hands on the bed.

I couldn't help it. I leaned in and captured her lips with mine.

Vesper's blood tasted absolutely divine on them as Aurelia tried to match the pace with which the hunter was fucking her with our kiss.

I pulled away, breathing heavily.

She gave me a smirk, and then in one move, she did something that would forever be ingrained in my mind.

She collected our mixed saliva in her mouth and spit it directly on Vesper's clit.

"Now the three of us," Aurelia said as she circled her fingers around the swollen bundle of nerves. "Can be all together."

"Fuck, I'm gonna come," Vesper whined, her voice muffled by Aurelia's cunt.

"Not until I'm done, you're not," Aurelia replied with a breathless laugh. "Work harder, Little Mouse."

I paused my fingers and leaned forward to lick from Vesper's entrance to her clit, still covered by Aurelia's fingers.

"Just. Like. That," Aurelia moaned. She jerked forward in pleasure, her mouth opening and her eyebrows pushing together.

Fuck, she looks delectable when she comes.

I quickly lifted my head and took one of her nipples in my mouth. When I bit it, she let out an explosive cry.

I began to fuck Vesper again but never let go of Aurelia's nipple.

"So close, so close," Vesper whispered.

"Beg for it," Aurelia ordered, her voice heavy with need.

Vesper didn't even try to fight it this time.

"Please. Please. Please. Please. Pleas—"

She was cut off by her own deep groan.

I let go of Aurelia's nipple, and she immediately pushed me backward. She climbed on top of me, her face coming to my neck, her hand already inside my pants.

"You passed your trial run," she whispered. "Can I bite you?"

I gasped when her fingers made contact with my clit.

"Please do, Princess."

I groaned when her fangs cut through my skin, but it was swallowed as Vesper came to the end of the bed and pushed her lips to mine.

Aurelia tasted sinful on her tongue.

Yes. Yes. Being between them was Helma's gift to me.

I asked for a way out, but the gods gave me something even better.

Aurelia slipped her fingers into my entrance, fucking my cunt with her vampire speed, and I couldn't help but arch into them, groaning into Vesper's mouth.

My entire body was hot. Aurelia's venom was working through me, making my magic go haywire, spreading out around us as it desperately sought a way out of my body.

It's too much.

Aurelia unlatched herself from me, her lips at my ear.

"Come for me, my lovely witch."

I couldn't hold back. I came with a whimper. I shook. I convulsed. I couldn't stop my body from moving as wave after wave of orgasm pulled me under.

My entire body heated. Pleasure that started in my core spread outward and tingled as it traveled through me.

Vesper pulled away, a wicked smile on her face, and Aurelia was quick to join her, both looking down at me.

At one time, I might have been afraid of what I'd gotten myself into.

But not anymore.

These two had been hand-selected by the gods for me, and I'd be damned if I ever let them go.

Vesper

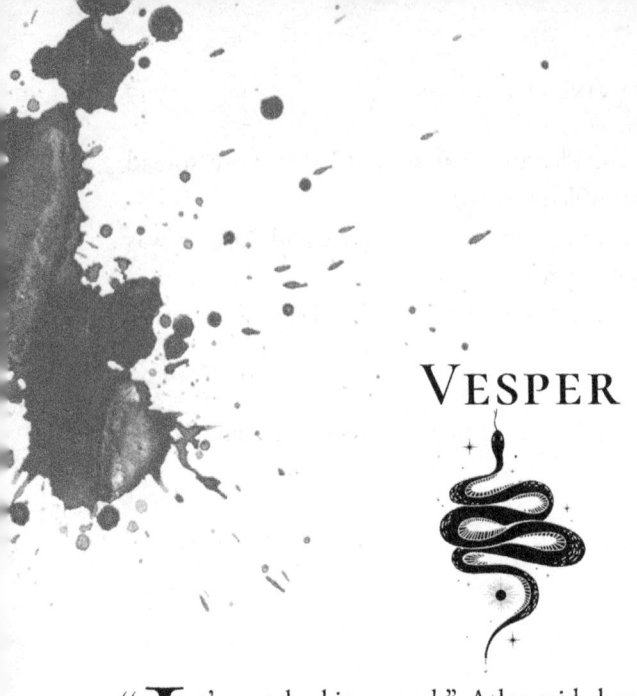

"It's not looking good," Atlas said, her eyes fixated on Aurelia, who sat to her right.

We had taken up a secondary dining room, with Atlas citing that the main one would be full as her clan used it for their social blood drinking and eating. Apparently the overconfident ruler was not as uncompromising when it came to her clan members and allowed half-humans.

But we weren't to mingle with the others. At least not yet. The one she took us to was private and only for her important guests.

Which only includes Aurelia.

The vampire practically ignored us as soon as we came out of the room.

I knew what she was after. Knew she had a soft spot for the princess. I didn't know *why*, but I could respect it. After all, it had saved us.

But that didn't stop the jealousy from burning in my chest.

Cedar and I were forced to her left, forgotten. Aurelia looked at us a few times but mainly focused on the vampire as she went over just how fucked-up our situation was.

I tried not to get too shocked when Cedar's hand found mine underneath the table and gave it a squeeze.

The air had shifted between the three of us since the night before. It wasn't just the sex. The world around us had changed as well. We might be running—from the council, the organization, and likely from the coven as well—but we were together. An unlikely trio, but we finally felt...complete.

"A war, you think?" Aurelia asked. "If I show myself, I can claim the throne—"

Atlas shook her head. She reached over, her hand trailing Aurelia's arm in a supposedly comforting gesture that made me want to snap at the vampire.

Aurelia's eyes snapped to mine, a bit of playfulness in them as she felt just how jealous I was through the bond.

"If the state of the palace is as what's rumored to be, you may not have a claim to it anymore. Vampire law states that whoever brings down the vampire in charge will become the next leader."

I didn't know much about vampire law, but from the look on Aurelia's face, Atlas seemed to be telling the truth.

How can I fix this? I wanted nothing more than to help Aurelia stake her claim, but I could do nothing but sit there helplessly.

"The council wouldn't let that happen, would they?" she asked.

Atlas's eyes shifted to me quickly before moving back to her. Cedar froze beside me and tapped my hand as if to say, *You saw that too, right?*

"The council only interferes when vampires break their laws," she explained. "Your brother challenging your father and beating him isn't that. Maybe if he were working with the hunter organization or even the witches to bring down vampires, they'd intervene, but this is normal everyday vampire law. He is allowed to do it."

A silence fell over us.

"Your father is strong," I said. "Even if he were to challenge him, it doesn't mean he'd win. And you could still stake your claim to the throne—"

"It's unlikely to work." Atlas waved her hand in the air, effectively dismissing me. "News of his *legitimate* son has spread. He is just as able to take the throne as Aurelia is, but if he stakes his claim, you'll have to defeat him. It's not a matter of whether he can defeat your father anymore; it's can you defeat *him*?"

We all knew the answer, and it was enough to silence the room. The tension was so thick it threatened to choke me. But even so, Aurelia didn't look fazed. She just stared at Atlas, her gaze unwavering.

Can she? After what we saw?

He had killed three witches without so much as a blink. He had been training, and so had his people, and it was laughable to even entertain the idea that he would fight fair.

"How likely is a war between the families?"

Atlas shrugged.

"Whispers in the underground say the other families want no part in this mess," he said. "Others, a few select families, say they will use the chaos to crumble your father's empire and take his people and fortune. All that's missing to sweeten the deal is *you*—the perfect Castle woman with an undeniable bloodline."

The bloodline comment caused Aurelia to freeze.

"Do you know the rumors?" she asked, then paused. "Let me rephrase. Have you always known?"

Atlas shrugged. "I've been around a long time. I've heard them, but they mean nothing. To me at least."

"They meant enough for them to sell her off," I interrupted. They both turned to look at me.

"Prince Icas believed it enough to arrange it with her father," Cedar said. "I would say it's pretty damn important."

Aurelia's gaze fell to the table. "He's dead now."

"Because of me," I reminded. "I saved Aurelia when you couldn't."

My jealousy had gotten the better of me with that last comment. Atlas all but snarled at me.

"Be careful, hunter," she growled. "Or I might just think you're being ungrateful that I saved your ass back in the coven. You're lucky I even brought you."

"Why did you?" I asked and leaned forward. Cedar's hand was

squeezing mine, telling me to cool it. "You made it clear you didn't want me here."

"I'm starting to regret it," she answered. *She's deflecting.* I opened my mouth to fight her, but Cedar beat me to it.

"Icas was one small fish in a big pond," Cedar said. "We should prepare for the other vampire families to come after you."

"I'd be more worried about the hunter here trying to finish the prophecy before I worry about any of the vampires," Atlas said, her tone accusatory.

Anger roared to life inside me.

I'm going to shove my sword through her chest.

"I would never," I spat.

"But you did stab her, no?" Atlas asked, her head tilting to the side. "Sounds to me like you were pretty damn close."

"It was a cover," Cedar said. "A stupid one, but it worked. It got us away."

"And into a coven that almost killed you."

None of us had a response.

"The seer said we didn't have to kill her," I said after the silence got to be too much. Aurelia's eyes shot to mine, something unreadable in them. "Even said she could save herself."

"Is that so?" Atlas asked, her eyes wandering to Cedar then back to the princess.

Aurelia held my gaze. Something thrummed to life in the bond. Guilt? Sadness? I didn't know, but it left a bitter taste on my tongue. She let out a noise of agreement before turning her attention back to Atlas.

"Name the families that want to come after me."

"Your brother, darling. You don't need to worry—"

"Don't play with me, Atlas," Aurelia threatened. "The throne is and always will be mine. Tell me."

"I will not be even entertaining this idea," Atlas said as she shooed a vampire away.

I paused at the door, peeking into a meeting I was obviously intruding on.

The vampire in front of her was a well-dressed, aristocrat-type with a slight accent. He bowed his head to the vampire, his hands gripping the front of his suit tightly.

Most likely a right hand. Someone who didn't have the power or the authority to stand up to her.

"The other families are talking, but not just them—the clans as well," he said, his voice shaky. "You've had too many enemies for too long. You need to tie yourself to someone or risk all-out exile. The council has been watching, and they likely will ste—"

"And you think what I want is a musky old vampire who's been around since before the modern toilet was invented?" She let out a scoff. "I am doing just fine. If anyone has issues with me, they can—"

"That's the thing," he said. "If they do, you'll have to fight them. You're running out of options. If you want to keep friendly relationships and your people safe, you need Sir Burton."

Atlas looked like she was going to behead the man.

I cleared my throat, even though they both knew I was there. Atlas waved him off again.

"I have another engagement," she said. "Leave or I will force you out."

He took it with a sigh and left, sending me a glare as he passed.

"What was that?" I asked. "A new way of doing vampire business?"

Atlas let out a scoff and shook her head.

"An arranged marriage," she said. The shock must have been evident on my face because she let out a laugh. "You'd think they'd have had enough after a hundred rejections, but one comes every month now, all but begging me."

"Why would they care?" I asked and sat down on the chair in front of her.

The anger from our time in the dining room all but fizzled into a slight dislike. As jealous and annoyed as I was, she was right. She was the one who saved us.

"Because they all hate me, but no one wants to go to war with me," she said. "I have people, land, money, and no ties to other vampires besides Aurelia. Getting married to me ensures they are safe."

I let out a hum.

"Then why didn't you marry Aurelia when her father was trying to sell her?"

Atlas leaned back in her chair with a smirk.

"You think I didn't try to save my friend? You were so quick to judge but never thought to ask if I actually did," she said. "Her father despised me. Good fucking riddance to the cunt."

The air was knocked from my lungs. *So it's true.* But she acted like it was still a possibility that he was alive in front of Aurelia.

Just another thing we're hiding from her.

"Why didn't you just tell her the truth?" I asked.

"Why didn't you?"

I had no answer. I was just as guilty as she was. I wanted to protect Aurelia. Maybe even placate her. I was afraid that if I let her in on the secret too early, she might blow it with her rashness.

What a horrible lover I am. I should trust her over anyone else...but I also know her better than anyone else.

"I've come here to ask—"

"For us to keep you, I know." She cut me off with a sigh and a wave. "Your attitude won't change my decision. You're already here; if the council comes because I took in new clanspeople, we will deal with it then."

Relief exploded in my chest. She had been clear last time that the council was watching and she wouldn't be able to accept new people.

Yet she was going through with it. For Aurelia, but I couldn't disregard the fact that her kindness extended to Cedar and me.

"What would they do?"

She shrugged.

"Fine me? Kill a few people? Who knows, but in return you have to promise me something."

I nodded. "Tell me what you want, and I'll try my best."

"Keep Aurelia here," she said, leaning forward. Her face was more serious than I'd ever seen it. "I see something brewing behind those eyes. I don't like it. Keep her busy here, and I will make sure you and your witch are safe."

I swallowed thickly.

Would Aurelia really try to leave?

It was a stupid question. Anyone with a single brain cell could see how badly Aurelia wanted to go back to her palace.

"Deal."

Cedar

Keep Aurelia busy.

Vesper had a single request, but it was difficult when faced with someone like the princess.

Her sexual appetite was immense, especially now that she had both of us. Her attitude? Even worse now that we were stuck in Atlas's home.

It had only been a few days, but the vampire had insisted that we stay inside for fear that either the council or the organization would see us.

A bit paranoid, but somehow I felt that her fears were not unfounded.

Even the coven still posed a risk, and if it meant keeping everyone safe, I would do it.

"Please, *break*," Vesper whined as Aurelia straddled her for the third time that night. I sat back on the pillow, watching as Aurelia's hands started to run up the vampire hunter's body.

Vesper's pale skin was lined with bruises and smeared with blood, and she was shaking from the onslaught of orgasms we'd given her.

But it still wasn't enough for Aurelia.

Vesper's eyes caught mine. She was pleading.

Since she's asking so nicely, I guess I'll be forced to help out.

I crawled across the bed and positioned myself behind the princess until our naked bodies were pressed together. My hand was in her hair. My lips at her ear.

"Abusing our toy now, are you?" I murmured, yanking her head back. She let out a guttural moan.

"The witch has come out to play," she said with a laugh.

I sent my magic out, letting the red vines wind around her thighs and body. I made sure they weren't touching her too harshly, but it would be enough to cause a slight sting.

"Does the bratty princess like a bit of pain with her fucking?" I asked, my eyes traveling to Vesper.

She got the hint, and in an instant, her hands were stroking the princess's cunt.

Aurelia's hips jerked against her hand, but my vines kept her in place. She let out a hiss when she moved a bit too much and one started to burn her.

"If my brain was working properly right now, I might think you two are distracting me," she said. Her sentence ended on a hitch as Vesper pushed her finger into her pussy. I couldn't see it from my position, but I felt it in the way Aurelia sank onto them.

"From what?" I asked.

"We're safe," Vesper said, moving from beneath the princess's legs and turning to her. "We have all the time in the world to explore." Her tongue flicked out to lick Aurelia's rosy nipple. "To play." Aurelia let out a gasp as Vesper kept using her fingers.

"Don't act like you don't like it," I murmured as she began shaking.

Aurelia was coming up on her fourth orgasm, each one coming faster than the last.

I prayed this one would wear her out.

"Harder, Vesper," she moaned.

I tightened the vines around her.

"Fuck! *Krae—*"

"The goddess would shy away at the sight of how sinful you look right now," I murmured.

"Tied up, begging for a vampire hunter and a witch to make you come," Vesper continued. "What a magnificent sight."

"Fuck the both of you," Aurelia hissed.

"But you are, baby," I cooed.

"Hurry up," Aurelia whined.

"Just for that, I'm going to rethink giving you that orgasm. Vesper, stop."

Like the good little hunter she was, Vesper stopped completely, looking at Aurelia with a wicked grin. Vesper loved to give in to the princess's every whim, but like all hunters, she was a rule follower to her core and couldn't resist a command. *Or a praise.*

"Good hunter."

"I swear to Krae, if you don't make me come right n—"

Vesper leaned forward, her lips colliding with Aurelia's, who'd started to thrash against my vines. She was trying to break free, even as the magic burned her skin.

Testing a theory, I pushed my hand between her legs, pushing in a finger alongside Vesper's.

She was sopping, and her cunt pulsed every time she brushed against one of my vines.

Vesper took her finger away, and her hand started moving, likely rubbing the vampire's clit.

Aurelia moaned into her mouth.

"Say sorry," I whispered in the princess's ear. She ignored me entirely. "*Vesper.*"

The hunter stopped.

"Fuck, okay. *Please* make me come," Aurelia whined. Vesper started again, slow strokes on her clit. They were enough to keep her on edge, but not enough to give her the relief she wanted.

"That's not what I said," I all but sang. "Try again."

When she didn't, I tightened the vines further, and I let out a hiss as her pussy clenched around me.

"Faster, Vesper," I ordered.

"Come on, *Princess*," Vesper pleaded in a low voice.

"Damn it," Aurelia said. Her body was shaking, her voice sounding almost like she was going to cry. "*I'm sorry.* Please make me come."

Vesper's eyes sought out mine. *She's asking me for permission.* The satisfaction that ran through me knew no bounds.

"Be a good princess and come for us," I said. "Will you give us the honor?"

"Come for us, Aurelia," Vesper commanded breathlessly.

The vampire couldn't hold back any longer. Her body seized against me. Her moans got caught in her throat. I pulled away just in time to see her eyes roll back in her head.

Perfect. I'd never get enough of seeing either of them come apart.

I called my magic back and placed Aurelia on the bed as she recovered. Vesper was at her side in a second, wrapping her arms around her.

I lay down as well, my head against Aurelia's back.

"Are you hiding something from me again?" Aurelia asked.

My heart dropped. I didn't like hiding things from Aurelia. It felt like a betrayal. Especially after everything.

But we had to.

"No," Vesper said.

"Cedar?"

She turned to look at me. *Please don't look at me with those eyes.*

It was for her own good. We both knew what she'd do. But no matter what, it still felt awful to hide it from her.

"Are you?" I asked, meeting her gaze.

When she didn't say anything, my stomach sank.

"Don't do anything reckless," I whispered. "For *us*."

She paused, then gave me a slow nod.

Vesper's hands ran up Aurelia's body until it got to the feather now hanging on her neck.

"I've loved you since this," Vesper whispered. "Don't make me worry anymore, okay? My heart might not be able to take it."

I had to look away from the scene; the vulnerability of it was too much for me.

"My heart almost didn't make it when you stabbed it," Aurelia shot back. There was a silence. "But I loved you then too, Little Mouse."

And me? Is this love?

No one asked me or pressured me for an answer, but I was pretty sure I didn't need it.

Actions spoke louder than words after all, and I was planning to prove just how much both of them meant to me.

I just needed time, and I was praying that Aurelia would give it to me.

"And this one?" I asked, tracing the scar that led up to the back of her neck and disappeared into her hairline.

Vesper leaned back against me, water sloshing as she stretched her legs in the long tub.

"I don't really remember, but I think it was my school's annual battle royale," she explained. "The point wasn't to kill anyone, but you got extra points if you did."

The bathroom was nicer than any place I'd ever stayed at. The only one that could compare was the one in the princess's bedroom, but I'd only seen it while she was bleeding out.

Not exactly the best time for an interior design assessment.

The bathroom was quiet; Aurelia had gotten out of the tub not long after she realized we weren't fucking.

"What a fucked-up school," I murmured and leaned forward to place a kiss on her scar. "All mine did was take away all our magic until it felt like we were dying."

Vesper turned to look at me.

"That's fucking harsh," she said.

"So is killing your classmates!" Aurelia yelled from the next room.

"I know for a fact her schooling had a few beatings as well," Vesper grumbled.

"Starvation, actually!"

I couldn't help but laugh at just how fucked up the three of us were.

Each of us came from wildly different worlds. Humans. Vampires. Witches.

Yet somehow we weren't that much different. All the people in our pasts had been willing to hurt and traumatize us to get their way.

All it did was solidify my feelings for them even more.

They understand me.

Vesper grabbed my hand and gave it a kiss. I returned it by kissing another one of her scars.

"What about this one?"

"You can talk about scars later! The water's getting cold and it's dangerous for humans. They get hypothermia or some shit."

Vesper let out a chuckle; I couldn't help but join her. We slowly got out of the bathtub, putting on loose pajamas and going back into the bedroom, where Aurelia was waiting in the middle of the large bed.

She gave us a smirk and moved beneath the covers, a sign that she wanted us to join her.

Vesper was the first to crawl into bed on her right side; I took her left.

I let out a hiss as her cold feet pushed against my skin.

"Humans can't get hypothermia that easily. Besides, I rarely get that cold," Vesper said and placed a kiss on Aurelia's shoulder before wrapping her arms around her waist and placing her head next to hers on the pillow.

I let my arm fall over the two of them and lay my head down with a sigh. My eyes fluttered closed. Their warmth and company were so comfortable.

Nothing I'd ever imagined I'd get.

"It takes a lot to get hypothermia," I murmured. "And it's a bitch to recover from. You get so cold that any bit of warmth against your skin feels like fire."

There was a pause, then Vesper's hand came to grab my own under the covers. My eyes fluttered open, but neither was looking at me.

"How do you know what it feels like?" Vesper asked.

"Were you left out in the cold, witch?" Aurelia said, a slight joking tone to her voice. "Harsh, even for your coven."

She was trying to lighten the mood, but she was so close to the truth it had my chest tightening.

I could still feel the fire coursing under my skin as I was forced under a hot shower.

"Training—for the White Lotus. I started young but wasn't exempt from the harshest training, which included being outside in the forest in freezing temperatures."

"Not surprised," Aurelia said with a huff. "They're fucked over there."

"Your parents let that happen?" Vesper asked.

I gritted my teeth. *Is this okay to talk about?* I didn't want to ruin our warm moment.

"They were gone before then," I said. "I thought they'd abandoned me and the high priest took me in. But..."

I wasn't sure if I wanted to continue.

"It's okay if you don't want to say it." Aurelia turned her head to make eye contact with me and lay her hand on my belly.

"The high priest might have killed them," I confessed. "I probably witnessed it, but my mind blocked it out. I'm not sure. It was a dream I had right before the seer sent me the vision, so I don't know what's real or not."

The silence between us made me feel like I had said too much.

"I guess we're all a little fucked up, huh?" Aurelia said with a scoff.

Vesper let out a sigh.

"I guess it figures. Maybe that's why we're good together. Thank you for sharing, Cedar. I know it wasn't easy."

My throat threatened to close.

"No, it wasn't."

Violent relief ran through me.

They're not going to reject me.

With a content sigh, I cuddled into Aurelia. This could work. *We* could work.

It was better than I could have ever imagined.

I wished I could stay in the warm, happy bubble forever.

Aurelia

I *can save myself.*
But the more I spent with Cedar and Vesper in Atlas's compound, the less it felt true.

I guess that was why the universe decided it had to remind us.

It has been a calm morning; Cedar and Vesper were getting their breakfast, and I was sitting on the side, watching as they had their human moments.

I was lost in thought.

About my brother. About my father. About what I needed to do to save us from the cold iron grip of the prophecy.

Those two might have been content staying in the compound, but I knew we were on borrowed time. And the pressure of being the only one able to save my own life was wreaking havoc on my psyche.

And then, it all changed.

Atlas barged through the doors to the dining room. Not a hair on her head was out of place, but her look of sheer panic gave her away.

I stood quickly, my hands flying out to the witch and human at my side.

The sound of fast-paced footsteps rang down the hall.

"The council! They are—"

She was pushed aside by vampires in uniforms. I recognized their black and white suits and family crest on the left lapel immediately.

The council. They've come for me.

Vesper and Cedar were up in an instant, both maneuvering to stand in front of me. *To protect me.* The two people in this world who were supposed to want me dead the most were protecting me. *Again.*

The vampires charged at them, wasting no time.

"Don't you dare think about touching—"

But Vesper's threat was short-lived. When they got to her, they used their vampire speed to force her to turn around and put her hands behind her back. Without weapons, there wasn't much she could do.

They're not fighting her. They hadn't even tried. *They're...arresting her?*

My entire world crashed.

"Vesper Monroe, you are under arrest for breaking vampire law and colluding with the vampire hunter organization for the attempted assassination of Aurelia Castle," one of them said, their voice booming across the room.

No one spoke. Vesper and Cedar's thunderous heartbeats were all I could hear.

Vampire law only applies to vampires.

"What the fuck?" Cedar said, speaking my thoughts out loud.

Panic like never before had my body moving before my brain could make sense of it.

"You can't touch a human," I said and rushed forward. "Plus, I'm right here; I'm fine—"

"Back up," another commanded, sending me a glare.

"Atlas!" I called for the vampire's help, but she just looked back at the front door.

"Interfere, Atlas Nox, and we will charge you for harboring the fugitive," the one holding Vesper said. "If you comply, we will overlook your...*transgressions.*"

Atlas's lips pressed into a thin line.

I could hear the thoughts running through her head. I had been in her shoes once as princess and I would be thinking the same.

Protect her or risk my people?

But selfishly, I wanted her to protect Vesper.

"You can't interfere with humans," Vesper growled and attempted to free herself.

They pulled her to the door like she was a kid throwing a tantrum, straight-faced and with ease.

"The human government won't stand for this!" Cedar yelled, following them. I was quick to follow as well, but they didn't stop, not even when they walked right out the front door.

There were three cars and at least ten vampires waiting for her. My jaw dropped at the sight.

How did this happen? Why did the council send so many?

Both Cedar and I descended the stairs after them, but we were stopped by two vampires with reddened eyes before we could reach the front door.

"She's human," Cedar said, her voice trailing off at the end as if... she was doubtful? *Impossible.*

One of the vampires smirked.

"No, she's not," he said. "Which means she's subject to vampire law."

I reared back, my teeth bared.

"Who told you that lie?" I hissed. "I've tasted her blood. I would know—"

"Straight from the Castle family," he replied, his eyes narrowing. "As it turns out, some blood she left at the palace has been tested. She's a quarter vampire, which is enough for her to fall under our jurisdiction."

Father? He would never think of—

I swallowed thickly.

It had been him. Not Father. Which meant...

I gripped Cedar's arm as we watched the council take Vesper toward their car.

She turned back toward us, her eyes set. I could feel the panic through the bond, but her face showed determination.

"Wait for me," she whispered. "I'll figure this out."

"Vesper, wait—"

I tried to follow her, but more vampires moved in an instant to cover my path. One even went so far as to reach for me.

"Don't you fucking touch her," Cedar growled, her arms circling my waist and pulling me to her.

"Touch her and I'll fucking kill you, you hear me?" It was Vesper this time. She was turning around in their grip, attempting to fight them off.

Don't.

The word was at the tip of my tongue, but I couldn't let it out.

They forced her against the car, one opening the door as the other fought to keep her still.

"You'll regret it if so much as a hair on her head is harmed!" Vesper let out a growl. "Cedar! Protect her for me."

"Don't worry! We will figure this out—"

"Please!" The desperation in Vesper's voice had my heart breaking. She held our gazes even as her head was forced down and she was pushed into the car.

There was nothing we could do. We stood there watching as the car left. The vampires in front of me lingered, getting in their own vehicles last.

I felt impotent. I thought about screaming for fucking Atlas and demanding to know how the fuck she allowed this to happen.

But I knew.

She would always put her clan first.

My brother is calling me back to the palace, making his move before I could.

I didn't have time to think about what I'd do next anymore.

The universe had decided for me.

Arms wrapped around me, hands covering my mouth.

I stifled a gasp once I recognized the smell.

Slowly, Cedar lowered her hands.

"How did you sneak up on me?" I asked, turning to look at her.

The room was dark, but with my vampire vision, I could make out the annoyed expression on her face.

I had specifically chosen the middle of the night to stalk the grounds so she would be asleep. Last I'd checked, she had been, in our bed, her body curled around Vesper's pillow.

All I had done was change and put my hair up, but somehow she had concealed herself well enough to stop me from sneaking out our bedroom door.

Ever since Vesper had been taken, my mind was in a frenzy.

I wanted to go to her. Wanted to save her. Plead her case.

It only made it worse that our room smelled like her.

I tried to lie down with Cedar, but without her, it felt wrong.

My brother was calling me. I had been too slow, so he decided to speed up the process.

He had likely killed Father by now, but I needed to see it for myself to make sure.

"I hid myself with magic and waited for you to walk past. I was worried you'd left already," she said. "You must not have noticed in your hurry."

I balled my hands into fists, ready to fight the witch.

I took too long scouting the perimeter.

"So you're going to stop me?" I asked.

"I'm going after Vesper," she said. "I want you to stay here. I know you're trying to sneak out to get to her."

I ground my teeth, not wanting to tell the witch what I was truly planning to do.

"How'd you know I'd sneak out?"

She gave me a look.

"You're you," she replied. "I've been around you long enough to know you'd go ballistic on the council for what they've done."

I wanted to. I wanted to rip all their heads off for taking her from me. I could feel Vesper's panic through the bond, and it made it even worse.

"How are you going to do it?" I asked. "Your coven will come after you at some point."

Sha gave me a wicked grin that in any other scenario would have had my heart skipping a beat.

"That's the point, Brat," she said, throwing around the nickname that *should* have made me feel better. "They'll be a good distraction, and I'll swoop in and save our lovely little hunter."

"Hunter-vampire hybrid," I joked, but it fell flat. "Be careful, okay?"

"What? We fuck a few times and you care about me now?" she asked, though it was less of a joke and more like asking for reassurance.

My lack of response gave her the answer.

I care about her too much. About both of them.

I didn't try to stop her as she brought her lips to mine. I grabbed her shirt and kissed her back greedily, knowing it might just be the last time I felt her against me.

Her warm tongue invaded my mouth, and I moaned against her taste. This time, it was just the two of us.

My hands threaded through her hair. With hers at my hips, she forced us together as she kissed me so deeply it made my head spin.

I don't want to leave. I don't want to do this.

But there was no choice.

I have to be strong.

I continued to kiss her until we were both shaking with a need we'd never get to satisfy.

She pulled away, breathless.

"Believe in me, okay?" she asked.

I nodded and leaned into her, inhaling her scent. Committing it to memory.

She didn't know that, as soon as she stepped off Atlas's grounds, I would be quick to follow.

But we would be going in opposite directions.

Vesper

Magical chains were attached to my neck, wrists, and feet, weighing me down to the ground.

The vampire guards at my sides pushed me forward into a room that looked similar to the Castle family throne room, but instead of just a throne, there were also benches off to the side where multiple vampires sat.

In the middle was a long aisle leading up to the throne, and I was pushed onto a circle-shaped indent in the ground. It lit up as soon as I fell into it, runes similar to the ones I'd seen in the coven written around the outside.

Since when do vampires and witches work together?

"Vesper Monroe," a woman said as we walked down the long aisle. She had a regal-looking coat on, claws tipped in red, and long silver hair, as well as a smirk on her face and an air of superiority as she looked down on me.

Could be a relative of Atlas. Their egos definitely match.

"Who are you?"

There were a few gasps at my insolence. She silenced them with a wave.

"I go by many names. I'm sure you can think of one."

"Nope. Never heard of you. And one name would suffice," I said in a bored tone.

"I'm the head of the vampire council," she said. "Kyan Le Rouge, conqueror of demons, ruler of—"

"Kyan, thanks; I think there's been some type of mistake—"

She was in front of me in seconds, her bloodred eyes digging into mine as her clawed hand came to grip my chin.

The smile on her face had my blood running cold.

"You are a vampire," she whispered. "Even if there is only a tiny percentage of it in you. That means you are under *my* rule. The humans won't save you, so I suggest you leave the attitude at the door."

I filled my mouth with spit and spat it directly on her face.

The crowd erupted.

Kyan merely wiped it off, but her smirk stayed on.

"And here I was going to give you a chance to plead your case." She stood slowly, motioning for the guards to grab me. "Indentured servitude. Give her to the Leclair family as a gift for their daughter."

Horror washed through me.

"You can't do this! I'm not a vamp—"

But my struggling was useless. I was taken out of the fucked-up courthouse and dragged down to the dungeons kicking and screaming to await my fate.

I let out a groan as I was thrown to the ground yet again. Unlike the clean floor of the courtroom, this one was filled with blood and other grime I didn't want to know about.

"You'll get blood every other day until your escort arrives to take you to the Leclair family," one of the guards said as they locked my cage.

I pushed up on my hands and knees.

"I'm human! I need food—"

They hit the bars of my cell, a sinister smile twisting their face.

"Council head's orders."

They left without looking back. Pained screaming echoed down the hall and caused me to jump. My heart raced. My mind was in a frenzy.

How the fuck did this happen?

I couldn't be a vampire. There was no way...

Do you even know what the blood does to humans?

The look Gabriel and Tate gave me flashed through my mind.

It's common in the organization.

There had been no indication. My entire life I had never once thought I was anything other than human.

I sank back to the ground, dread filling me.

And prayed to god Cedar or Aurelia would come save me soon.

Aurelia

He was there, just like I thought he'd be. *Adrian Castle.* The youngest of the Castle family and the person who threatened everything I loved in this world.

Everyone was talking about how he had taken over the palace, and now I got to see it for myself.

He was sitting on Father's throne, one leg over one armrest, his propped-up elbow on the other. He had been waiting for me, and as soon as I pushed through the doors of the throne room, a smile lit up his face.

Two of his lackeys were behind him, watching me intently for any wrong move.

Images of my nightmares hit me like a truck, filling my head with my mother's bloodied face and her handmaiden's as they both reached out for me.

It hadn't been long since I'd been here, but I'd barely recognized how it felt to walk on the plush red carpet that led up to the throne.

Forgotten the smell of my own palace as it had been replaced with Vesper's and Cedar's.

This isn't my home anymore.

My people were here, but it lacked warmth. Lacked belonging.

It made my stomach churn.

There was a trail of blood that led from the doors to the bottom of the throne. My father was on his knees in front of my brother. The once all-powerful king was withering away.

They're starving him.

His eyes widened when he saw me.

"Aurelia..."

"Welcome, sister," he said and stood. "Ignored my message to stay away, huh?"

"That went out the door when you tattled on us to the council," I said, taking slow steps to the throne.

My father stiffened, but he just threw his head back, his booming laugh echoing throughout the room.

"Maybe you did get some of your mother's genes after all," he said and stood.

"Father was stupid to throw you out," I said, causing him to raise an eyebrow at me.

"Aurelia—"

"Silence!" My brother kicked my father's back, sending him sprawling forward.

Satisfaction unfurled inside me.

I might not have been able to give him what he deserved, but at least someone could.

"Oh? I see that little smile of yours. Here." My brother yanked my father's face back by his hair. "Now's your chance, dear sister. Say anything you want. I've kept him here just for you."

A lump formed in my throat.

"You killed my mother," I told him. "Was it because she tried to save him?"

My father shook his head.

"Listen, Aurelia, don't let him do this. I would never—"

My brother grabbed his hair tighter.

"Tell the truth."

It shouldn't have pleased me as much as it did to see him fear my brother.

"Okay, yes," Father said quickly. "I couldn't have it getting out—"

"You made my life hell," I growled, taking one step at a time. "You groomed me to be your perfect mini-me. Sold me. Did you know what the Solei family wanted to do to me?"

I let out a scoff when his face told me he did.

"Of course." I shook my head. "How did you steal her from them?"

"Oh, I know this one!" My brother sounded like an overexcited child. "You forcefully blood-bonded her! Assaulted her and got her pregnant so the Solei family would reject her, isn't that right?"

Bile rose up my throat. My body was threatening to collapse under the pressure that was building in me.

No. No. No. No. Not Mother.

Her smiling face flashed before my eyes. She was too kind. Memories of us together filled my mind. Her warmth. Her smell. Her love. Her last words.

How could someone ever—

I dug my fingernails into my palms. *I'll kill him. Right now.*

"Aurelia. Wait."

My feet had already started moving before I had a chance to think through my actions.

"Oh, not so fast," my brother said, and in one swift movement, tore my father's head from his body.

I froze, unable to comprehend what I was seeing.

His body fell to the ground with a thud. My brother held his head in his hand and, with a smile, sat down on his throne.

He's dead. Just like that. The person who'd fucked over my entire life. Killed my mother. Dead in one second.

But he couldn't have gone without me knowing that earth-shattering truth.

Mother loved me. I knew she did. There was no doubt about it. But there was a sour taste in my mouth at the realization of what my father had done to her.

How could she love me after that? How could anyone?

As if reading my mind, my brother gave me a sympathetic look.

"He never loved you. He valued your ability to bear children. To be controlled. Father knew he wouldn't be able to control a son. He *never* wanted to give up his throne." He let Father's head fall to the ground. "Even in the end, he fought. Do you know he even offered up his stepdaughter to me?"

My eyes wandered to where my stepmother and stepsister were huddled together, more of his lackeys on either side of them.

I thought maybe seeing their fear-stricken faces would excite me, but it didn't. It disgusted me instead.

"Thank you," I said. "For dealing with that bastard."

My brother raised a brow. "You're welcome, dear sister."

"I've come with...an offer. Something better than fighting. And after taking care of our father, I feel as though you deserve nothing less," I said before kneeling on the ground. Coldness seeped into my skin from touching the hard stone.

"Oh?" He leaned forward. "And what is that?"

Sweat rolled down the back of my neck.

"The families will rebel. I have information that they are preparing to start a war," I said.

"You think you're telling me something I don't know? This won't save your sister."

"No," I said and lifted my chin. "But there's something that can save you, this family, and also ensure that there will be no war."

He raised a brow.

"I offer myself," I said. "To be used for the family. For its growth and safety."

"Are you asking what I think you are, sister?"

The gleam in his eyes gave me hope.

"Marry me off," I commanded.

VESPER, AURELIA, AND CEDAR AREN'T DONE YET!
JOIN THEM IN...

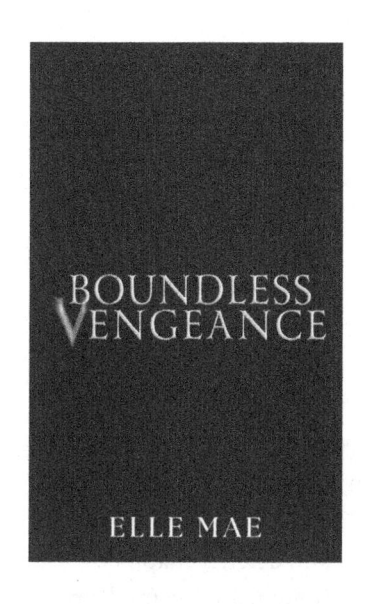

Vesper

I didn't know what was worse.

Getting kidnapped by the vampire council or being forced to serve a random vampire family.

No, wait, it was my bonded going off and getting *married* while I could do nothing about it.

Cedar and Atlas may have gotten me out, but I'll stop at **nothing** to save Aurelia from her doom.

Aurelia

I can save myself.

Once I deciphered what the seer was saying, I knew exactly what I had to do, *the thing I was born for.*

It will save us all, so why can't they understand?

They know my heart and soul better than anyone else, but if they insist on trying to ruin my plans,

I might just have to teach them a lesson or two.

Cedar

Getting involved with them might be the most dangerous thing I've ever done.

Being thrown between powerful vampire families and a bastard vampire heir was definitely *not* on my to-do list.

But I couldn't let them face it all alone.

Maybe I would have been better off rotting in the coven, but they showed me a world I never thought was possible.

I'll bring us back to our happy little life together, *even if it means getting my hands dirty.*

Preorder book 3 on amazon now!

Want to be in the know? Join my newsletter for publishing updates and free shorts!

Join my Patreon and you will get access to all stories BEFORE they are published.

If you join now you will get free stories and deleted chapters!

There is also a tier for NSFW art that is exclusive for my Patreon members

Check it out here or go to https://www.patreon.com/ellemaebooks

Want exclusive NSFW art?

For NSFW EC art (and other series) join my Patreon!
I also update my novellas on there every other week and they are the FIRST to get ARCS of all my newest releases!
Check it out here or go to https://www.patreon.com/ellemaebooks

About the Author

Elle is a native Californian who has lived in Los Angeles for most of her life. From the very start, she has been in love with all things fantasy and reading. As soon as Elle found out that writing books could be a career, she picked up a pen and paper. While the first ones were about scorned love and missed opportunities of lunchtime love, she has grown to love the fantasy genre and looks forward to making a difference in the world with her stories.

Loved this book? Please leave a review!

For more behind the scene content, check out my Patreon or sign up to my newsletter!

https://elegant-mountain-68199.myflodesk.com/y8a9duflae

𝕏 x.com/mae_books
📷 instagram.com/edenrosebooks
g goodreads.com/ellemae

Made in the USA
Monee, IL
11 March 2025